Conspiracy

Other Books by R. A. Stokes

The Nehemiah Project
Riches and Prosperity

Conspiracy

By R. A. Stokes

MountainFirePress

To Jesus Christ, my Lord and Savior: Thank You, Lord, for putting this story on my heart. May this book serve to further Your kingdom and glorify Your name.

To Mary Jo—my wife, companion, and friend: thank you for your many years of love, friendship, and support.

"We glide along the tides of time as swiftly as a racing river and vanish as quickly as a dream."
(Psalm 90:5 TLB)

Chapter One

On a breezy April morning, Tanner Johansson pulled his car into the parking garage, descended a ramp one floor to ground level, and then walked briskly to the high-rise building a block away. An arch of pastel colors settled on a pillow of large white, billowy clouds following the thunderstorm that lasted no more than twenty minutes but left puddles on the sidewalk that Johansson deftly stepped over.

As he crossed the street, he glanced at the sign with gold numerals and letters: "58 Brickell Avenue." A doorman wearing a clear, lightweight rainsuit over an impeccably ironed black and gold uniform with matching cap, nodded as Johansson walked under the canopy and entered the revolving door entrance. He walked into the lobby, flashed an identification card at the front desk receptionist, took several steps through a turnstile checkpoint, proceeded on to the elevator, and then got off on the twelfth floor of the Emerald News Media conglomerate high-rise building.

The receptionist looked up and smiled. "May I help you, sir?"

"I'm Tanner Johansson. I have an appointment with Mrs. Martindale."

"Of course. Right this way, Mr. Johansson."

Moments later, he stood in an open doorway and scanned the executive suite, a large office overlooking the city through a wall-to-wall window just behind an elegant cherry-colored mahogany desk, and an adjacent wall covered with plaques and small shelves holding gold-colored statuettes.

"Knock, knock."

A woman glanced up. "Can I help you?"

"Agnes Martindale?"

"Yes, and I've never forgiven my parents. Everyone here calls me Aggie. How can I help you?"

"Tanner Johansson. I was told to report to you."

"Mr. Johansson," she said, peering over her glasses, slowly letting the name roll off her tongue in the same manner one might reference a distant place or scene from years past. "I've been expecting you. Sit down, please."

Agnes Martindale, an attractive, well-dressed woman of fifty, peered over her glasses as Johansson sat down. "You don't look like a beat reporter. You don't look like you've ever gotten your hands dirty."

Johansson lifted his chin and smiled. "Well, looks are deceiving, I guess," he said, with a hint of sarcasm.

"Your first show will be a week from Friday. Take the next few days and get oriented to the set. Meet the producer and staff members, get accustomed to the production protocols, find out what's acceptable and what's not, and then you have a week to get your first show down. You've got three months, max, to show me what you've got. After that, if the ratings aren't there, you're back on the street. Understood?"

"Nothing like a little support out of the chute. Thank you for the warm welcome."

Agnes Martindale shook her head. "I'm extremely busy. I'm only giving you this chance because I was told to. Don't press your luck. I've seen countless young wannabes come and go."

"I don't plan on being back on the street. I expect to be in your top time slot in three months."

"Bring me an outline Monday morning, a week from today, on where you'd like to go with the show. Ten o'clock sharp. I'll give you an hour to convince me. Don't be late, and please be prepared." She wasn't about to give a small-market reporter, already far too confident for his limited journalistic background and stature, any more credence than he could handle—or that she could handle, for that matter.

"Any questions for me?" she asked.

"I'm sure I'll have some before the day is out."

"Write them down. After Monday's meeting, we'll have a one-on-one at nine o'clock each morning. You'll have thirty minutes to brief me on your show and ask me any questions you might have. I expect you to be punctual. I have a rapid-fire schedule from the minute I arrive until I leave each night."

Aggie pushed an intercom button on a red desktop phone. A voice answered instantly. "Yes, Mrs. Martindale."

A tall, slender young woman with shoulder-length red hair, appeared in the doorway of an adjacent office to Aggie's suite.

"Cynthia, this is Tanner Johansson. He's joining the Miami team from the Land of Enchantment, where's he been working in Santa Fe. Mr. Johansson, this is Cynthia my assistant. She can usually help with any questions or concerns if I'm not available.

"By the way, Cynthia is considered the most fashion-able dresser in the studio." Aggie's eyes glanced at the blue windbreaker and Levi's jeans Tanner was wearing. "But, we're informal for the most part. I'm sure you'll fit in.

"Cynthia, please show Mr. Johansson his office."

"Yes, ma'am. Right this way, please."

Agnes Martindale didn't mention the memo that Cynthia had received from Aubrey's personal assistant: "Give Johansson a room with a view." Incredible, she thought. He was skiing in the Swiss Alps and took the time to relay a message on behalf of a beat reporter from New Mexico.

"I look forward to getting to know you, Mr. Johansson," Aggie said smugly. "Welcome to the team."

Chapter Two

Although not as elaborately furnished as Aggie's suite, Tanner's office on the twelfth floor of the Brickell Avenue office building held spectacular views toward the eastern seaboard. A splash of rainbow colors following the brief thunderstorm settled on a magnificent palette of blue sky, blending gracefully over the distant waters. A maple-colored wood grain paneling covered the north and south walls of the room, and, like all the suites facing the bay, a full floor-to-ceiling window filled the twelve-foot-high east wall. A luxury executive desk of maple-colored wood grains with a perpendicular matching side wing was symmetrically placed in the center of the room. A small couch with two chairs and an end table were situated to the south of the desk. The north wall was filled with a matching glass cabinet and bookcase, traditional furnishings filled with books and decorative items of various sorts. A polished, intricately carved oak hatstand and coatrack stood to his right as he entered the room, the crest of the six-foot-high rack holding five curved pegs with rounded ends.

Tanner placed a worn black attaché case at the base of the hat stand, pumped his fist in the air, and said, "Yes!" to the otherwise empty room.

Johansson was a handsome man with wavy golden-brown hair, loosely parted on the right side with his hands, sans comb, that hung halfway down his ears and at times fell over his forehead. He had a sharp nose, prominent cheek bones, hazel eyes with a tint of green, and an almost always earnest expression on his face. Close family members said the facial expression was a feature he was born with. His countenance had changed little over the years. Amara had said he was "dashing" when they first started dating years before, but professional associates referred to him as brash and arrogant, at best aloof. Johansson's driving ambition lent itself to an intensity that, using a sports analogy, meant running over his opponents rather than running around them. The strategy routinely left injuries in the wake. His sister, older by a year, and his only sibling, had often said when they were growing up, "There's a reason you don't have a lot of friends in this life, Tanner. Do yourself and everyone around you a favor—lighten up!" His six-foot-two, one-hundred-and-ninety-pound frame was twenty pounds heavier than the lanky build he had as a high school and college track and football star. A dual scholarship—he was a wide receiver in football and ran the 400 and 800 meters in track—had paid his way through college and looked impressive on his résumé when he landed his first reporting assignment for a small newspaper in Kansas. His early jobs zigzagged from Kansas to Texas to Nebraska to Colorado and then to New Mexico where he met Amara, her late father of Spanish descent, her mother born in Cuba. Tanner and Amara were married at twenty-five and fifteen years later had a son and two daughters, fourteen, thirteen, and twelve years old.

Johansson had been to Miami for Emerald News Media award banquets, trade shows, conventions, and occasional meetings over the years, but had spent little time on the three floors of Emerald's high-rise office suites and recording studio. The opportunity had come with a salary increase, a generous moving package, and most importantly, from his standpoint, his own show. The narratives had been running through his mind for months now—long before the offer had come. Now he had the chance to show what he could do. Amara was happy to be near her mother, they had found a reasonably priced home in Coral Gables, near Fontainebleau—unaffordable at any other time in their married lives, but the home they purchased in Santa Fe ten years earlier had sold at a price well beyond their expectations. They were ten miles—a half hour commuting distance—from the office suites and studio on Brickell Avenue, four miles from Miami Beach, and just over ten miles from the small Spanish Mediterranean bungalow where Amara's mother lived on the edge of Little Havana.

Looking at the skyline, Johansson could scarcely contain his excitement. He had not expected the cynicism he'd encountered in his initial meeting with Agnes Martindale, but that's okay, he thought. He had no expectations when he came. He would give it his best; if it worked out, great. If not, he had always been able to find a job. But certainly, he hoped it would work out.

Johansson was as passionate as he was ambitious, with convictions ranging from criminal justice reform to a disdain for career politicians. He could never shake the horror he felt watching documentaries of Antanimora Prison in Antananarivo, Madagascar, the South Cotabato Jail in the Philippines, or La Mesa Penitentiary in Tijuana, Mexico. The in-turn inhumanity to the world's perceived most inhumane was staggering to him, but closer to home the jail and prison conditions in the United States were reprehensible. State-after-state, the worst-of-the-worst conditions existed in metropolitan jails and prisons throughout the country.

"I'm not soft on crime," he would say. "I believe we should support our local police officers, not castigate them. But we have a broken criminal justice system. Many prisoners remain behind bars, in part, because of failed government oversight. How can the 'land of the free' and the 'home of the brave' have the highest incarceration rate in the world?"

There was a dichotomy in his views. Johansson held no sympathy for hardened, dangerous criminals. "The perpetrators of violent crime are getting what they deserve," he often said. "I'm not talking about them," he would qualify. "I'm talking about nonviolent offenders who have been forgotten in a failed criminal justice system. I will never trivialize serious crime, but where possible I will be large on compassion and reform."

In respect to gun control, he understood the argument against military-style weapons, but Johansson was strongly Second Amendment. His anti-bureaucracy views would never allow for greater government control than it already exhibited over the nation's citizenry. In his view, the dramatic increase in societal violence was driven by drug abuse, broken families, and the accepted glamorization of violence in media—television, movies, and gaming.

In spite of some progress, systemic injustices remained, and he blamed political leadership. "I want to share a story about a man named Dennis Hope, a prisoner in Texas who was kept in solitary confinement for twenty-seven years. What was his crime? Burglaries and armed robbery. Serious offenses deserving lengthy sentences, to be sure, but no one died in the course of his crime spree. Where is the equal application of justice in this sentencing? I'm not arguing for a light prison term, but twenty-seven years in solitary confinement? How does that happen in the United States of America? What kind of leadership allows that?"

Even worse were the stories of those who had been wrongly convicted. He donated money to the Innocence Project, an organization instrumental in the release of more than two hundred wrongly convicted men and women, scores of former prisoners released after

DNA testing and other scientific methodologies proved innocence.

Johansson's mind was racing with a seemingly endless tranche of exposé vignettes when his thoughts were interrupted by Cynthia, who was standing in the doorway with a young man.

"Excuse me, Mr. Johansson. I'd like you to meet Mitchell Carmichael. Mitchell is a senior editorial research assistant for Emerald. He's been assigned to assist you with editorial content, production matters, and anything else you may need in putting together your show.

"Mitch," Cynthia turned to the young man and continued the introduction, "this is Tanner Johansson. Mr. Johansson has been with the company for a number of years now, but he's new to the Miami area. I'm sure the two of you will work well together."

Cynthia smiled, turned, and left the room, leaving Mitchell standing awkwardly in the doorway.

Carmichael was a young man about thirty with a slender build and short dark hair, neatly cropped at the sides with a tussle pushing up at the front, wire-rim glasses, and a pleasant, innocent looking demeanor.

"Come in, come in. Please sit down. Tell me about yourself, Mitchell."

"Mitch is fine, sir. Or Carmy."

"Carmy?"

"That was my wife's nickname for me before we were married. Now it's generally, Mitchell, meaning she wants my undivided attention."

"Kids?"

"No, but we're working on it."

"How long have you been with Emerald?"

"I'm approaching four years now. The first two years were in production, and then I was given this editorial gig, position, I should say. I have quite a bit of technical experience—everything from cameras and lighting to sound and digital overlay—I majored in computer engineering in college, but I love the editorial research I'm doing. I won't let you down, sir. A to Z—give me the topic, and I'll give you more information than you wanted.

"By the way, Cynthia asked me to show you around. At your convenience, I'll be happy to give you the grand tour. The twelfth floor has all the big shots—no offense, sir. Most of the editorial and production team employees are on the tenth floor. I have a cubicle toward the middle of the first row when you get off the elevator, just an FYI. The production studios take up most of the eleventh floor; storage and equipment rooms are also on the eleventh floor. Oh, I almost forgot, the cafeteria is on the southeast end of the eleventh floor. It's open from 5:00 a.m. to 10:00 p.m."

"How's the food?"

"Outstanding, sir. Seafood, Chinese, Japanese Bowls, Italian, Mexican, American cuisine, of course. All of the cuisine choices are divided up into small stations, each with its own mini kitchen and staff. It's pretty amazing, sir. For most of us, it's one of the highlights of our day."

"I appreciate that, Mitch. I'm racing to get to an

appointment that I'm afraid I'm going to be late for, but let's meet in the morning."

Mitch turned to leave but then said, "I love your office, Mr. Johansson. It's a first at the network for an unknown news anchor—" Mitch caught himself. "I'm sorry, sir, I didn't mean to be disrespectful in any way."

Tanner smiled. "I'm far too excited to be offended, Mitch. We're gonna hit the ground running and make a name for ourselves. You're part of the plan. I'll be in touch."

Chapter Three

The following Monday at ten o'clock in the morning, Johansson sat at a large, opulent-looking hardwood table in the conference room adjoining Agnes Martindale's suite on the opposite side of the room from Cynthia's office.

The conference room adjoining Aggie's suite held an eight-by-twenty-foot, cherry-colored mahogany table—part of the furniture set that included Aggie's executive desk—complete with high-backed, ornately carved chairs with plush seats and cushioned backs surrounding the table. The wall adjacent to the window overlooking the skyline, Brickell buildings, Biscayne Bay, and the Atlantic Ocean in the distance, was filled with a floor-to-ceiling bookcase holding volumes of news commentaries spanning the two decades since Emerald News Media's inception as a news organization.

This morning, seven days after their initial meeting, Tanner Johansson and Agnes Martindale were the only staff members in the boardroom-style meeting room.

Johansson spoke passionately for fifteen minutes, occasionally waving his arms, periodically reviewing his notes, painstakingly elaborating on nuances to his presentation as Martindale listened with a stoic look on her face.

Johansson ended his talk, pursed his lips, lifted his chin, and looked confidently at his boss. "What do you think?"

"We don't traffic in conspiracy theories," she said wistfully.

"Conspiracies? What does that mean? I have an extreme skepticism of people in power. And I believe history supports me on that. Where do you want me to start?"

Aggie stood up and turned toward the window, squinting at the rays of sunshine now resting on the desk and wall behind her. It was a splendid April morning, a cloudless sky of blue creating a watercolor backdrop to the buildings separating Emerald News Media from the ocean five miles away.

"Johansson, I didn't get this view peddling conspiracy theories. I can't believe we're having this conversation. Your first week on the job and you're bringing me a story that will . . ." Aggie hesitated but then continued. "I told Ed this wasn't going to work," she said, shaking her head. "Small town politics in the southwest and national news commentary from Miami don't mix."

"I'm not a rookie. I'm a forty-year-old professional journalist who has been on the street for fifteen years. I know the pulse of everyday people. I've received countless accolades, multiple awards . . ." Johansson stopped and looked intently at Aggie who had moved to the head of the table and sat back down. "I even got kudos from Aubrey. Obviously, you knew that before I interviewed with Collins."

"Have you forgotten something? I'm the executive producer. You're the new, at this point completely unknown, television anchor. I get paid to maintain journalistic standards. I decide what stories get published."

"And what's my role?" Tanner said, not trying to hide the disgust he felt.

"Your job is to deliver monologues that won't have the entire journalistic world looking at us as if we were kooks! Don't you understand that, Johansson? I'm getting impatient with this conversation." Aggie stood up again and started to stack several folders on top of each other, as if she were preparing to leave the room.

"Wait! I have a proposal to make. I'll change the sequence and start with a story that, at this point in time, is now indisputable. I've got a million stories racing through my mind. Plots from one end of the globe to the other. Most of them have already happened, so now we have history to validate. The opening feature will be the tip of the iceberg."

"Tip of the iceberg? Great! Now you want to turn the station, and me, I might add, into the laughingstock of mainstream media *and* cable news. No thanks."

"Hear me out. You said at the team meeting on Friday that you were open to a special edition piece from time to time. A compilation of stories on trending topics. Give me thirty days. I'll put together a series of narratives that will burn through every media outlet in the country."

"Johansson, I don't even know why I hired you. Actually, I didn't hire you. Ed Collins hired you—against his better judgment too. All right, thirty days—I can't believe I just said that." Aggie rolled her eyes and shook her head. She had a look of incredulity on her face. "Wasted payroll, probably," she added.

In an uncharacteristic moment, Aggie's tone softened. "Your credentials are good. I like some of the scripts I reviewed from your last assignment. I do want this to work. If for no other reason than Aubrey wants it to work. I'll agree, but here's the catch. You bring me a riveting piece to kick this off, which, by the way, I have no confidence that you will, or you agree to working on stories that I give you. Agreed?"

Tanner smiled broadly. In his mind's eye, he was crossing a finish line with arms raised in victory.

"You got it," he said.

Chapter Four

So you think it couldn't happen to you? Let's go back in time for a moment. Picture this scene, friends: within twenty-four hours, every mainstream media outlet is crying, 'Conspiracy theory!' Listen to what the *Daily Richmond Examiner* or the *Whig* or the *Dispatch* might have said: 'Today, right-wing extremists are claiming that the military has conspired to murder Indians, the very people who have signed a monumental, fair, and equitable treaty with this great republic, the very tribes who have willingly been relocating to mutually agreed upon lands where they can begin new lives with their wives and children. President Martin Van Buren, an honorable man of dignity and renown, has been disparaged mercilessly by extremists for his noble work in carrying out the treaty brought forth by his predecessor, President Andrew Jackson. To malign these great patriots to our young nation of noble townsmen is nothing less than dastardly. Men and women of this great land, stand erect for our freedoms, which are being undergirded by the most sinister and fiendish of foe!' "

Johansson paused and looked thoughtfully at the camera. "Friends, do you know how many Native Americans died on the Trail of Tears? Do you have any understanding of the treaties that were broken by the United States government leading to the relocation of these indigenous peoples? Do you know how many thousands of Choctaw, Muscogee, Chickasaw, Cherokee, and Seminole died of starvation, disease, or extreme cold during the winter of 1838–1839?

"Let's switch gears for a moment. Some of you are looking around the country today and asking, 'How trustworthy is my government?' Well, fortunately we're not in America of the 1940s. Yes, the America of FDR and the New Deal and a boom of economic productivity brought on by the manufacturing of ships, airplanes, and munitions—those 1940s. I'm referring to the period of history when the United States government decided to round up Japanese Americans, remove them from their homes, freeze their bank accounts, and put them into fenced detention centers in California, Idaho, and other states.

"None of us have forgotten the sacrifices of Abraham Lincoln, Harriet Tubman, Martin Luther King, Jr., and the countless scores of abolitionists who labored for civil rights for Black Americans. But how many remember that Abraham Lincoln was the sixteenth president of the United States, sworn into office on March 4, 1861, and that prior to Lincoln there were fifteen presidential terms, each administration governing parallel with a congressional House of Representatives and United States Senate?

"As we remember the brave abolitionists who fought for the freedoms of Black Americans, who can forget the horror of the transatlantic slave trade, a criminal enterprise that began well before the inauguration of George Washington in 1789 and continued until it was officially banned by the United States government in 1808, albeit American and British ships continued to traffic human beings illegally until the 1860s? In a cacophony of infamy ranging from the utter squalor in the lower decks of cargo ships, to men being thrown overboard during stormy seas, Black men, women, and children suffered atrocities that should never have been written in the history pages of a civilized nation.

"To say that conditions in the lower decks of the cargo vessels was inhumane, leaves me searching for words in a thesaurus incomplete in describing the greed of shipmasters and merchants at every rung of the slave trade.

"Over six hundred thousand people died during the Civil War, fighting over the declaration of our Founding Fathers that 'all men are created equal.' Yet who would recognize those words in the media outlets of the day, newspapers opposed to Lincoln with voices decrying efforts to abolish a practice too often buried in the history of infamy?

"Picture an editorial headline, prominently placed just below a paid advertisement for a 'Young, strong, male, experienced in all manner of planting, picking, and horse stable cleaning,' from the prominent, pro-slavery newspapers in the days before emancipation, writing, 'Abolitionists and disruptive social anarchists have feverishly undertaken a cause not unlike the tyranny of the French one hundred years ago when our cherished colonies were brutally attacked by those who would have toppled our fledgling republic. Today, forces are arrayed once again, this time against the livelihoods and very way of life of law-abiding citizens who want nothing more than to earn a living by the toil of their hands, and raise their families with the help of their own rightful property. To war against these good men and women, and against the ship captains and crews of the enterprises who braved the winds and seas, and toiled through sleepless nights from the African coasts to this great continent, is nothing less than traitorous, a rebellion of the most serious nature, rendering the worst of punishments for these nihilistic, perfidious rebels.'

"None of us have forgotten the indignities of slavery, from the treachery embedded in the transatlantic slave trade to the discrimination found as recently as the 1950s in the Jim Crow laws.

"What we need to remember is the division of good versus evil, the divide between right and wrong, the chasm separating just and unjust—yes, still today, the breach between free or slave—that remains in too many places across the globe, is upheld by the expansionist neocons, and covered up by the duplicity of a modern-day supporting cast of media accomplices, complicit in the same manner that even Northern newspapers like *The Boston Gazette,* the *Hartford Courant,* and the *New York Post* were in the days of slavery.

"Folks, the mainstream media uses terms like conspiracy theory, election denial, science deniers, and on and on, to make you feel insecure about questioning the official government narrative. It's all propaganda. What I'm going to do in the coming weeks is *prove* to you . . ."

Several weeks later, Tanner closed his show by saying, "For the past two months, our segments have focused on suspicious, historic events that, at the time, when questioned by journalists and other inquiring minds, were labeled conspiracy theories by the establishment. These so-called conspiracies are now well-documented history. In other words, what were once branded as dangerous, conspiratorial narratives are now established facts, and our program has worked to expose that. Over the coming months, we're going to bring these cover-ups closer to home. Stay tuned. Tanner Johansson, until next week."

The following Saturday morning, Johansson slowed to a walk and stopped at a bench along the running path at the end of his three-mile jog. His mind was racing with details about an upcoming news segment he had titled "Failed Government." As he placed his foot on the end of the bench and began to stretch his leg, he noticed an old man sitting at a nearby bench. The man was huddled over as if he were trying to shelter himself from a cold wind, but there was scarcely even a breeze on this muggy, sunny morning. The man looked up at Johansson and smiled. "Good morning."

"Good morning, sir. I guess I was preoccupied for a minute. I hardly noticed you sitting there. I've been coming to this park every Saturday morning for the past two months, and this is the first time there's been anyone sitting on that bench at the end of my run."

"Well, I've been coming here for the past seven or eight years, and I've sat at this same bench almost every week. The difference is I'm an hour late this morning."

The old man smiled, stood up, and moved toward the bench Tanner was standing at. "Ezra Townes," the man said, extending his hand. "And if I'm not mistaken, you're the young journalist who has the cable news world reeling, if I can describe it in that manner. I mean that in a positive way."

"Not sure that's the case, but thank you for the compliment." Johansson gently took hold of the old man's hand and introduced himself. "Tanner Johansson. Nice to meet you, Mr. Townes. By all means, sit down."

"Ezra, please. I'm old, but not that old."

Ezra smiled warmly and sat down on the end of the bench opposite Johansson. "Thank you for your segment on the Trail of Tears. It brought back memories of my childhood that I hadn't thought of for years."

"Are you of Native American descent?" Johansson asked.

"No, but as a child I read countless books about the American Indians. In grade school, the teacher handed out a three- or four-page pamphlet called the *Weekly Reader.* You could order paperback books for about fifty cents, if I remember right. That was back in the late fifties, early sixties. Good books, great stories with traditional values. My favorite author was Paul Hutchens. He wrote the Sugar Creek Gang series, which chronicled the adventures of a group of young boys. The stories had a strong Christian theme."

Ezra paused and looked thoughtfully in the direction of the pond. "Those were different times," he said, with a hint of sadness in his voice.

"The local library had a great number of books about the American Indians," he continued. "I loved reading about the Seminole Tribe—they were in Florida. The Muscogee were from the southeast; they were called the Creek Nation. I worked my way across the country— from the plains to the southwest to the northwest—the Blackfoot, the Sioux, the Apache. I read every book I could get my hands on. I've forgotten most of what I learned, but I remember my favorite American Indian was Chief Joseph of the Nez Percé. I never understood the suffering. Reading the stories had a profound effect on me as a young boy."

"I appreciate you sharing with me, Ezra. Thank you," Tanner said.

"Well, I guess I should be going. I'm meeting one of my daughters for lunch. I have a couple of errands to attend to in the meantime."

Ezra stood up to leave but seemed to lose his balance

and teetered for a moment. Tanner sprung up and gently steadied his arm. "Are you okay?" he asked.

"My left knee gives out every once in a while, but I'll be fine. Thank you."

Ezra began walking slowly toward a small paved parking lot not far from the bench the men had been seated at. As he approached his car, he turned and waved.

"All the best with your new show, Mr. Johansson. I hope we meet again."

Chapter Five

I think we have a fascist government," he said with a smug, dry tone. "They'll manufacture a crisis before the next election, trust me."

"It's nice to know you have an opinion, Johansson."

Agnes Martindale was a refined, confident, assertive woman just short of her fifty-first birthday. She had a smooth, svelte face, penetrating blue eyes, and deep burgundy-colored hair that hung midway down her back. On newsroom meeting days, or when conducting managerial staff or television anchor performance reviews, she tied her hair up in a bun and peered over glasses encased in a stylistic blend of red and black colored frames. She was astute, scholarly in her approach, and to most of the Emerald News Media team, intimidating.

"It's unheard of that anyone with your experience would be handed a weekly show. You should be grateful."

"These people are so corrupt they'll do anything to stay in power," Johansson said with a slight smirk. "I am grateful. I'm only repeating what every conservative talk show personality has been saying for the last three and a half years, but I'm going to expand on it: if the government tells me to do something, I do the opposite."

"You have a very cynical point of view. Johansson, what are we even talking about this morning? I'm happy with the feedback we've gotten on your show. The ratings have been good. What's with the constant badgering?

"Let me ask you something," she continued. "Why are you always so contemptuous? Did you have a bad childhood? Did your parents not love you? I know an excellent psychiatrist, if you're interested."

Moments later, they were interrupted by the presence of Ed Collins, Vice President of Emerald News Media Group. Dressed in a neatly tailored black cashmere suit, offset with elegant red pinstripes running vertically on the jacket and trousers, Collins wore a crisp white cotton shirt with gold diamond-shaped cuffs and a ruby colored tie. He had shortly cropped gray hair, almost like a crewcut from 1965. Collins walked with a swagger and held an air about him that left no room for debate; to the staff of Emerald News, rendering an unsolicited opinion, however well intended, was risky at best.

"I knew you had promise after our first phone interview, Johansson. I'm pleased you're off to a good start. Aggie has given you a lot of accolades since you arrived. She doesn't give out compliments very often, never when they're unwarranted, so that tells me you're doing things right."

Tanner glanced at Aggie who had her lips pursed

together tightly. She made eye contact with Johansson for an instant and then looked away.

"We're never asked to do anything unethical here, but my peers at other networks engage in questionable activities twenty-four seven," he said with a pompous cadence to the words.

Yep, I'm sure you're innocent, Johansson thought.

"I like to keep things on the up," Collins said with a broad grin, his perfectly straight, snow-white celebrity teeth, surgically placed from a renowned orthodontist in Stockholm ten years before, providing an awkward contrast to his tanned, slightly wrinkled sixty-year-old face.

"I like what I've seen in your early shows. Just don't go overboard. We have a lot of eyes watching us. Not just your audience."

With that, Collins abruptly turned and left.

Aggie, who had been sitting at her desk with her hands folded in her lap while Collins delivered his address, straightened up in a display of almost perfect posture, placed her hands on the desk, and looked at Tanner with a somber expression on her face. She had long, slender fingers which she was now gently tapping—her forefinger, middle, index, and little fingers moving in sequence as if she were playing scales on a piano.

"If Ed only knew the stress you've caused me after three months on the job," she said wistfully.

"Thank you for the accolades. I'm happy to be making such a positive impression," he said dryly.

An hour later, Tanner's mind was racing through

a montage of upcoming news segments when Mitch Carmichael knocked on the door. "You wanted to see me, sir?"

"Yes, good morning, Mitch. I need a summary of Operation Paperclip, Operation Mockingbird, Operation Washtub, and Operation Mongoose. I just sent you an email with the list."

Johansson looked at his assistant and rolled his eyes. "Creative, aren't they? You'd think they could come up with a code name with a title other than 'Operation' in the heading."

"I'm on it, sir. How much information do you want?"

"None of these segments will be long. Mockingbird was a CIA wiretapping scheme, Mongoose involved subterfuge by the CIA in Cuba, Paperclip involved the United States Government bringing sixteen hundred scientists and academics from Germany to the U.S. immediately after World War II. How many were Nazis who were given immunity? We can only guess. Whatever the official narrative is, look for the real story. Washtub was a covert operation between the United States Air Force's Office of Special Investigations and the FBI. Dig in, let me know what you find. I'm looking for stories that were met with denial when they were first publicized, but now everybody that has studied the charges knows they're true."

"Like the so-called Russian collusion hoax that kept the country off-balance for three years."

"Exactly."

"I never bought into it for a second, sir. But some

of our extended family—my wife's and mine—vote Democrat, and they bought it hook, line, and sinker."

"What do they say now?"

"They don't talk about it. Like it never happened."

"Of course."

"Yes, sir."

"Okay, so you understand. You know what we're looking for. Suppressed stories. Cover-ups that if the public had been aware of at the time, there would have been mass hysteria."

Mitch was wearing a plaid shirt and navy-blue corduroy trousers, an attire that seemed much better suited for a cold spring morning in Michigan or Wisconsin than muggy, tropical Miami in late July.

"Not being arrogant or anything, sir. I was a chess champion in high school. I'm strategic too. I'm all over it."

"I'm not even sure we're going to use them. With everything else in the queue, I don't know that we'll have room. I'm running out of time for my slot, but I hate to leave them out. If we do use them, they'll be short. More examples of government propaganda that turned out to be true."

"Yes, sir. You know the old saying, 'Where there's smoke there's fire.'"

The next morning, Tanner picked up the single-page summary from Mitch and scanned through the headings:

Operation Paperclip: German scientists in World War II given prosecutorial immunity from U.S. Government;

Operation Mockingbird: Government eavesdropping on American journalists;

Operation Washtub: Subterfuge agents, Alaska intel gathering;

Operation Mongoose: Cuba regime-change spy operation;

Mitchell's report closed with the words, "The CIA initially denied each of these operations, calling the reports 'anti-government propaganda.'"

Par for the course, Tanner thought. What else would we expect?

That afternoon, following a quick lunch in the twelfth-floor dining room, Tanner opened his inbox and clicked on an email from Mitch:

I thought I'd follow-up on your previous request for the "Operation (fill-in-the-blank) intel briefs." Please see attached. Several other stories you might be interested in.

Tanner opened the attachment, which started with an introductory line from Mitch:

I've formatted the briefs to include the nuances listed below. Please let me know if there's any additional information you're looking for.

Governmental Agency:

Alleged Conspiracy / Wrongdoing (Crime):

Time Frame / Locale:

Response:

Summary:

Tanner gleaned through the document:

Project MKNAOMI: CIA, Army Biological Laboratory, Fort Detrick, Maryland; Summary report taken from the National Archives; Internet link, "Summary Report of CIA Investigation of MKNAOMI"— Note: This was a successor to the CIA's mind control initiative (i.e., CIA brainwashing operation).

Project MK-Ultra: CIA heart attack gun;

Church Committee: Frank Church;

Testimony of Nayirah: False testimony before

Congress to bolster Iraq War efforts;

COINTELPRO: FBI counterintelligence program;

(Note: This is a big one, Tanner. Speed forward to real time and the FBI's efforts to cast spurious allegations against domestic political and human rights organizations.)

Naval Ship Maddox / Gulf of Tonkin: False narrative accelerates U.S. involvement in Viet Nam War. See U.S. Naval Institute; Naval History "The Truth About Tonkin." (https://www.usni.org). Especially incriminating is former Secretary of Defense Robert McNamara's quote: "I learned early on never answer the question that is asked of you. Answer the question that you wish had been asked of you. And quite frankly, I follow that rule. It's a very good rule."

Operation Big Buzz: Mosquitos weaponized;

Mitch's report concluded: "As you can see from the supporting National Archive documents, the CIA conducted internal investigations into each of these operations."

Sweet, Tanner thought. Investigating their own crimes.

On Thursday morning, Tanner looked into the camera and summarized his talking points for Friday night's show. "So, there you have it, folks. Events that at the time were branded as so-called 'conspiracy theories' but are now established historical facts. Don't be fooled, friends. We're surrounded by the same level of deception now that we were then, but the primary difference is the mainstream media is complicit with the perpetrators of these crimes. Don't sit back and do nothing. Pick up your phone and call your congressional representatives. And then at the next election, vote most of these people out of office. They're the ones allowing this to happen!

"Stay tuned. Next week will be riveting. Until then, this is Tanner Johansson exposing lies and putting a spotlight on corruption and governmental malfeasance."

The taping that morning had included three separate segments from the list of CIA operations, as well as references to lung cancer and pharmaceutical companies.

"To the cynics in my audience—and I'm talking to representatives from all the legacy media outlets from RST, UVW, and XYZ who are only watching the show tonight because I have strong ratings and you're trying to figure out why—I suppose you believed the tobacco companies when they said that cigarettes weren't harmful," he said derisively. "You probably believed Big Pharma before they agreed to pay 50 billion dollars plus in state settlement funds as recompense for the opioid crisis.

"I have a question for every member of your alliance: How much money do you have?

"Why?" you ask.

"I want to know so I can tell you about the choice land I have for sale that's guaranteed to have mineral deposits. Trust me. I have a great deal to offer you.

"Friends, today, when you hear a mainstream media voice say, 'So and so's a conspiracy theorist,' or you hear an established politician say, 'This is nothing more than a conspiracy theory,' take a deep breath, let out a heavy sigh, and tell yourself, 'It must be true.'

"Have a great evening, folks. This is Tanner Johansson signing off until next week."

Chapter Six

A collage of thoughts and images raced through Tanner's mind as he ran along the Miami Beach Boardwalk: skipping rocks on the twelve-acre pond in Swan Park; his last encounter with Ezra; the bench the two men always sat on; the Arecaceae palms lining the walkway; the Anatidae Swans; the gaggle of geese congregated near the edge of the pond; a lone Great Blue Heron somehow separated from its flock; his now weekly Sunday afternoon runs along the boardwalk; the beach; the bustling coffee shops; beach umbrellas; sandcastles; the same woman with sunglasses reading a book at the same spot at the same stretch of sand for the past three weeks in a row; children playing in the sand; and young and old alike walking peacefully along the waters' gentle tide.

It was a splendid morning and a block of billowy white clouds hovered over the water today, though it had been a cloudless blue sky last week. Tanner thought about the recent Saturday afternoon family trips to

Everglades National Park, Biscayne Bay, Flamingo Park, and Vernisha's delight when she spotted a flamboyance of flamingos waddling through the grass.

"Flamboyance is the term to describe 'flock,'" Tanner explained.

"Very good," Amara said, smiling at her husband.

The brisk three- to four-mile runs along the walking path in the park—or the longer often eight- to ten-mile runs on Sunday afternoon along the boardwalk—were exhilarating and reflective, periods of relaxation juxtaposed over a relatively intense physical workout, but the times were rarely, if ever, free from thoughts of upcoming news projects or the ideology that accompanied his work. As he ran, Johansson's thoughts flashed from the scheduled segments in next week's program to conversations with Aggie and Ed Collins.

At last month's team meeting, Collins had sauntered into the twelfth-floor, ninety-seat, banquet-style conference room just as Aggie was summarizing her presentation, an itemized list of managerial action-plan directives. She looked up at Collins and said, "Is there anything you'd like to add, Ed?"

"Boys and girls," he said with his typical, condescending, 'I'm superior to each of you and don't ever forget that' phraseology, "I have two lines on my business card: Executive Director of Programming and Senior Vice President of Operations. I didn't get a dual title because I'm a sweetheart guy. I have two titles because I get things done. I make things happen, guys and gals.

"I expect the same from each of you," he added, with a pompous tone.

That afternoon, following a budget review with one of the Emerald News Media CPAs, Frank Jurgens, Aggie and Johansson crossed paths with Collins in the hallway. "Thanks for the motivational spiel at this morning's meeting, Ed. I know Tanner was impressed." Aggie turned her back to both men and rolled her eyes.

"Always here to help," Collins replied. He then looked at Johansson and grinned. "Just call me daddy," he said.

Later that week, Tanner sat at a table in the cafeteria, seated alone as was often the case, contemplating upcoming programming narratives while scarfing down a quick lunch, when Brandon Williams, Senior Sports Producer for Emerald News Media, walked up and extended his hand. "Can I join you?"

"Sure. Why not," he said, as more of a statement than a question.

Williams sat down and placed his lunch, a tray with a gourmet burger, fries, and soft drink, on the table.

"You're too young to remember, but the heavyweight champion of the world in the early sixties was from Sweden. Ingemar Johansson beat Floyd Patterson for the title in 1959 at Yankee Stadium and then lost the rematch the following year at the Polo Grounds. His name is spelled the same as yours."

"I'm familiar with Johansson. I was a fight fan growing up."

"Maybe you're related?"

"Maybe," Tanner replied. "I guess we're all related if we go back far enough. Do you remember the second Sonny Liston, Cassius Clay fight? The one with Clay standing over Liston, screaming, 'Get up!'" Tanner asked.

"Of course, I've watched it many times," Williams said.

"Was it fixed?"

"Absolutely. At the time, the whole boxing world knew it was fixed. Why?"

"Just giving you a little perspective for the next time you watch my show."

Johansson ended his weekly monologue by saying, "Some of you are thinking, 'That's all well and good, Tanner. You're telling us about things a century removed or two continents away. That could never happen here.' Well, folks, stay tuned. Next week we're going to bring things closer to home."

"Everybody worth knowing will be there—politicians, lobbyists, prominent CEOs—all the quote, unquote, 'beautiful people' in Miami. Not to mention all of our local competition. The company limo will pick you up at six-thirty sharp," Aggie had told Tanner. "I asked Aurelio to pick me up first. I'd like to see your neighborhood."

That evening, the limo arrived at 6:29 p.m. on the dot. Tanner opened the door, then turned back and gave Amara a kiss. "See you about ten. Eleven at the latest. I'll make sure I'm out of there early."

Tanner walked toward the limousine, a 1999 Rolls-Royce Park Ward edition, as Aurelio opened the driver's door, walked to the passenger side of the vehicle, and opened the rear door for Tanner, who sat down in a beige-colored leather seat opposite Aggie who was looking through a tinted window at the Johansson home. "Cute," she said. "Charming little place."

"Amara and I are thankful. It's larger than the house we had in Santa Fe."

"You'll have lots of choices if your ratings keep climbing."

"We're satisfied."

"Fame and fortune have a way of broadening one's horizons, Johansson," Aggie said and laughed.

"What does a limo like this cost?" Tanner asked, stretching his legs forward as he sat down in the spacious interior, glancing at the plush blue carpet, champagne-colored ceiling, and glossy, wood grain cabinets with beverage holders and foldout tables extending from each side of the partition separating Aurelio and a front passenger seat from the back seat compartment he and Aggie sat in. Centered between the tables, a lustrous, matching, marble-colored media console held a 12-inch television screen, radio, and cassette player.

"It was very reasonable. I negotiated the price. Not as much as you'd think," Aggie said without giving a number.

"I told one of the producers I was going to the banquet tonight and that the company limousine was picking me up. He said, 'Company limousine? That's Aggie's private limo. Picks her up in the morning, takes her home at night.'"

"You may not feel it's important, Tanner, but you'll learn. Besides, I've earned it. It's one of the perks I have for running a tight ship. Ed and Aubrey are very generous when things go as planned. Take that as a lesson."

Thirty minutes later, the limousine pulled into a circular driveway at 128 North Bay Road in Miami Beach, at the home of Sergio and Maria Cassiopeia, third generation heirs of the Spice family business empire. The 12,558-square-foot house had a white slanted exterior wall and large, granite block stones running between five and twelve feet high along the length of the entryway side of the home. The walkway was adorned with immaculate landscaping, surrounded by areca palm hedges and a row of royal   palms separating the estate from the adjacent property. At the end of the sidewalk, manning the front entryway to the home, a polite, professional looking doorman, wearing a bellhop-style uniform, stood on one side of the front door, directly across from an armed security guard in street clothes, whose stoic look balanced out any notion of mistaking the welcoming posture of his colleague for the acceptance of impropriety of any sort.

"The house sold for $38 million a few years ago. It would probably go for $55 mil today. You should see their place on Fisher Island," Aggie said, after being greeted by a familiar hostess, who said, "It's always nice to see you, Mrs. Martindale."

Agnes Martindale was as popular as she was glamorous, long being part of the "in-crowd" of Miami's movers and shakers. Her presence commanded respect from her peers in the media world, as well as from business executives in the greater Miami area, and she generally received preferential treatment from local politicians. Always impeccably dressed with matching bracelets and necklaces and earrings—tasteful displays of fashion and affluence not unlike one might see in a gathering of heads of state and other prominent settings such as the home of the Cassiopeia's—Aggie Martindale carried herself with an air of self-assurance and asserted herself in a confident, cerebral manner that seldom took a back seat in any social setting. But she was gracious and accommodating to those in positions of service.

"Thank you, Brittany. Oh, I love your hair! How did you get it to lay that way? You look wonderful this evening, dear."

"Thank you, Mrs. Martindale. You're always so kind."

"Impressive," Tanner managed to say, instantly regretting the comment, and silently chastising himself for a disingenuous accolade made for an estate, social setting, and caste of guests he disdained.

The home was an eclectic display of opulence and fashion. A stately dining room with two intricately designed crystal chandeliers imported from Prague, held a thirty-foot-long oak table, the walls decorated with French impressionist paintings by Monet on one side, and Renoir's *Dance at Le Moulin de la Galette* and Gustave

Caillebotte's *Paris Street; Rainy Day* on the opposite wall. Even distinguished guests among the high society caste of Miami would whisper, "These are originals," even though Mrs. Cassiopeia would say, "Oh my, no! These are as fine of prints as you can find, but the originals are at the Art Institute of Chicago and the Musée d'Orsay in Paris, respectively. If they ever come available, I'll be first in line."

Aggie and Tanner worked their way through several rooms of luxury and elegance toward the backside of the home, oceanfront rooms filled with windows and sliding glass walls and panoramic views of the Atlantic Ocean, exiting to a waterfront terrace where groups of people mingled at small cocktail tables, sat at lawn chairs, walked leisurely along a twenty-foot-long buffet line, some congregating in front of a guest home and adjoining sunroom. The living room was a hi-tech, contemporary display of black and white and silver and gold beams, and ceiling décor with colored artwork of squares and triangles and circles and an assortment of geometrical shapes and patterns. Playing through a sound system— that tonight, for this party, was live throughout all of the rooms that guests had access to, as well as the poolside area on the veranda and patio area—was a playlist of jazz guitarist songs from the thirties and forties.

"Stay with me, Tanner. I'll do the introductions. Everybody knows my loyalty to Ed and Aubrey. But neither of them would ever forgive me if you were recruited right under my nose. You're the new kid in town making a name for himself. I don't expect you'll get any job offers with me hovering over you."

"So, I'm more valuable than you let on?"

"The compliments would come a lot quicker if you weren't always so contrary, Johansson. Come on, let me introduce you to the powers that be. Oh, and by the way. Stay out of trouble. There are more temptations lurking in the shadows at these parties than you could ever imagine."

"That's why I stay in the sunshine," Johansson said with a charming, albeit rare, smile.

The two began mingling through the crowd stopping every five or six feet to acknowledge a guest, couple, or small group.

"Mr. Jennings heads up a lobbyist group in Washington. They have offices in New York and Chicago, and of course, beautiful Miami."

Jennings extended his hand. "I've seen your show Johansson. Interesting perspective."

"Not a fan, obviously," Tanner said to Aggie as they moved out of earshot.

"Pro-choice lobby. I didn't say that in the intro. No fights tonight, Tanner. Please," Aggie replied, emphasizing the word "please."

Johansson and Aggie worked their way through the estate house, mingling among the party's guest list, a privileged class of cultured society, stylishly dressed cosmopolites, highbrow, nose-in-the-air jet-setters peering over designer glasses dangling by gold chains.

"Tanner, I'd like you to meet Lawrence Abernathy.

Lawrence is the anchor for one of the O'Day-affiliated weekend shows in the greater Miami metroplex—"

"Statewide, Aggie," Abernathy interjected.

"Of course, Lawrence. How could I have missed that important detail? The station has made great strides with you at the helm."

Abernathy stood erect, lifted his chin, and looked intently at Tanner with both the wariness and confidence of someone looking at a rare tiger species through a three-inch-thick glass wall.

"Lawrence, this is Tanner Johansson. I'm sure you've seen his new show. Tanner has made quite a name for himself since he arrived in Miami."

Neither man extended his hand. Abernathy's stare shifted to a patronizing smile. After an awkward sixty seconds of Aggie asking Abernathy about his family, Aggie said, "Nice to see you, Lawrence. Say hi to Mattie for me."

Johansson and Aggie turned and moved toward a round table with finger foods and other hors d'oeuvres when Abernathy, suddenly emboldened, called out, "Hey, Johansson, kudos on the weekly soliloquies! I look under the bed at night, but you take fearmongering to a new level!"

Abernathy nodded in the direction of a nearby circle of associates and laughed uproariously. He could still be heard laughing as Tanner and Aggie maneuvered through a group of ladies just beyond the table, the leading talebearer in the group, an elderly woman with stark white hair and an ankle-length maroon-colored designer dress, loquaciously comparing the Spice family's fortune to the wealth of a neighboring industrial tycoon, famous for the manufacture and distribution of textiles and linens worldwide.

"Don't give him a second thought. He'd give anything to have your ratings and audience reach," Aggie said, tugging at Tanner as they approached the party's host.

"Mrs. Cassiopeia, this is our new anchor, Tanner Johansson. He's in the Friday night slot at 8:00 p.m. Tanner, Mrs. Cassiopeia is the matriarch of Spice Foods, founded by her grandfather, the renowned Albert Kostopoulos. You may have driven by his former estate in Palm Beach."

"You're as good looking in person as you are on television, Mr. Johansson," the woman said, peering over spectacles with a thin gold chain draped around her neck. "You'd make more money in the movies than Emerald News pays you, I should say. No offense, Aggie."

A cocktail server approached Tanner and Aggie as they moved toward a small group of men and women

huddled near an elaborately designed whitish, tan-colored firebrick barbecue pit.

"Our competition. Be nice, Tanner."

Aggie went around the circle, introducing the members of the group one by one, editors, producers, writers, and two newscasters.

"You're off to quite a start, Johansson," said a tall, distinguished man Aggie had introduced as Dade

McDaniel, Vice President of Programming for XLZ News in Richmond with an affiliate station in Orlando.

"We were number one in the eight o'clock time slot for 182 weeks in a row, or was it 183, Frances?" he said, looking at a woman whom Aggie had introduced as Director of Operations for the network.

"Until you came along," he continued. "Nothing wrong with a little competition to bring out the best in us, right, Frances?"

Frances, clearly uncomfortable, looked down, but then for an instant glared at Tanner with the look of a longtime manager who had been passed over for a promotion by a young, preppy-looking, twenty-three-year-old just out of college.

"He's bringing out the best in us, Aggie," McDaniel said with gusto, followed by a loud, boisterous laugh.

"I'm sure you'll recover, Dade," Aggie said, in a congenial, lighthearted tone. "Always nice seeing you, Frances."

Aggie glanced around the circle. "We'll let you get back to business," she said.

Tanner lifted his chin and flashed a condescending smile at McDaniel as they moved away from the circle.

Minutes later, Tanner glanced toward the boathouse just steps away from the sunroom and noticed a man looking intently in his direction. The man wore a white T-shirt, navy-blue blazer, tan-colored slacks, and a 1920s-style beret cap. Suddenly, the man stepped forward two steps, raised his arm slowly to shoulder level, and then brought his hand forward in pistol formation aiming straight at Johansson's gaze. The man's left eye was closed and his right eye narrowed as if he were looking through a scope. His open eye peered intently at Johansson, and then, as quickly as the exercise had begun, the pistol formation became a thumbs up, he smiled broadly, nodded his head, and smirked just as two young couples walking from the dock eclipsed his face from Tanner's view.

What was that all about, Johansson thought, slightly unnerved. "Who was that?" he asked Aggie, aware that his voice had wavered slightly when he spoke.

"His name is Max Bennett. He never misses a party. He claims to work for a lobbyist in Bethesda, but everybody knows he's intel. Don't say anything within earshot of him. Try not to get close if you can help it."

"Intel? Seriously? What's he doing here?"

"He probably likes your show," she said with a tight, nervous smile.

"I suppose," Tanner said cynically, trying to disguise a slight pang of uneasiness that momentarily engulfed him. "Is he dangerous?"

"What do you think? You didn't hear this from me. Just watch your back."

Earlier in the evening in the midst of a cacophony of voices, some supportive, others suspicious, Aggie commented, "This place is a microcosm, Johansson. With all your recent success, your critics are just beginning to come out of the woodwork. I'm sure you've thought this through. I just hope your wife can handle it. You'll have detractors and enemies galore."

At nine o'clock sharp, after mingling through a seemingly endless stream of Miami's stylishly dressed, privileged class of—in Tanner's mind—highbrow, nose-in-the-air, cosmopolites undeserving of any admiration, and after stopping and indulging at a dessert bar with dishes of crème brûlée sprinkled with raspberries, and small cups of chocolate and strawberry mousse, Aggie said, "Let's go. We're leaving early before the loose comments gain traction and go off the rails. After an hour of drinks, everybody's courage starts building. After two hours, friends and foe alike make themselves known.

"You'll be flowered with all types of suggestive, not-so-subtle comments and other forward advances. I'm going to help you stay on the straight and narrow. I'd hate to see you stray and blow up a good thing."

"Not a chance. I'm married to the most beautiful woman in the world."

What should have been a thirty-minute drive back to Tanner's house, was delayed by an accident at Monroe and Thirty-Second Street, which brought the drive to a complete standstill, disrupting Tanner's pensive mood following the party.

"I noticed you didn't have anything to drink tonight," Aggie commented. "Good for you."

"Never smoked or drank. My dad would have killed me."

"Are you serious? You've never smoked or drank? Not

once? That's remarkable!"

"I played sports in high school and college and always had jobs after school and on weekends. My teammates on the football team viewed me as a loner, kind of an outcast. I didn't really hang out, so I stayed out of trouble. I'd see kids smoking, but they weren't the ones winning track meets or scoring touchdowns. It just never appealed to me. I wanted to win. The other thing is, I didn't want to spend the money. I bought my first car when I was sixteen. That's where my money went."

"You're a good-looking guy. I'm sure you dated," she said matter-of-factly.

"Some. A little. Not much, actually. I came across as aloof and distant—don't know why." He looked at her with a wry smile. "I guess I turned a lot of people off. To this day, I have no idea why."

Aggie closed her eyes and nodded. "Of course, you don't. Yes, I'm sure it's a mystery to you."

"I had tunnel vision. I knew what I wanted careerwise. Or it least I thought I knew. My dad was an engineer. He built bridges and other complex architectural structures. I was going to follow in his steps. The reporting jobs just kind of happened."

The limousine pulled up in front of Tanner's home at exactly ten o'clock.

"This is the most cordial conversation we've ever had, Tanner," Aggie said, as Johansson exited the limo door. "I feel as if I've just had a conversation with a real person who has feelings."

Before closing the door, Tanner leaned down and said, "You realize that I could return the compliment?"

"Meaning?"

"I may have missed something, but I've yet to hear anyone at Emerald News accuse you of taking an interest in their personal life."

"Yada, yada. Get out of here, Tanner. I take care of the ones who can't take care of themselves. The little guys. The rest of you don't need my help. My job is to hold your feet to the fire and make sure you toe the line.

"I should have stopped after 'real person,'" Aggie said, waving him away. "Good night, Johansson."

Early into Tanner and Amara's marriage, his parents had visited them in Santa Fe. On their first night in town, the Johanssons went out to dinner at a popular prime rib joint. On the drive back to the young couple's home that evening, Tanner's dad quipped, "Beef's not the same in New Mexico as it is in farm country. Cattle don't respond to green chiles like they do corn." A lighthearted moment for most, but Tanner avoided lighthearted moments. Relaxed, playful moments meant letting his guard down. His empathy was conditional. He was self-examining when confronted with suffering. *Why didn't I do more?* he often asked himself. He was introspective when his children were born, determined to give his family every advantage he could. But he was only occasionally reflective about his own direction and purpose. He had tunnel vision for his causes, a take-no-prisoners approach to coming out on top, and a relentless pursuit of what he felt was truth.

Johansson held a biting cynicism toward virtually every governmental institution on the face of the globe. His distrust covered supervisors, middle managers, executives, members of the legal profession, medical practitioners, and any other person in authority that exerted control over the common man. Leftist news organizations and liberal, progressive journalists commanded a particular disdain. Coaches in high school and college had often described him as uncoachable, but he won track events and caught passes on the gridiron, so they left him alone. He trusted his parents; he had a fierce loyalty to his wife and kids. Whether it was rejection by friends in junior high, and in turn going through high school and college with no close friends, or some other psychological incident from the past that Johansson didn't acknowledge, he was usually on the fringe of relationships, seldom inside a circle, arm's length from any emotional bonds. He recognized Ezra as honest; he liked Mitch. There was a cautious and dubious respect for Aggie, only reluctantly acknowledged over a juxtaposition of skepticism.

Tanner walked briskly up the driveway, unlocked the front door, and entered the darkened vestibule, overcome by an overwhelming sense that he had shared far more about his life than he was comfortable with.

The following Monday, tired of the small talk every time he got on the elevator, Tanner took the stairwell one floor down to the cafeteria when he crossed paths with Art Goodrich, Managing Director of Media Relations.

Goodrich rolled his eyes when Tanner finished the

story. "She's about as conspiratorial as you are, Johansson. High drama every time someone blinks the wrong way. That's Aggie. That's probably why the two of you hit it off so well."

Tanner had a surprised, puzzled look, prompting a reply to his questioning expression. "Don't let her fool you. She loves the adversarial discourse as much as you do.

"You've been here for what, three, four months now? The entire team knows the two of you have a contentious relationship. She loves every minute of it. She's been with Emerald News for twenty years. Every step she's taken to the top," Goodrich said with a bemused glitter in his eyes, "has been met with, 'Yes ma'am.' Not a peep from anyone until you came along. My hat's off to you, Johansson."

"What can I say? It's the charm, comes naturally," Tanner said, with no real emotion. His surprised expression moments before was now replaced with a stoic look. "Thanks for the insight."

The two parted, Tanner still unsure what to make of the playacting from Max Bennett.

Chapter Seven

Ladies and gentlemen, the title of my monologue tonight is 'Broken Government.' I take no pleasure in what I'm about to say, but none of us are helped when we refuse to acknowledge the truth. The system is irreparably broken. And no, I'm not talking about places like North Korea where the masses view their leader as a supreme being. I'm not talking about Third World nations where governments come and go, where dictators are toppled only to be replaced by an even worse despot. I'm not talking about Middle East nations that suppress human rights or Communist countries that imprison political opponents. I'm talking about the United States of America, the place where our Founding Fathers produced the Constitution and Bill of Rights, documents we hold in high esteem.

"A few days ago, a viewer wrote in and said, 'Tanner, why are you so disparaging of our government?'

"Let me spell it out for you, friends. The system is broken. Our politicians have failed us due to a crippling entanglement of bureaucratic regulations, free-for-all spending, and incompetent oversight.

"Let's go back in time: Remember when cigarette commercials plastered every television screen in the country? With messages telling you how glamorous it was to smoke this brand or that? Some brands were even endorsed by doctors. I actually heard a government apologist say that the FDA hadn't yet recognized the harmful effects of smoking. Seriously? A decade after developing and dropping the atomic bomb, medical science was ignorant of the effects that toxins have on the lungs? These are the so-called experts?

"Let me tell you how wrong the people running this country are. Do you know that 99 percent of antibiotics, medicine we need to fight infections, are manufactured in China? What type of legislators would allow that? I suppose, people who are beholden to their donors. If Big Pharma gives you x number of dollars for your reelection campaign, you may not want to cross them during your time in office. So here we are, dependent on China, a foreign nation that by some accounts is the greatest threat to our democracy we face, to manufacture and distribute antibiotics. What happens if a war breaks out over Taiwan and we suddenly find ourselves at war with China? Should we say, 'No worries; even though we're now adversaries in war, China will still supply our prescription needs?' Right, of course, they will.

"Some of you are thinking, 'Okay, so why aren't the

pharmaceutical companies manufacturing antibiotics in the United States?'"

Tanner paused, pursed his lips together tightly, and rubbed his right thumb rapidly against his middle finger and forefinger. "Money, friends. Profits from antibiotics don't fill the coffers for anybody. There's no money in antibiotics, so Big Pharma doesn't produce them. They're content to let China have control over a critical aspect of our national health, and Congress, in a seemingly state of paralysis, fails to act.

"Since we're on the subject of China, let's talk about America's farmland. Why is China allowed to purchase our farms and croplands? Could we as citizens, or could the government of the United States, purchase land in China? I think you know the answer to that. Free enterprise doesn't mean allowing foreign entities to jeopardize our national security!

"Question: Which electronics component is used in every computerized operating system in the world? I'm referring to laptops, handheld devices, cell phones, the automobile industry, the military, medical technology equipment, the list goes on. The answer is semiconductors, and yet we're woefully dependent on Taiwan, the country we could find ourselves at odds with China on. What happens if China invades Taiwan and interrupts our ability to import these chips?

"How many of you are comfortable with China building a spy center in Cuba? Are you even aware that it's happening? Do you remember the Bay of Pigs? Has this recent danger been splashed over every mainstream media outlet in the country? Of course not! It doesn't fit their narrative. Our mainstream news agencies have become government co-ops, propaganda outlets, indoctrination centers for weak-minded listeners who accept anything they're told.

"I won't say on the air that you're naïve or unintelligent, because my executive producer would say I'm disparaging my audience, even though we know I'd only be speaking to a small fraction of naysayers who are tuned in to the show for no other reason than to find fault. What I'm talking about this evening doesn't apply to most of you because to the vast majority of my listeners tonight, common sense is a virtue you learned as a child, and to your intellectual staying power, you've never forgotten it.

"It doesn't take a physics instructor to understand that we have an emergency at our southern border.

Since the last administration took office, eight million immigrants have illegally crossed our border and been sent to municipalities throughout the country, in some instances disrupting community services and facilities at the expense of the local citizenry.

"To the affluent, liberal progressives who welcome this influx, here's my question: What if your neighborhood was affected? To those of you among us who live in expensive homes, perhaps with a spectacular mountain view or a nice view of the foothills, maybe you live near the ocean or by a beautiful lake, or maybe in a historic neighborhood with tree-lined boulevards, let me ask you this: What if a migrant shelter was built right down the block from where you live, and suddenly your cozy, secluded lifestyle was disrupted? Would you be as generous with your immigration ideology if your own neighborhood was affected?

"We all feel compassion for people seeking a better life. The entire populace understands that the United States was founded by immigrants. But who doesn't feel revolted by a system that terminates the livelihood of several thousand military personnel for not taking the Covid vaccine and then allows an unmitigated saturation of unvetted migrants to be interspersed throughout the country with no consideration of the health risks? Or national security risks, for that matter. None of us are amiss to the inconsistencies in these policies. Anyone paying attention sees what's happening. The hypocrisy is off the charts.

"I'm discussing, 'Why our system is broken; why our politicians have failed us,' if you're tuning in late, friends.

"Let's talk about government spending. I wish we had time to read, in depth, all the reports tabulating the wasteful spending our legislators are responsible for. These documents are public record, and I encourage you, as a loyal patriot, to do your homework and research this information. But here's a smidgeon: Do you remember that our government left billions of dollars of munitions and other military equipment in Afghanistan in the course of that disastrous withdrawal? We left behind tanks, helicopters, explosives, high-powered fully-automatic machine guns, and artillery shells. Billions of dollars! Who benefited from that waste? Defense contractors, of course! Ultimately the equipment needed to be replaced.

"On a routine basis, the legislative branch has out-of-control earmarks attached to government-spending appropriation bills. No one can operate a household that way. No one can operate a business that way. And yet, this is what we allow our political leaders to do.

"What should our response be? Obviously, vote them out of office! In the meantime, blow up their phones and send emails demanding change. Demand term limits. Demand a prohibition against serving in the administrative branch or Congress and then joining the boards of Big Pharma or any company associated with the military industrial complex.

"Someone might ask, 'So, who would run for office with no benefits?' The answer is, thoughtful, mindful patriots who understand their role, which is to create legislation that cares for the people, upholds the infrastructure of the country, provides a safe environment for the citizenry, enacts common sense governance, and understands that this is not a lifelong career. Listen, the salary is good even without the millionaire-making perks. Most people would be happy to earn $174,000 a year for being a member of Congress, even if they have to rent a small apartment in D.C. Along with the influence and prestige, it's not a bad gig if you can get it.

"Finally, let's talk about our national defense capabilities. Do we have an Iron Dome missile defense system?

Answer: no, we do not. Multiple sources have been reporting for the past decade or so how vulnerable we are to a bad actor detonating a nuclear bomb in our atmosphere and taking out our electrical grid. Is our government all over this? Are representatives working diligently to create a suitable defense system for this potential catastrophe? Answer: unfortunately, not. Recent polls show the approval rate for Congress at 12 percent. Why? Because our congressional leaders are so impotent that even the most basic, common sense national defense needs don't get prioritized. We need substantial, foundational change, and we need it now! Will it happen, ladies and gentlemen? Should we expect to see this change forthcoming in the days ahead? Is it just around the corner? I wouldn't bank on it, friends. To coin an old cliché, 'They're not like us.' They continue to prove Ronald Reagan's famous quote about the nine most terrifying words in the English language: 'I'm from the government, and I'm here to help.'

"There's more to come. Trust me. In the meantime, this is Tanner Johansson signing off. See you next week, friends."

At nine o'clock the next day, Tanner sat down across from Aggie for their morning meeting.

"It's nice to know you'll have a job lined up in Washington if you decide to change careers, Johansson," Aggie said sarcastically. "I'm sure the House and Senate will be battling to see who gets to host an honorary dinner party for you."

"I'm not trying to win a popularity contest."

"Obviously."

Aggie glanced at her computer. A new email from Ed Collins populated on the screen:

Congrats, Johansson hit #1 last night. Keep it going!

Aggie smiled to herself. Her bonus had just doubled.

Following a light drizzle from an hour before, the eventide held a stunning sunset of mystery and grandeur. Streaks of light pierced the blend of reddish burgundy-colored clouds creating an artist's palette splashed across the otherwise gray sky.

Five miles inland, Tanner's run, interrupted by the earlier rain, had slowed to a leisurely walk along the Miami beach boardwalk south of Surfside and Eighty-Seventh Terrace, where he had left his car and started out on what was supposed to be a ten-mile run. His thoughts turned to Ezra and their last meeting at the park.

"You said you were from Iowa originally?" Tanner asked.

"Yes, the northwest part of the state. A small town in the Iowa Great Lakes area."

"Is it still home? Do you ever think about returning?"

"In years past, I used to think about moving back, but as time went on the thought was always associated with a realization that I'd be going back to die. It's a good place, but no, it's not home anymore. This is home. My daughters are here. The ocean is nearby. I love this park.

I'll be here unless the Lord says otherwise.

"What about you? You said your family was in Santa Fe for quite a few years. Any interest in New Mexico?"

"There are some beautiful places there, but at this point in my life I would never move to a blue state. The COVID-19 restrictions solidified that. New Mexico was in the upper tier of Covid tyranny, along with New York, New Jersey, California, and Michigan." Johansson paused and looked intently at Ezra. "I would never again subject myself to that level of government overreach."

"I understand," Ezra replied. "Things were quite different in Florida."

"You referenced 'the Lord.' Are you a religious man?" Tanner asked.

"I'm a Christian. Not a perfect man, by any stretch, but Jesus Christ is the most important part of my life."

Tanner nodded respectfully. "My wife is a serious believer as well."

"And you?"

Tanner looked down and ever so quietly said, "There are a lot of things I'm not sure of anymore." Johansson gazed off toward the pond and then turned back toward Ezra. "My producer never fails to point out the flaws of politicians on both sides of the aisle. 'Who's to say who's right?' she says, typically playing an advocate and trying to counter my narrative."

"I have a spiritual view on this. If we don't have Judeo-Christian values, we have no society," Ezra said. "If Christianity isn't true, then there is no truth. If I were to ever reach that point, I don't need help from a man's philosophy. I can come up with my own opinions by myself. But let me say this clearly: I believe with all my heart that Christianity is true.

"As far as political parties go, ask yourself this: Is there an issue of good versus evil that would define which party is on the side of truth and which party supports evil? What party best represents Christian values, and which side opposes biblical truths? If we lose Judeo-Christian values, we have no society," he said.

"Again, I'm viewing this through a spiritual lens. Perhaps not in Third World countries, but certainly in the West, I believe countries often get the leaders they deserve. Any nation as self-centered and apathetic as the United States has become cannot survive. And when I say, 'apathetic,' I'm referring to a profound apathy among the masses that allows every traditional value we've ever known to be turned upside down.

"I heard your interview with the two right-to-life guests a few weeks ago, and you came across as very sympathetic. You also stated you were pro-life. I can tell you how to get abortion banned."

"I'm listening."

"Organize protests. Peaceful protests, of course. I'm not suggesting otherwise. But imagine millions of people converging on every major courthouse in the nation demanding that lawmakers outlaw this barbaric infanticide.

"Why doesn't that happen?" Ezra asked and then continued. "Thirty years ago, I would have said the reason was apathy. But the country has changed. It's more than that. Far worse than apathy, we've reached a point in society where half the country now thinks that abortion is okay. In some municipalities and states the percentage is much higher. Collectively, the American people accept abortion on demand. It should be resoundingly outlawed, but the support is not there.

"Liberals like to say, 'I go by the science.' Well, I've examined the science, and it's clear that life begins at conception. At seven weeks the baby's heart is beating, and after twelve weeks we have a fully formed child in the womb. At twenty weeks critical organs have been formed, and babies can hear their mother's voice. The fact is the United States has the most extreme abortion laws in the free world. Alaska, Colorado, the District of Columbia, Maryland, Minnesota, Michigan, Oregon, New York, New Jersey, and New Mexico have no restrictions on abortion. Vermont and Michigan have even enshrined the right to abortion—or, 'reproductive freedom' to coin the euphemism they so infamously like to employ—into their state's constitution.

"Europe prohibits abortion after fourteen weeks from conception. Our laws resemble China and North Korea. There is no denying it. The country has changed."

Ezra straightened up, and for a moment his eyes flashed a sudden indignance not seen moments before. "I feel passionately about this. Abortion is a barbaric practice. It's only possible if people are under a spell.

"Maybe we're getting what we deserve," he added.

"A society that resists the truth and no longer knows right from wrong . . ." he began and then paused, sighing deeply. "Do you realize what happens to countries that abandon truth? Countries that at one time had strong Christian values and a large population of true followers of Christ? Do you know that when those nations backslide and fall away from God's laws, that they're worse off than they were before? Jesus told of a man who was delivered of an evil spirit, but later, finding the man unoccupied, the spirit returned with seven other spirits more evil than himself. China, Russia, South Wales, now the United States, at one time had a Christian heritage but then abandoned the faith.

"The Bible says, 'Righteousness exalts a nation, but sin is a reproach to any people' (Proverbs 14:34 ESV). When you choose the side of evil, the consequences are terrible."

The old man paused and looked down. "Actually, that's true in every aspect of life, whether choosing leaders or allowing sin to go unchecked."

That evening, Tanner sat quietly at his desk and reflected on Ezra's words: "We're at a time in history when the future of our country will be determined. Nations rise and fall over the span of millennia. The earliest settlers from England, the Pilgrims and Puritans, were devout Christians, and many of the Founding Fathers were Christians. There was an understanding that they would prosper by God's grace, but there was no expectation of their survival without Him. The United States today bears no resemblance to that period in history."

From the time the children were infants, Amara refused to let the kids watch television, citing the violence and profanity. She was right, Tanner thought. He had long believed that the dramatic increase in societal crime was directly correlated to the influence of Hollywood, violent video games, and the worst drug abuse in the nation's history.

"What a travesty that abortion is one of the most divisive issues in the election. What kind of society incentivizes abortion? What an indictment against the American people," Ezra had said.

"You're an insightful man. I admire your convictions. We are in a different place spiritually, and I say that respectfully. Sometimes I wish . . ." Tanner's voice trailed off and he looked thoughtfully toward the pond, trying to determine what to say next, shifting his eyes away from Ezra's penetrating, almost piercing gaze, but the kindness in Ezra's eyes drew Tanner back, like a lost vessel at sea moving into the view of a rescuing ship.

"You offer a fresh perspective every time we talk. I do appreciate that, very much. Thank you," he said.

Ezra's eyes sparkled, and he smiled warmly. It was the happiest, most joyful expression from anyone other than Amara and the kids that Tanner could remember.

Ezra had an average build, brown eyes, a youthful face belying his age, a full head of silver hair with shiny streaks of gray and white lines, ruffled and disheveled looking on days that he wasn't in church or didn't have a doctor appointment, which was most days, and a look unheard of during his business management career. But there was no one to impress, Ezra often thought, so why be concerned?

Long after Tanner had left the park, Ezra sat on the bench with his head bowed, praying quietly. "Help me, Lord, please, even at this stage of my life to be the man you want me to be. Remove the veil of self that so often blinds me. And please, reveal Yourself to my new friend."

Chapter Eight

People who think it's okay to abort a baby moments before birth, have zero credibility with me."

"We're talking about early-stage abortions, Johansson. You're not a woman. You have no idea the challenges facing women today. I'll continue to make my views known at the ballot box, just as I should."

Tanner looked at Aggie with a stunned, almost horrified expression. "Help me understand this. So, you're a Democrat?" he said incredulously. "You're working for Emerald News Media, and you vote blue? Are you kidding me?"

"I didn't say that, but what if I was? I have bills to pay, Tanner. Ed offered me a job when I needed it the most. I knew where he stood, and he knew where I stood. The station was a lot more apolitical in those days. There's no sense in starting over at this point. Ed's been good to me. Besides, it's a well-kept secret. I would appreciate it if we could keep it that way.

"One other thing, Johansson. There are ideologues,

and there are realists. I fall with the latter. Nothing wrong with that. As they say, 'Different views make the world go round.' "

The discourse would typically have emitted, at minimum, a series of rapid-fire questions followed by their own summary statements and conclusions, or depending on his mood, a diatribe of sorts, but Tanner had an appointment which meant keeping the meeting short. As he turned to leave, he caught himself. "Nice take. I like that line: 'Bills to pay.' "

"Property tax, Tanner. If your ratings keep climbing, you'll understand that." Aggie paused and looked at Johansson, pursing her lips and lifting her head. "If you don't screw up along the way. By the way, I love the tie, Johansson. Very nineties."

"It was a gift from my dad after I landed my first gig. He said it was his favorite tie."

"Your dad had good taste, but the year is 2024, not 1995, Johansson."

Later that week, Tanner began his show by reading several comments and questions from viewers who had called or written into the station:

"Do you think the last presidential election was stolen, Mr. Johansson, and if so, what's the answer to prevent this from happening again?"

"Everyone who has been following mail-in balloting knows it was rife with fraud. Do I question the results? Of course, I do. Along with every other discerning American who's paid attention to the political scene for the last three years. What's the answer, Dean? Tight controls on mail-in balloting, the elimination of ballot harvesting, yes, you heard me correctly, no drop boxes—which we haven't had in the previous 230 plus years of presidential elections—and then a requirement for voting precincts to have their votes counted the night of the election. It can be done, Dean, but it requires good management. Something that's terribly lacking in too many states.

"Ralph Barnett writes in and says, 'You routinely point out the ineptitude of government officials, singling out Congress in particular. But what's the solution?'

"I spoke about this the other night, Ralph. The obvious solution is term limits. A seat in Congress should not be a career occupation. Following a congressional term, there needs to be a moratorium on serving on corporate boards. A term in Congress should not be a power platform. It should represent a time of service for making common sense, sound governing decisions untethered to political longevity. The salary in itself is good. Most Americans would be happy earning $174,000 a year for serving two years in the House or six years in the Senate. Maybe both branches should be six years. But then you do your job for that six-year period and then go home and run the family business or go to work in corporate America. But you don't stay in Washington and build on a platform of influence and monetary gain. So, the next question, Ralph—I knew what you were going to ask—is, why won't this be enacted? Because they won't vote on it. Why let go of a good thing if you don't have to? But we're not helpless, Ralph. If every voting citizen in the country demanded term limits, we'd have term limits.

"Susan Keller from Scottsdale, Arizona writes in, 'My husband and I enjoy your show. We think the term "conspiracy theory" is obsolete. It appears to us that we only have actual conspiracies. The question is, do we find out the truth today, a year from now, or ten years from now?'

"I couldn't agree more, Susan.

"A viewer, Eric Downey, writes in, 'Tanner, why don't you try to be a little more ingratiating to your audience. Wouldn't that reap dividends for your ratings?'

"Thanks for the question, Eric. My dad was an engineer who designed bridges. He had a reputation with his subordinates for being blunt and to the point. He used to tell people, 'I'm not here to win a popularity contest but to keep people safe.' Same thing. I don't care if someone likes me or not, Eric. My job is simply to tell the truth about what's happening.

"A viewer writes in, 'Help me understand why I should listen to a multi-million-dollar cable news anchor any more than I would listen to the autocrats you so rightly expose and condemn. Aren't you cut from the same cloth, Tanner?' The letter is signed by Jen Perry from Indianapolis, Indiana.

"Thank you for the question, Jen. If I were making a multi-million-dollar salary, you may or not have a point. In other words, if I were a philanthropist and gave away 90 percent of my earnings, you would probably hold me in high esteem, regardless of what I made. On the other hand, if I lived like a Hollywood actor surrounded by luxury and splendor at every turn, you'd have reason to question me. With that said, here's the bottom line: Until four months ago, I was a small-town journalist reporting on local government affairs in New Mexico. I was thirty years old when my wife and I bought our first home, and we needed help from my parents for the down payment. My wife and I have three kids. I won't tell you what my salary was all those years, but believe me, it was modest. To be fully transparent, Jen, I did get a raise after taking this new position, and in fairness, I'm up for a contract renewal in light of the program's success. But it will be a long time before I forget where I came from. Trust me on that.

"Finally, folks, I have a note from Lewis that says, 'How do you characterize the pundits who say there's no proof in what you're saying?'

"Ridiculously naïve, Lewis."

Tanner closed the segment with the following:

"Obviously, I can't see you. I'm in the studio, and you're in the privacy of your own home or wherever you might be watching this telecast from, but raise your hand if you remember when common sense was a governing theme for elected officials in Washington." Johansson laughed playfully. "Hmm, anyone with raised hands? Not many of you, I suspect. Yes, unfortunately for the nation, common sense seems to be just that—a distant memory for those of us who have to painfully endure the decisions coming out of Congress and this administration. Well, hop on board and fasten your seat belts, friends. We're heading to Common Sense Boulevard. Together, we're going to work to restore sound governing decisions.

"To the naysayers out there, let me close by saying, 'You figure it out.' Until next week, Tanner Johansson."

An hour later, Tanner sat down with Aggie reviewing notes from the taping. "I liked the comments from the man named Eric. Apparently, he doesn't understand how endearing you are in real life," Aggie said.

"So, we do have something in common?"

"He said he was a regular viewer. I don't know how he's missed your charming personality."

"Eric obviously isn't aware of the ratings," Tanner said smugly. "Speaking of ratings, I haven't heard any complaints from you or Collins. When did you say we were meeting on my new contract?"

"Get outa here, Tanner. Have a good day."

Chapter Nine

A number of pundits have weighed in. Several conservative news outlets have run segments over the past year, but there's still no closure. It doesn't appear the CIA is any closer to releasing the files than it was three years ago."

"Is there anything new? I hate to rehash the same old same old."

"The only thing new, and it's not really new, but last year on a podcast, RFK Jr. stated publicly that he had dinner with Mike Pompeo in Las Vegas, and intimated there were other shadowy figures present that he wouldn't reveal. He claims Pompeo told him privately that his one regret during his time at the CIA was that he didn't get rid of the top layer of CIA officials who he claimed didn't respect the Constitution."

Mitch looked down at his tablet, scrolling through his notes searching for additional details that might add to his report. "Actually, I thought this might tie in with a piece on the continual unwillingness of our governmental agencies to be forthright with the American people."

"Give me an outline. I'll send it back with questions."

The next week, at his nine o'clock meeting with Aggie, Tanner spoke passionately about Eisenhower's speech warning about the dangers of the military industrial complex, John F. Kennedy's threat to the CIA and the assassination that followed, and then finished his narrative by saying, "The Warren Commission has been discredited by everyone who has paid attention to this cover-up. Everybody knows this."

"Well, I don't know it, Tanner, and I like to think I represent the pool of people you refer to as 'everybody.'"

The following Saturday morning Ezra Townes sat at the park bench, leaning over with his head bowed and his forearms resting on his legs, when Tanner approached the small clearing facing the pond. On either side of the walkway, flower beds of pentas, lantanas, and marigolds displayed an array of late summer colors, filling the lush square mile park with tints of orange and red and pink and blue and purple and yellow and every imaginable shade in between. Madagascar periwinkle, citrus, and fig trees spotted the park with vibrant shades of browns and greens. Hydrangea trees, royal poincianas, magnolia, and sabal palmetto palms surrounded the twelve-acre pond and small cluster of benches, pavilion, and parking area that Ezra had arrived at earlier.

The old man looked up from his prayer and smiled.

"I was hoping you'd be here. Please sit down."

The men spent the next few minutes discussing Ezra's two daughters, Tanner's weekly show, their mutual appreciation for the beauty of the park they both enjoyed so much, and the sultry humidity on this beautiful but hot, muggy morning.

"I didn't like the politics, but I loved the mountains and appreciated the dry air," Tanner said. "I miss New Mexico in that regard. Not sure I'll ever get used to the humidity."

"I'd be honored if you would share a little bit about your family," Ezra said.

"I think I've mentioned that my wife's name is Amara. Her father is from Spanish descent—her paternal great-grandfather emigrated from Spain; her mother was born in Cuba. She grew up in Santa Fe, New Mexico where I was a beat reporter for a number of years. We were both in our early to midtwenties when we met. She was working as an aide to one of the House members I used to cover. I thought she was the most gorgeous woman I'd ever seen. She looks like a Spanish-Cuban aristocrat. Whenever I wanted to talk to the House member in question, I had to go through her. I finally got up the nerve and asked her to dinner, and she said yes. We were married six months later."

"Kids?"

"Yes, a boy and two girls. Mateo, he's named after his grandfather, goes by Matt, is fifteen. Floramaria, Flor, named after her grandmother, is fourteen. They just had birthdays a week apart. Obviously, Amara named the kids. Vernisha, another Cuban name, turns thirteen in a couple of months. So, we'll have three teenagers, fifteen, fourteen, and thirteen. Our first child, Aarah, we lost in a miscarriage. Her name means, 'I will see God.' We were both devastated, but we're thankful to God for the three children we have."

"You said you were thankful to God. When we last met, you expressed uncertainty about your beliefs. Are you a Christian?"

Tanner gazed off toward the pond, took a deep breath and sighed, and then looked back at Ezra, who sat quietly, respectfully, awaiting his reply.

"I grew up Protestant. My parents, and my sister and I, attended a Lutheran church when I was a kid, and I went to a small parochial school for a while in junior high. I don't consider myself religious. Amara was a practicing Catholic when we first met. I used to attend Mass with her sometimes." Tanner had been looking thoughtfully at Ezra as he spoke but now looked abruptly back toward the pond. "Not often," he added, "but I did go occasionally. In the early years of our marriage, it was more ritual and creed. She uses the word 'relationship' now when describing her faith in God. At one point she began attending a Protestant church in Santa Fe, and now she attends a small nondenominational church near the home we live in. She tries to get me to go with her, and I should, if for no other reason than for her and the kids, but work has been so intense . . ."

Tanner paused again. "In all fairness, I'm not sure

what I believe anymore."

Ezra looked down, closed his eyes, and seemed to be praying, as Tanner said softly, "I'm just not sure."

"Thank you very much for sharing. I've been praying for you and your family, and I will continue to do so."

Tanner nodded and said quietly, almost in a whisper, "Thank you."

The following Saturday, Ezra was walking toward the bench when Tanner arrived at the end of his morning jog. "You're early," Ezra said, smiling warmly.

The men sat down and Ezra starting talking. "I've been thinking about you and your family. I know you have a lot going on. Actually, I think the whole world is overwhelmed, to put it lightly. Between raising a family, trying to please the boss, working to pay the bills and put bread on the table, the average person has days when he or she can't see straight. He knows when he listens to the liberal media ruling class, that what they're telling him isn't right. He knows he's being fed propaganda, but he feels powerless. What's he going to do? He's just trying to survive. It's like you're running on the railroad tracks trying to stay ahead of the train. If you slow down and look over your shoulder, you get run over."

The old man paused and looked at Tanner. "You know all that. You're in touch with your viewers."

"Yes, but thanks. It's good to hear someone else say it. It makes me feel like I'm on the right track."

"I have a daily prayer list of people I pray for, mostly family and friends. I mentioned to you last week that I added you to my list. I'm not trying to sound pious. We all need prayer."

"Thank you so much. I appreciate your concern."

"One more thing, if I could. I know you indicated you had doubts. That you didn't know what you believed anymore. Would you mind if I sent you a Bible verse now and then?"

Tanner raised his chin and looked inquisitively at Ezra.

"I won't blow up your phone. Just a verse here and there as I feel led. If you don't want to give me your number, I understand. I can't imagine the calls and texts you must get every day. I generally get a text from one of my daughters or my doctor's office, that's about it." Ezra smiled warmly.

"Ezra, we've only known each other for a few months, but I feel like you're a true friend. Getting a Bible verse from you as you feel led would be special. It would be an honor."

Chapter Ten

D on't give me that 'aha' look, Johansson," Aggie said, brows raised, eyes flashing a red-flag signal that Tanner ignored.

"So, you think there's equal application of the law?" He looked at her with a smirk. "Let's use Hillary Clinton's private server as a litmus test. She was doing government business on a private server. After it was discovered and an investigation was underway, she destroyed over thirty thousand emails, BleachBit the hard drive of her computer, and took a hammer to her Blackberry phones to destroy the evidence. And Comey said that no reasonable attorney would prosecute this cover-up? Are you kidding me?" Johansson questioned, raising his voice in disbelief while lifting his hands in the air incredulously.

"Do you know what would have happened to you or me if we were government employees conducting business in the same manner as Hillary? Let me tell you what would have happened. We'd be in exile like Edward Snowden or locked up like Julian Assange prior to his release. There's no question about it. We'd be talking through a peephole from Attica or Great Meadow Correctional Facility."

"Calm down, that's an anomaly." Aggie rolled her eyes. "But I suppose your audience will cheer."

The following Monday, in the course of her morning walk-around, Aggie stopped at Tanner's office and stood gleaming in the doorway.

"Well, I guess you already know that your Clinton rampage went off the charts. After the spike in ad revenues the last three weeks, I thought maybe the ratings were peaking but apparently not. Ed was happy. I couldn't be prouder of you, Johansson. In spite of your adversarial tone every time we meet.

"By the way," she continued. "You mentioned Edward Snowden during your show. You realize that most conservatives hate Snowden?"

"I wouldn't say 'most.' I consider myself conservative, but who said I represent conservatives?" he shrugged. "Assange and Snowden exposed information that the electorate needed to know. The public isn't a bunch of serfs bowing to nobility."

"You understand that you're being associated with the extremist arm of the Republican party? If you go too far to the right, you lose your credibility. I don't need to tell you that once that happens you become a liability to the network."

"I thought you stopped by with commendations. Apparently not."

"Every supervisor you have had since you were hired on by Emerald News Media gave glowing reports on your work, but every single one, without fail, described you as difficult and hard to manage. After having you on board for close to five months, that's still a mystery," she said, with biting sarcasm.

"We're not the largest media conglomerate; we're not the smallest either," she continued. "But we've never had an unprofitable year, and that speaks volumes about the loyalty of our advertiser base. I intend to keep those relationships intact."

"I see the numbers. In case you've forgotten, I attend the monthly financial meetings. Year-over-year advertising dollars are through the roof. I wonder why," he said curtly.

"We appreciate what you bring to the table, Tanner. No one's disputing the impact you've had on revenues. I just don't want to see you go off the rails. You fall off, I follow along with you. That's the way it works. Forgive me for having a vested interest in your success."

Not to be outdone, Tanner slammed home his final point. "Are you looking for my resignation? Is that what you're getting at? I've got three different networks I can be on tonight, if that's what you and Collins want. Every one of them pays more than I'm making now," he said with a smirk, and started to stand up.

Aggie, who had been standing in the doorway the entire time, had a rare look of concern on her face.

"Tanner, sit down. That's not what I'm saying. We

love your work. Well, I do, anyway. Don't worry about Ed. All he sees is green, and you're giving him that. I just don't want to see you take a great opportunity and mess it up by associating yourself with the Freedom Caucus, the far right MAGAs or whatever their name is today. These people are lunatics. You know that."

"Lunatics, seriously? You're obviously missing the entire point of my show. The country needs radical change if we're going to maintain democracy as we know it. Not mere change, but radical change. Question: How bad is it? Answer: we have a corrupt intel community, a corrupt Department of Justice, a corrupt Military Establishment, a corrupt Department of Health and Human Services, a corrupt Department of Homeland Security . . . where do you want me to stop? Some of the far-right voices may seem extreme; they're firebrands, I get it. So what?"

"There are journalistic standards we need to adhere to," she countered.

"Journalistic standards? Are you kidding me? Look, the mainstream media networks aren't nonprofit organizations. They are *for* profit. Who are their donors? I'll tell you who they are. Big Pharma. If Pfizer gives one hundred million dollars to ABC, do you think ABC commentators are going to turn on them? Not a chance."

"I'm going to say it again. We don't peddle in misinformation, Tanner."

"Misinformation?" Johansson laughed, shaking his head with an incredulous look on his face. "Our media and government agencies are the biggest perpetrators of propaganda and misinformation in the history of the republic. Ninety percent of Washington D.C., and that includes the mainstream media, vote Democrat. Do you think these people are objective? Do you believe these people maintain so-called journalistic standards?"

Johansson lifted his chin, flashed an arrogant smile, and in a condescending manner that seemed to pierce through the room like a blast of wind off Lake Erie, continued. "I have some land in the Everglades that I guarantee has mineral deposits. Not just copper, iron ore, silver, and gold, but there's oil too. Any interest? I'll sell it to you for a good price."

"You don't trust anyone, do you? Good day, Tanner."

During his segment that Friday, Johansson spoke passionately as he delineated the number of times Democrats had opposed election results, and then followed up his monologue with a montage of mainstream media voices decrying the propagandist line, 'Election deniers.'

Tanner ended the segment by saying, "My own network does it too."

At their nine o'clock meeting on Monday morning, Aggie was furious. "My own network does it too?

What are you talking about?" she demanded.

Over the intercom, playing loudly and clearly throughout the tenth, eleventh, and twelfth floors of the Emerald News Media office building, a cheerful voice interrupted the employee workday with a special announcement detailing the record ratings from Johansson's Friday night show.

Johansson smiled at Aggie. "It was a great idea you had to set that up."

"Congratulations, Johansson. Again, just try to keep me off the firing line. Please, Tanner."

"Corrupt decisions are made by governments every day. Why do you think that what I said is implausible?" he asked during a meeting the following week.

"It can't happen here," Aggie replied, emphasizing the words with a tone of conviction in her voice.

"Why do you believe them? How could you possibly believe voices that are so clearly partisan?"

"Why do I believe them? What kind of question is that? I believe them because they're the experts."

"Experts?" Johansson laughed derisively. "There are no experts," he said with a sneer. "Do you remember the 'transitory' phrase? The one involving inflation? The descriptive term our so-called financial experts used to describe the fact that retail prices nationwide were increasing at an alarming rate? Or maybe you mean the experts who said that Covid came from a wet market? Oh, wait! You probably mean the ones who said that if you get the vaccine, you can't get Covid. Or how about the ones who racked up $34 trillion in national debt with no end in sight? Those experts?" Johansson started laughing. "I'll trade common sense for so-called 'expertise' any day."

On the taping that week for Friday night's show, with Aggie standing arms crossed in the production room,

Tanner hit home his point: "A business associate of mine, who will remain unnamed, believes that 'experts' are guiding governmental policy. Really? I said. Philip Tetlock, Professor at the University of Pennsylvania, did a twenty-five-year study that measured predictive outcomes. Who were his subjects? So-called, experts. Academics, economists, business executives, politicians—all so-called experts in their respective fields. The study used eighty-two thousand pieces of data, and what did Tetlock find? He found that the so-called experts were right about half the time.

"That's a flip of a coin, friends. We don't need experts who get it right half the time. You and I can do that on our own."

On Saturday morning, Ezra was sitting on the park bench when Tanner walked up. The sun shone brightly in the Miami skyline to the west, but clouds to the east hovered menacingly just above the eastern line of palm trees bordering the park.

"I grew up in Iowa. After moving to Florida, I realized that I'd been living in a climate with gray skies five months out of the year. Overcast, partly cloudy, every time I was anyplace and the sky was gray, I would say, 'Those Iowa skies.' They seem to be everywhere now. I think there's a graying of America underway."

"I'm doing a piece on global warming. What are your thoughts?" Tanner asked.

"Well, first of all, I'm seventy-five years old. I've read the Book of Revelation many times over the course of my life, and I can tell you right now, the world doesn't end from global warming."

The following Thursday morning, Tanner looked into the camera for Friday night's show. "Okay, so what about the science? Let's talk about the science. Let's talk about the so-called climate change experts, the self-appointed global warming ambassadors. Do you know how many failed climate change predictions have come from the mouths of climatologists and other global warming alarmists? Do you know how many doomsday global warming timelines have come and gone? In the 1960s we were supposedly heading for a new ice age. Fifty years later, the planet's burning up. The science has been wrong time after time, the proponents of this propaganda have been wrong over and over again.

"The first guest on my distinguished panel, Mr. Sebastian Conners, is the president of *Truth in Reporting,* a leading publication documenting failed climate change predictions. Mr. Conners, welcome."

"Thank you, Tanner. I'm going to make a bold statement, an address geared primarily to college-aged students. Young people, write this down: 'On September 15, 2024, Sebastion Conners and Tanner Johansson spoke about climate change. Conners said that in ten years there would not be one discernible difference in the state of the world due to global warming.'

"Science is continually evolving, young people. Scientific journals and academic papers are filled with theses that were once held as scientific fact but were later proven wrong. Write it down and reference your notes in ten years. Thanks for having me, Tanner."

"At this time, I'd like to introduce my next guest, Professor Arnold Peabody from the Institute of Molecular Studies and Technology. Thank you for being on the show, Mr. Peabody. What's your message for the audience tonight?"

Peabody glared at the camera and began his diatribe. " 'So you want to ban fossil fuels? Do you realize what we get from fossil fuels?' That's your argument, right? Of course, I do, Johansson! We get gas-guzzling combustion engines and diesel-fuel-polluting semitrucks filling our atmosphere with toxins! You told me that my views would be unfiltered. I could say anything I want. Well, here's my message to you: Tell your climate change deniers to go back to school!"

Without waiting for an introduction, Micah Stone, whose name quickly flashed across the screen, jumped in. "I'm glad you identified gasoline and diesel fuel as the culprits here. Let's take a deep dive for a minute. What do we get from fossil fuel derivatives? Let's start with home health care products like makeup, eye shadow, and lip gloss. Sorry, ladies, you won't be doing up your face before heading off to work this week. Soap? Sorry, guys. Your wife may be repulsed next time you want to give her a hug. How about the plastics that are part of every tool handle you've ever worked with, men? Sorry, guys, no more building and repairing for you. Vacations? You're joshing with me, right? You need tires on your automobile to drive to the Grand Canyon. Any idea where the compounds that go into tire manufacturing come from? How about driving in general? Did you learn in science class that asphalt is made from fossil fuel derivatives? What about the electrical wiring or the plumbing pipes in your home? Any idea how conduit materials are made? Or where the elements come from to make these components? You guessed it. The materials come from fossil fuels, ladies and gents. But hey, who needs these nonessentials? Throw your car keys away and go sit in a dark corner of your living room until Mr. Peabody says it's okay to resume life as we know it.

"Mr. Peabody, what concentration of carbon dioxide, how many parts of CO_2 per million does your research corroborate? I'd like to point out that a recent study on climate change by Professor—"

Peabody interrupted. "Now you're going to quote rogue scientists from unaccredited universities in the—"

"In the beltway, Mr. Peabody. Universities in the beltway. Which Midwest state are you going to disparage?"

The camera shifted to Johansson. "In closing, friends. Should we have concern for our environment? Of course. But that doesn't mean we defy common sense and destroy Western Civilization in the process. We're decades away from fossil fuel independence. Yes, you heard me correctly. Decades, plural. If green energy is the goal, transition into it by harnessing the country's one-hundred-year supply of natural gas, a relatively clean, inexpensive energy, but don't destroy the economy by going to war against fossil fuels.

"The environmentalists are the same fat cats who like to express concern for 'future generations.' How about concern for the nine million people, many of them children, who die from starvation each year? How about concern for the hundreds of thousands of people killed in wars each year? I don't see these high rollers raising the alarm bells for these victims of societal ills. Why is that? It's because these people have no real convictions. The egotistical oligarchs at the vanguard of this movement see themselves as royalty, as monarchy, as princes and kings. Preaching to the masses about climate change and riding on private jets doesn't faze them one iota. They're royalty ruling over their minions. These people have the ultimate sense of entitlement. In the end, what we're battling is progressive left-wing lunacy. Unfortunately, they have an agenda that's far beyond whether or not we drill for oil.

"At this point, if they concede anything, they've destroyed a multi-billion-dollar industry. But wait! This isn't about money. Climate change is an existential threat! Friends, who talks that way?" Johansson asked scornfully. "It's like when the Treasury secretary used the word 'transitory' to describe inflation. Before you knew it, every public official in D.C. was using the word. Embarrassing!

"My question to you is, Who would believe anything they say? Global warming is for people who need to believe in something. People that are blind.

"Until next week, friends. Tanner Johansson signing off."

Chapter Eleven

H ere's the brief, sir."
Johansson looked at the summary heading:

Matthew Graves, Department of Justice Lawyer

"Who is he?"

"I tried to give you a brief synopsis, which you'll see on the second page, but in a nutshell, Graves is the DA that critics say slow-walked the Hunter Biden investigation. I sent you the bullet points, sir. Five minutes ago."

Tanner turned back to his laptop and opened the email:

- Hunter Biden joins Burisma;
- Prosecutor General Viktor Shokin opens investigation into Burisma corruption;
- Joe Biden works with Ukrainian President Petro Poroshenko to get Shokin fired;
- Joe Biden brags about getting Shokin fired;
- 51 intel officers sign off on a document suggesting

that the laptop story may be Russian disinformation. (Note: For nuanced timelines, financial transactions, and officials named in the report see https://oversight.house.gov/the-bidens-influence-peddling-timeline/)

"The timelines are laid out chronologically in an online report from the Committee on Oversight and Accountability."

"Should have been a slam dunk," Tanner mused.

"It was the Republican House that put the story together. According to Democrats, it was partisan every step of the way. By the way, it was two years after the initial reporting before the mainstream media picked this up," Mitch added.

"One more so-called conspiracy theory that turned out to be true. We'll work the intel letter into another segment, but at this point, everybody and his brother have reported on the laptop. What else do you have?"

The following day, Mitch sat down in a chair next to the side wing of Tanner's desk. "Here's the summary, sir. Three pages of hard facts, just as you asked."

Tanner shuffled several files on his desk, glanced at a text on his phone just after the dial lit up, and then looked up at Mitch who waited anxiously, unsure of Tanner's mood this morning.

"Sorry, I'm up to my neck, Mitch. Meetings this morning with Aggie and Collins, taping the show this afternoon, and then I'm trying to get out of here early. Hopefully, leave about four. It's my anniversary. If I'm late for dinner . . . well, you understand."

"Congratulations on your anniversary, sir. I'll leave the file on your desk."

"No, read it to me. I'll catch the nuts and bolts of it while I'm organizing."

"Yes, sir."

Mitch reached for the manilla folder he had placed neatly on the desk moments before, removed the pages, and began reading:

"Setting: Chapel Hill, North Carolina;

Protagonist: Dr. Peter Daszak, President, EcoHealth Alliance;

Study: Gain of Function research;

Funding Body: National Institute of Health (NIH) headed by Dr. Anthony Fauci;

Synopsis: Allegedly, NIH funded EcoHealth Gain of Function research at the Wuhan Institute of Virology in Wuhan, China. This is the lab where many now believe the Coronavirus (COVID-19) originated. At this point, innumerable voices and organizations, including the FBI, I might add, believe the virus escaped from the Wuhan Lab. The wet market theory espoused by government officials has largely been discredited.

Initial NIH response: Denial;

Recent developments: Emails from Dr. Fauci appear to show NIH's knowledge and complicity. I should note that funding for this research has stopped. Rand Paul has exposed this and asked the DOJ to investigate."

"Good luck with that," Tanner interjected as he stuffed several folders into his briefcase. "By the way," he added, "did you personally extrapolate any of this? In other words, did you add anything questionable in your summary?"

"No, sir. It's all public record. Most of this has been reported on by multiple news organizations."

The next day, Tanner opened his inbox and went straight to an email from Mitch, sent twenty minutes earlier.

Good morning, Tanner. Hope your day is starting out well. We had talked about doing a segment on the Covid lockdowns from the average American's point of view. You wanted me to find something from an ordinary man on the street. Somebody who experienced the government overreach first hand, and what his perspective was. I did find something you might like as a 'post-pandemic, in- hindsight' piece. It might be more than you were looking for, but I'm sending you this essay (accompanying attachment) for your consideration. More thoughts at the end of my email.

Moments later, Mitch walked into Tanner's office and sat down. "I hope I'm not interrupting, sir."

"Not at all. I was just getting ready to read the essay you sent. Read it to me, if you would, Mitch. I'm buried. I need to multitask, but I'll catch the gist."

Mitch opened a manilla folder and pulled the article from the bottom of a group of neatly organized papers, each bound by a small gold-colored clasp and separated by a handwritten page of notes, and began reading.

"The title of the essay is, 'One Hundred Million American Lives.' It was written in 2020 during the height of the pandemic. It's a couple of pages long, but I'll hit some of the highlights. Here goes: 'How do the country's leading health institutions reverse their position overnight on something as basic as wearing a face covering to protect the transmission of spreading a virus? Whether you believed in masking or not, it's staggering that prominent members and representatives of U.S. and international medical and scientific governing bodies would reverse their position, virtually overnight. The virus is serious, without question, and it's tragic for all who contract it. And for those with underlying health issues, preexisting medical conditions, weakened immune systems, people in certain age groups, people in areas of the country that have been hit particularly hard—the most vulnerable—these people should be segregated to prevent them from contracting or spreading the virus. But there are a number of things that have taken place over the last two to three months that should be of grave concern to every American. There were early signs that should have alerted all of us as to the uncertain science we were hearing. In late March or early April, members of President Trump's Task Force, along with the World Health Organization, were telling the American people that they didn't need face masks. One leading WHO official, after giving his narrative against the use of face masks, actually suggested that face masks could be detrimental.

"Three points about these conflicting positions:

"One. It's beyond incredible that world health officials would defy common sense and create a narrative against the use of face masks—including a suggestion by one WHO official that use of a face mask might actually be detrimental. Something as basic as covering your face, your mouth, your nose, from the spread of a virus would be discouraged?

"Two. It's staggering that prominent members and representatives of U.S. and international medical and sci-entific governing bodies would then reverse their position, virtually overnight.

"Three. It's frightening that the American people sim-ply do whatever they're told. The term that comes to my mind is 'Pied Piper.' How do the country's leading health institutes reverse their position overnight on something as basic as wearing a face covering to protect against transmitting a virus?

"And then, in the course of this, the economy shuts

down. And if your business isn't deemed essential, the doors are closed, and you're out of business. My wife works at a local Walmart store. During the early stages of the shutdown in March and into April, when paper product aisles were being rampaged, Walmart became a bigger hub than ever. Cashiers had perhaps 150 people a day go through their lines, some of them coughing, sneezing, hacking away with colds and whatnot, and yet if you owned a small gift store or floral shop—maybe you had six people walk through your store between nine in the morning and two in the afternoon—you're closed down. But Walmart and other grocery stores became bigger hubs than they were before the pandemic started. Why didn't you hear about massive outbreaks of COVID-19 among Walmart employees nationwide?

"So, we shut down the national economy and quarantine a large segment of the population, and today there are forty million plus people unemployed. Europe and the United States followed the Chinese model—not the Swedish model, I might add.

"This is not about disregarding science, but the models which have been used to create public policy were clearly flawed, and the American people have been given a tremendous amount of misinformation. In January we were told that the virus couldn't be transmitted person-to-person. In early April, leading health experts reversed their position on face masks—literally overnight. Now we're hearing that the virus can't be easily contracted from hard surfaces. There's nothing wrong with questioning people that claim to be experts when their positions change as rapidly as they have over the past two and a half months.

"Anders Tegnell is Sweden's Chief Epidemiologist. Tegnell, early on, came to a different conclusion than Dr. Fauci, the CDC, and the WHO on several key observations involving COVID-19, and Sweden made the decision not to lockdown their economy like the United States and much of Europe. Results? The *Washington Examiner* reported on a recent Johns Hopkins University study that compared Sweden's mortality rate to the United States, showing Sweden with 39.26 COVID-19 deaths per one hundred thousand people; the United States with 29.87 deaths per one hundred thousand. The United States with extreme lockdown measures had just under ten deaths less per one hundred thousand than Sweden that didn't lock down. Sweden had just under one additional death per ten thousand people than the United States had.'"

Mitch looked up from the paper and said, "I should note that the author's website provides an update to these numbers."

Mitch resumed reading. "Again, the virus is serious, and I would hope that no one would diminish that; our hearts go out to those who have died from COVID-19. Likewise, we're saddened by those who die from cancer and heart disease and a host of other medical conditions. We're caring people. We're saddened by the loss of life. But we can't have this discussion without addressing the effect the lockdown is having on millions of people who are now out of work. People who have been devastated financially. One estimate suggested that 500 million people worldwide will be thrown into poverty as a result of closing down our economies. Now forty million plus people are unemployed. A number of these people have a spouse; a number of them have children. So, in terms of family unit size, what does that forty million number represent? One hundred million? One hundred million Americans affected by the unemployment facing our country? Much of that unemployment is due to shutting down our economy. A number of these people, a number of these one hundred million people are going to have devastating life consequences. There will be addictions—drugs, alcohol—there will be spousal abuse, child abuse, clinical depression. Some people will commit suicide. Psychologists say that one of the most traumatic things to the human psyche is the loss of a job. We lose the ability to financially take care of our spouse, our children; we're unable to pay our bills. What if 1 percent of those one hundred million people experience devastating life consequences as a result of these financial hardships? One out of one hundred people. One percent of one hundred million is 1 million. One million people that experience devastating life consequences. Millions of families will be financially devastated by the time the economy completely opens back up—assuming it does. Do you know how many deaths there are in the United States each year from lung cancer? The number is 150,000. Do you know what causes 90 percent of those deaths? Smoking. Why haven't we outlawed cigarettes?

"Even though millions of families will be financially devastated in the months and years ahead—many of the jobs won't come back, and the stimulus checks will be short-lived—the elites and the liberal media continue to resist the economy opening back up.

"Americans have every right to protest the inequalities in what states have defined as essential services. You can't operate a hair salon, but you can operate a liquor store, and you can sell marijuana. Abortion clinics have remained open in most states. Of course, people are going to take issue with that profound level of hypocrisy.

"If the leadership class of our economy—and what I mean by that phrase is salaried business managers; members of academia such as college professors, administrators, high school principals, and other administrative personnel; city, state, and federal government officials; the pastoral community at large; in other words, folks that are used to being in charge—had lost their salaries weeks ago when the rest of the country was losing their jobs, there would have been a deafening chorus of voices demanding that we reopen the economy.

"If the elites, the liberal media, and blue-state governors had their bank accounts and monthly checks taken away, the national narrative would change overnight. Many of these people could stay at home for the next two years, and it wouldn't affect them financially.

"Where is the empathy for the millions of Americans who are out of work? It certainly appears that there's more to the shutdown than simply faulty models and egregious miscalculations by scientific health officials.

"Question: How do you control the masses? Number one, take away their guns. Well, that hasn't worked.

"Two, take away their liberties. At the top of this list is the freedom for Christians to assemble and worship God. That's been underway.

"Three, take away their jobs and make them dependent on government. That, too, has been in process.

"Finally, make sure they have an ample supply of alcohol and marijuana. Keep the populace from thinking too much.

"I want to make a point here, and I'm not suggesting that we're on the verge of becoming a fascist state tomorrow, but I would like to reference Germany of the 1930s. The changes that occurred in Nazi Germany were incremental over a span of several years. Most of the population was silent—at least publicly—and accepted and acquiesced to the daily, ongoing propaganda they were being fed. Our changes have occurred with remarkable speed, in weeks, not years. The indoctrination that has taken hold in the country is staggering."

Mitch looked up from the paper with an anxious look on his face. "Your thoughts?"

"Interesting. Can we get him on the show?"

Mitch looked down, his face flushed with embarrassment. "I'd rather not be on the show, sir. Public speaking isn't my forte."

"This is your piece, Mitch?"

"Yes, sir. I was beside myself when the lockdowns

first came down the pike. My wife agreed with me, but there were plenty of family members who thought I was being subversive. I feel as if I've been vindicated."

"Very impressive, Mitch. Nice job."

Tanner was impassioned when the cameras rolled for the COVID-19 segment's taping titled, "Looking Back / What Have We Learned?"

"This evening we're going to talk about the Covid cover-up. Ladies and gentlemen, here's what we know today. Listen carefully. Hear me out, friends. We had crowded, filled-to-the-brim football stadiums in 2020 during the height of Covid, and by all statistical data, zero deaths. What does that tell you about transmission? By the way, remember the wet market in Wuhan? The place where bats initiated the spread of Covid? The official government story that was propagated relentlessly, that in tandem with mainstream media discredited as misinformation the lab leak theory? Well guess what? Everyone who has been following this story for the past four years knows clearly that the preponderance of evidence supports the notion that the virus escaped from the Wuhan Institute of Virology. Most Americans have known this for the past four years. It took two to three years for the mainstream media to get on board—they had no choice: either tell the truth or risk losing what little remaining credibility they had left—but now it's almost universally acknowledged. You figure it out.

"What else did they tell us about Covid? If you get

the vax, you won't get Covid. False. If you get the vax, you can't transmit Covid. False. What else did they say? Don't be concerned, the vax is safe. Well, not for some. A recent European report suggests millions of deaths worldwide from the vaccine. No one disputes the increase in myocarditis in young men who were given the mRNA vaccines. All of these reports should have sounded deafening alarm bells and raised glaring question marks for our so-called health experts, but too often questioning voices were suppressed.

"If you went to the doctor after experiencing severe abdominal pain, and the clinic put you through a series of tests but then gave you a wrong diagnosis three or four times, you'd say, 'I think I need to get a second opinion.' You wouldn't waste a moment—you'd look for a new medical practitioner that very day. You certainly wouldn't go back to the doctor who misdiagnosed your condition.

"If an auto repair shop technician hooked your vehicle up to a diagnostics scanner and failed to read the data correctly, you'd say, 'You know what? Respectfully, I don't think you're qualified to interpret the report your equipment just generated. I think I'll take my car somewhere else.'

"If you boarded an airplane and were sitting on the tarmac waiting for the flight to take off, and the flight attendant informed you that the pilot didn't know how to read the instrument panel, but hey, no worries, he's successfully flown and landed a number of small planes at low altitude, you'd say, 'Let me off the plane.' You would never fly with that pilot until his flight logs revealed the accepted number of flight hours, and his test scores showed a mastery of every aeronautics gauge required and essential to modern aircraft.

"Friends, the sad realty about propaganda is that oftentimes people don't remember things well. The perpetrators rely on you to forget the false statements that were made three months ago because they know we live in an age of information overload. Most of us can't keep up.

"Ladies and gentlemen, I'm talking about people who are supposed science proponents when it comes to vaccine mandates but science deniers when it comes to the conception of human life.

"On October 8, 2023, the Washington Examiner ran an article with the headline: 'Will Rand Paul get an apology from Dr. Fauci after NIH's latest admission?'

"An apology? Seriously? If this was you or me, friends, an apology would be the least of our concerns. We'd be wondering if we had postage money to mail a letter to our spouse from behind the bars we were confined to for the next thirty years!

"You can talk all day long about Covid originating from a wet market in Wuhan. A lot of people are willfully blind. Not this guy!"

Chapter Twelve

T anner jogged along the boardwalk, his mind deep in thought, racing and churning with ideas for his weekly show. A block of pastel colors settled on the horizon, a watercolor sky with splashes of reddish-orange horizontal bands resting gloriously in the clouds, but Tanner didn't notice. Instead, he thought about the news briefs he had read earlier that morning before leaving the house. He had opened the news section on his phone to a smorgasbord of colorful pictures, attractive faces, and cotton candy news briefs, snippets of stimuli that he gleaned through quickly, but it was the headlines about himself that caught his eye:

"Cynical, Young Journalist Makes a Name for Himself on Emerald Media News Outlet."

He glanced at the opening paragraph of the story:

"Conspiracy theorist journalist gets reluctant (or

forced?) endorsement from media editor to give weekly broadcasts of historical events proving conspiracies. Each broadcast is a sixty-minute synopsis of now proven conspiracies. The show has become the No. 1 rated broadcast on cablenews, the first No. 1 rating for Emerald News Media since its inception."

Tanner glanced at a second article:

"A beat reporter is given his own show and sets out to report on so-called government conspiracies that turned out to be true."

The article started out, "Or so he says!"

Johansson's thoughts shifted to his upcoming contract renewal and then to his recent conversation with Art Goodrich about a fellow journalist from a competitive station who had been reporting on government surveillance.

"So, what happened to him?" Tanner had asked.

"He basically went off the grid. They were following every move he made. Not to mention all the standard tracking devices they were using to monitor him through his car and phone. They had a profile built up that would make a family tree look sparse. Search engine results, what he ordered online, where he ate, who he hung out with, unsavory habits. Use your imagination."

"He had a past?"

"No worse than most, but enough to cause him to

back off."

Rattled, but not completely undeterred, Tanner asked, "Do you know who Realty Winner is?"

"Of course. Another example of getting crushed by the system. Take care of yourself, Johansson."

The following week, Mitch was his usual punctual self for their morning meeting, a thirty-minute planning session that preceded Tanner's morning briefing with Aggie.

"What do you got, Mitch?"

"Here's the summary you requested, sir. Every major international war in the last thirty years where the United States didn't intervene. The numbers to the right of each listed war is the death toll—military and civilian. In order, top to bottom."

Tanner scanned the list:

Rwanda: Estimates vary, but Tutsi civilian deaths at the hands of Hutu rebels range from 500,000 to as high as a million. No intervention by the U.S.

Bosnia: Over 100,000 Bosnian and Serbs were killed with over 2,000,000 people displaced. The U.S. stayed out of the conflict.

Iran-Iraq: The Iran-Iraq War began on September 22, 1980, and continued until a United Nations Resolution ceasefire was agreed upon by both sides and commenced on August 20, 1988. The war lasted almost eight years with up to 500,000 casualties. No direct intervention by the U.S.

Pakistan-India: Over 7,000 Pakistanis and Indians were killed. More telling, Pakistan's democide in 1971 is thought to have left 1.5 million casualties. No intervention by the U.S.

Armenia: The United States Holocaust Memorial Museum website reports on the Armenian Genocide that took place early in the twentieth century: "The Armenian genocide refers to the physical annihilation of ethnic Armenian Christian people living in the Ottoman Empire from Spring 1915 through autumn 1916." The site also says, "At least 664,000 and possibly as many as 1.2 million died during the genocide, either in massacres and individual killings, or from systemic ill treatment, exposure, or starvation."

"Granted, Tanner, this was before the United States entered World War I, and the logistics at that time would have made our involvement complicated. I report on this as a backdrop for the following: In excess of 100,000 Armenian Christians in the Nagorno-Karabakh region of a disputed territory with the Republic of Azerbaijan—both Armenia and Azerbaijan claim territorial sovereignty—have been displaced from their homes by Azerbaijan military forces with an unknown number of civilians losing their lives. Not only has the U.S. not intervened, the media has scarcely reported on the atrocities."

On Friday night's show, Tanner was livid: "There you have it, folks: selective outrage, selective aid, selective intervention, and selective reporting. What's the common denominator? Have you ever heard the terms, 'dollar,' 'yen,' 'euro,' 'pound,' 'yuan,'—take your pick! If there's no money in it for the military industrial complex and no payback for their hands-out enablers—can anyone say, 'Washington insiders?'—then the incentive is gone. We don't give weapons to governments unless we get something in return!"

On Monday morning, as Mitch gathered his notes together and got up to leave, Tanner said, "I meant to ask you, did you get ahold of the film writer for *Corruption*?"

"I called, but he refused to talk to me. As soon as I mentioned the network, he hung up."

"What's he afraid of?"

"Being on your show, sir."

"What about the director for *Corruption*?"

"I'm trying to get him on the show, sir. His assistant is telling me he's booked up for the next year."

"He's making excuses. Why?"

Mitch fidgeted and tried to change the subject. "What do you think about running a story on—"

"Talk to me, Mitch. What's his hang-up?"

"He thinks you're caustic, sir."

Chapter Thirteen

D o you know how many deaths have been caused by American interventionism?" Tanner looked intently into the camera, his eyes piercing the screens of a million plus viewers.

"The title of my monologue tonight is 'Wars for the Ages.'"

Johansson opened his report with a reference to State Department policies during Henry Kissinger's tenure as secretary of state: "Opposition to Kissinger's legacy and a strong condemnation of his policies have circulated among Democrat voices following his death at the age of one hundred. The most damning critiques report on his war hawk agenda in Central America and Asia. The Nixon administration with Kissinger at the helm as secretary of state, were the architects of Operation Menu, the military's carpet bombing in Cambodia. Operation Breakfast was the name given to the start-up of the campaign. They justified their actions saying that North Vietnamese were hiding in Cambodia. Death estimates range from 50 thousand to 150 thousand, many, of course, who were civilians. As an ominous sidebar, I should note that undetonated cluster bombs are still present in Cambodia's countryside today. In 1977 this indiscriminate bombing would be illegal under Article 51, Protocol 1 of the Geneva Conventions.

"Operation Barrel Roll, another innovative 'Operation' title by this duplicitous group, involved the bombing of Laos from March 5, 1964, to March 29, 1973. Reports say that 260 million bombs were dropped on Laos in a military operation that became known as 'The Secret War.' The United States never officially declared war on Laos—or Vietnam for that matter. In the end, it wasn't just the Vietnamese that faced the brunt of Nixon, Johnson, and Kissinger's wrath. Cambodia and Laos civilians, along with their homes and farms, were devastated.

"At this point, I'm sure most of you know that the United States left eighty billion dollars in weapons behind in Afghanistan, in the course of the most embarrassing military withdrawal in the history of our country—yes, even more shameful than the Vietnam withdrawal. And who did we leave those weapons in the hands of? The Taliban. The very oppressors we fought for twenty years were given tanks, helicopters, planes, machine guns, and a host of armaments to carry out oppressive jihads against the Afghan people we fought to protect. When you give the enemy a cache of weaponry, one thing you can be assured of is more wars.

"What was accomplished in Vietnam? Let me begin

by telling you what we didn't accomplish. Vietnam is not a bastion of freedom, a nation of democratic values. Vietnam is a Communist country today. During the Vietnam War years, two million Vietnamese civilians died, over a million military personnel between the North and South are dead. Over fifty thousand Americans died.

"Afghanistan is now controlled by the Taliban, leaving in the wake, thousands of dead men, women, and children. I'll never forget the tragic image of young men falling off a military plane as we left Afghanistan.

"Today, Iraq is a fulcrum of human rights abuses and is subject to Iranian influence following a war that left tens of thousands of casualties, many of them civilians, some killed in airstrikes that were covered up by the United States government. The Watson Institute for International and Public Affairs states that, quote, '432,093 civilians have died violent deaths as a direct result of the U.S. post-9/11 wars,' unquote.

"Vietnam, Afghanistan, Iraq. You'd think we'd learn our lesson, friends.

"Now we're fighting a proxy war in Ukraine, a war that has killed thousands upon thousands of Ukrainians, devastated the infrastructure of the country, cost the American taxpayer billions of dollars, and brought the world to the brink of nuclear war. If you're gullible enough to believe that Ukraine will defeat Russia, please contact me after the show. I have a timeshare on a beach in Aruba that I'll sell you for a fraction of the cost.

"In seriousness, ladies and gentlemen, I understand

fully well that most of my audience has the discernment and common sense to recognize the fallacy in what our government is doing. My sarcasm and cynicism are directed at the progressive-left extremists who have taken up abode with a military industrial complex that has long reigned supreme in the minds of many of our ruling class.

"How many of you know how the Vietnam War started? Friends, the propaganda our government told us was a lie! The second attack in what we know as the Gulf of Tonkin never happened! The United States government fabricated the story and used it as a conduit to go to Congress and get approval for the war. What was Madeleine Albright's reflection on the death toll? 'It was worth it,' she said.

"You can defend these people all day long, or you can say, 'Something is terribly wrong with what the leadership of our country is telling us.'

"Allow me to share the history of promises made to Russia regarding Ukraine and NATO. After the Berlin Wall fell, James Baker met with former President of the Soviet Union, Mikhail Gorbachev, and said the following: 'Neither the President nor I intend to extract any unilateral advantages from the processes that are taking place.' Baker went on to say, 'Not only for the Soviet Union but for other European countries as well it is important to have guarantees that if the United States keeps its presence in Germany within the framework of NATO, not an inch of NATO's present military jurisdiction will spread in an Eastern direction.' George H.W. Bush,

West German Foreign Minister Hans-Dietrich Genscher, former Chancelor of Germany Helmut Kohl, Francois Mitterrand, and Margaret Thatcher all made pledges or assurances to Gorbachev: Soviet security would not be compromised by NATO expansion. Where does this information come from, friends? These records are well documented in our own government's National Security Archive database. Ladies and Gentleman, detail is the art of performance. We have a media filled with revisionist history writers, but I believe in precise diction. Let our words mean exactly what we present them to mean.

"And now, in closing, I'd like to give you some final thoughts on the war in Ukraine: First let me say that I think Putin is a murderous thug. There's not an ounce of my being that carries the moniker, 'Putin apologist.' With that said, what was the United States' role in this? I'll tell you what it was. We wanted to weaken Russia, and so we set out to fight a proxy war against Putin through Ukraine. At what expense? A death toll of one hundred thousand Ukrainian men, women, and children, the utter destruction of Ukrainian homes and businesses in multiple cities, and the weakening of the United States in the process. Friends, as I noted minutes ago, Ukraine is not going to defeat Russia. The uniparty neocons who are complicit in this know that. And if they don't understand that, they're even more incompetent than I think they are. From Cyrus Vance to James Baker to Warren Christopher to Condoleezza Rice, to name a few, secretaries of state have engaged their Russian counterparts in diplomacy in an effort to avoid conflict, not encourage it. This war should never have begun!

"In the end, what's the plan? Wait for the entire country to be devastated and then negotiate terms? After putting billions of dollars in the coffers of munitions manufacturers?

"Wrapping up, friends, this concludes my segment on the tragic outcome for millions of people groups throughout the world at the hands of modern-day Babylon, Persia, Greece, and Rome. There is a great cost at being on the receiving end of the world's prosecutor, judge, and jury.

"Next week, I'll have a guest who advocates for war, but not just any war. Until next week, this is Tanner Johansson."

The following week, Johansson greeted renowned scholar and professor, Matthijs De Vries. "Good evening, sir. Welcome."

"Honored to be here, Tanner."

"You've written a book, titled, *History's Just Wars*, with the subtitle, *When War and Justice Unite*. Mr. De Vries, clarify for our audience, if you would, the premise of your new book."

"Thank you again, Tanner. I appreciate the opportunity to discuss the assertions laid out in my book. I'll start with a review of some of the worst atrocities over the last one hundred years and then bring my thesis to bare on the international conflicts raging across the globe this very hour, which I understand represent unjustified wars to a large swath of our audience tonight. In terms of civilian death tolls, Mao Zedong, the former President of the People's Republic of China, stands at the apex of the list. The Heritage Foundation reports, 'Mao Zedong has rightly been called the greatest murderer of the twentieth century, killing an estimated 65 million Chinese in radical Marxist experiments such as the so-called Great Leap Forward and the Cultural Revolution. Li Rui, Mao's personal secretary, admitted, "The deaths of others meant nothing to him." '

"Following the October 7, 2023, attack on Israel by Hamas, killing thirteen hundred civilians in the southern part of Israel, we're reminded once again of the horrors of Nazi Germany in World War II and the killing of six million Jews and millions of other ethnicities. No caring person can view the images from Auschwitz, Treblinka, Dachau, Buchenwald, and many other extermination camps and not be horrified at the evil brought about by Adolph Hitler and Heinrich Himmler, the Nazi Reich Leader considered to be the architect of the Final Solution, and countless other Nazi psychopaths. None of us doubt the United States' involvement in World War II, and furthermore, it's imperative that we remain steadfast in our support of Israel.

"In the former Soviet Union, Joseph Stalin's crimes are responsible for the deaths of millions of Russian dissidents and thereby classified enemies of the state. In respect to Norman M. Naimark's book, *Stalin's Genocides,* Princeton University Press writes, 'Between the early 1930s and his death in 1953, Joseph Stalin had more than a million of his own citizens executed. Millions more fell victim to forced labor, deportation, famine, bloody massacres, and detention and interrogation by Stalin's henchmen.'

"Moving to the Korean peninsula, Kim Jung Un, his father, Kim Jong-Il, and his grandfather, Kim Il Sung are responsible for the repression and deaths of millions of North Korean citizens over the past seventy-five years. Marked by some of the most inhumane and brutal ill-treatment imaginable, a spurious seven-decades-long shadow of death lays over three generations of North Korean families. Beginning with Kim Il Sung, placed into power by the Soviet Union and considered to be the founder of the Democratic People's Republic of Korea, human rights abuses included beatings, imprisonment, slave labor, and death for citizens who opposed the dictatorship of Kim Il Sung's Communist rule. Christians were killed to make way for a government that had no tolerance for religious freedom.

"Kim Il Sung's son, Kim Jong-Il, continued the tyrannical path of his father and was responsible for the persecution and repression of millions of his own citizens. From the disappearance of family members to slave labor in gulag-style prison camps to public executions, both Kim Il Sung and Kim Jong-Il are responsible for some of the worst crimes of the last one hundred years.

"In a 2004 report titled, 'An Act,' the 108th Congress reports a compendium of crimes unimaginable to free peoples in contemporary times. The report states that,

'The Government of North Korea executes political prisoners, opponents of the regime, some repatriated defectors, some members of underground churches, and others, sometimes at public meetings attended by workers, students, and public schoolchildren.'

"Kim Il Sung's grandson, Kim Jung Un, carries on where his grandfather and father before him left off. Under Kim Jong Un's reign, millions have died of starvation, been tortured, imprisoned, and killed at the hands of a dictator who governs with a ruthless and ironclad hand. Tragically, for the North Korean people, three generations of Korean families have been subjugated to some of the most egregious atrocities of the twentieth and twenty-first centuries.

"We were right to go to war against the Axis powers in World War II. It could be argued that other despots throughout history, and notably in the last century, were given free rein as the world stood by and watched while genocides unfolded and millions of civilians were killed.

"In the book of Ecclesiastes in the Old Testament, the writer tells us there is 'a time to every purpose under the heaven: a time to keep silence, and a time to speak; a time of war, and a time of peace.' There are righteous wars, Tanner. I agree with your guest; there are times in history when it would have been justified to topple evil rulers.

" 'So, what about Ukraine?' one might ask. Has Russia engaged in atrocities justifying our involvement? I would argue that they have. Many would disagree with me. Furthermore, I fully support Israel's right to defend itself. Israel's enemies have pledged Israel's destruction. These are not idle threats. I abhor civilian deaths, but there are no moral equivalencies at work here. As a case in point, an estimated 2,403 Americans were killed in the Japanese attack on Pearl Harbor with another sixty thousand military personnel dying in the Pacific Theater. Over eighty thousand people, mostly civilians, died when the United States dropped the first nuclear bomb over Hiroshima, with thousands more dying from radiation exposure in the months that followed. The bomb dropped on Nagasaki was responsible for approximately forty thousand more civilian deaths."

"Thank you, Professor De Vries." Tanner turned to his other guest. "Final thoughts, Mr. Douglas?"

"Part of the problem today is the American people no longer trust our government to make these judgments. They don't accept decisions by a leadership that they feel has lost its moral footing. I'll close my remarks by repeating what a close friend recently stated: 'Engaging in wars when we've lost our moral and spiritual compass is precipitous at best, cataclysmic and fatal at worst.'

"Sometimes in business we examine a range of outcomes when taking risks. We ask ourselves the question, What's the worst-case scenario, and can I live with the consequences? Tanner, there is no recovery from a third world war. Today the stakes could not be higher."

Chapter Fourteen

Johansson spent the evening and into the wee hours of the morning poring through Mitchell's notes. The next morning over a cup of coffee in the corner of the cafeteria, deep in thought, his mind racing over the format and content of his next show, Tanner looked up to see Aggie standing at his table.

"Can I sit down?"

"What if I said no? Would it make a difference?"

"It's always nice to see you too" she said, shaking her head. "Look, I have advertising time slots, scheduling considerations, reports to submit, and a hundred other things on my list today that you wouldn't understand. Or I should say, you couldn't care less about. I didn't ask because I enjoy your morning personality. My day includes planning for an entire team, and unfortunately what you do affects me. What are you working on today?"

"Do you know what the Great Barrington Declaration is?"

"One of those Rand Paul conspiracy theories?" She paused. "No, tell me."

"Your 'no' response reinforces where I'm going with this. Most Americans don't have a clue about the Great Barrington Declaration. Maybe one in twenty do. Actually, probably closer to one in a hundred."

"So what? You believe in far-right conspiracies.

What else is new?" Aggie said spitefully and laughed. "The elites are trying to take over the world, and they're using Covid. Give me a break."

"So, you know more than you let on. Let me ask you something. What level of due diligence have you done in examining the data surrounding the mRNA technology? Have you extensively studied the research supporting mRNA and the resulting spike protein concerns from the so-called vaccines? A better question yet would be, Do you have the scientific background that would enable you to do a forensic study of the data?"

"What's your point?" she asked impatiently.

"The point I'm making is that 99.9 percent—yes, my guess is one in a thousand—of the people who claim to quote, unquote 'follow the science' aren't qualified to make a scientific opinion as to whether or not the vaccines are helpful or harmful. Medical doctors make educated opinions, but most people simply accept what the NIH, the CDC, the FDA, or their family doctor tells them. So, the issue isn't truly following science. What we're debating here is judgment. You make a judgment as to whose medical opinion you think most represents science. You don't actually understand the science, but you believe representatives from the NIH and the CDC to be competent and truthful, or, conversely, you determine that opposing voices represent truth. In the end, you may or may not be following science. You, like the vast majority of the American people, aren't qualified to judge the so-called 'science.' The judgment you make is whether or not the bureaucracy is telling the truth or not."

"Don't condescend to me, Tanner. Your conclusion is wrong."

"Okay, so what was the point of our meeting?"

"Ed wants me to get more involved in the programming side of things. Have a little more input on what runs each week. Oversee the content before it airs. That type of thing. I agree with him."

Johansson looked at her with a blank expression.

"Nothing's going to change today. Just a heads up. At some point, I'd like a greater collaboration on some of the topics we cover."

Aggie stood up to leave. "Gotta run. Have a great day, Tanner."

On Saturday morning, Tanner sat at the park bench alone. Ezra had told him the week before that he wouldn't be coming this morning; he would be boarding Brightline and taking the train with his daughter, granddaughter, and two of his great-grandkids to West Palm Beach where Ellie was playing in a girls' softball tournament.

His thoughts were interrupted by a momentary glow from his phone, which he had placed on the bench when he sat down. He clicked on the text message icon and saw there were several new messages. The last line said, "Ezra Townes." It was the first text he had received from Ezra since giving him his number. Tanner opened the text and read the verse Ezra had forwarded:

> "Trust in the LORD with all your heart,
> And lean not on your own understanding;
> In all your ways acknowledge Him,
> And He shall direct your paths."
> (Proverbs 3:5–6 NKJV)

The book of Proverbs in the Old Testament has 31 chapters. The pages are filled with priceless wisdom. Lots of Christians (including me) have made it a habit to read one chapter a day. Just wanted to give you a gentle nudge.
Ezra

A second verse followed a few minutes later:

> "For the LORD gives wisdom;
> From His mouth come knowledge and under-
> standing; He stores up sound wisdom for the up-
> right; He is a shield to those who walk uprightly."
> (Proverbs 2:6–7 NKJV)

I appreciate our friendship. I'm praying for you.
Ezra

Tanner sat quietly, contemplating the verses Ezra had sent. He had memorized Proverbs 3, verses 5–6 when he was a child at vacation Bible school. He remembered the excitement he felt as a young boy learning lessons from the Bible, and the enthusiasm that came with sharing those stories and lessons with his sister and parents. But those memories had become distant and faraway, so long ago that they seemed like stories from another person's life. The Bible was taught at the parochial school he attended in junior high, but church was no longer part of the family's home life by the time he entered high school. What happened? he wondered. How had his life become so unsettled? How had the sense of well-being and contentedness he experienced in his youth evolve into such tightly held convictions and ideals—thoughts and emotions oftentimes agitated, frequently disquieted and restless, and always, it seemed, so far removed from the peace he felt as a child?

Tanner gazed at the pond, taking in the kaleidoscope of colors dancing on the surface of the water, brightened and sparkling from the morning sun. Across the pond an elderly couple sat on a bench, seemingly motionless as if they were captured in a moment of time in a 1920s still portrait.

Tanner thought about his youngest daughter, Vernisha, and the comment she had made the other night. "Why are you always thinking about work, Dad?"

On this Saturday morning, Johansson was unusually contemplative, thinking about time spent—or more accurately the lack of time spent—with Amara and the kids, various reporting assignments from the past fifteen years, the meaning of the Bible verses Ezra had sent, and Ezra's deeply held convictions, never far removed from the discourse the two men shared. He thought of Amara's quiet yet certain faith, and the testimony of each of the kids in the midst of attending youth groups in recent years, all three testifying to a personal relationship with Jesus. Layers of the past covered him like sheets of stacked blankets on a never-used guest room bed. What was he accomplishing? Was he making a difference in anyone's life? Did any of it really matter? Was he helping anyone?

He thought about the comment Ezra had made during their last visit in the park: "We seem to find lots of reasons why we shouldn't help but few ways on how we can help. I helped a man once who was in a tough spot. He said to me, 'I'm indebted to you a great deal.' I said, 'No, not at all. You don't owe me anything. No one does.'"

Ezra then said, "I've been given much more in this life than I'll ever be able to give back. I try to maintain a grateful heart."

Tanner's thoughts turned to the Navajo family in Santa Fe a few years before. He was standing in the waiting room of a used car dealership when a Navajo Indian family came to pick up their repossessed truck.

"They let you out, huh? Don't ever come in here threatening me. I'll have you thrown in again if you even look sideways."

"I have the money," the man said meekly.

The man behind the service desk stood up and pushed an invoice across the counter. "Twelve hundred dollars. Cash."

The Navajo man hesitated. "Twelve hundred? I was only behind two payments," he said haltingly. "My payments are four hundred. I missed two. You need eight hundred."

"I need twelve hundred. There's another four hundred for the tow truck, interest, and fees."

"I only brought eight hundred. That's all I have. I sold two cattle to get the money. Can I have my truck?" he said in a pleading, almost desperate tone.

The Navajo man's wife clutched her husband's arm, her eyes filled with fear.

"Twelve hundred. Come back when you have the money, but tomorrow the price goes up. The interest and fees accrue every day."

The man's face turned red. "We came to get our truck. Our ride's gone. We live out past Cochiti, between Peña Blanca and Kewa Pueblo. I want my truck. Please give me our truck."

"Alvin, let's go." The man's wife tugged at his arm. "Come, before anything happens." A little girl stood tightly against the knee-length, multicolored dress the Navajo woman wore. A boy about ten held the man's hand and looked fearfully at his father.

"Get out of here. Come back when you have the money," the man said scornfully and then turned his back to the family.

The couple and two children walked several steps toward the door. "We don't have a ride. He won't give us our ride," the Navajo man said to his wife.

Tanner followed the family outside and listened as they tried to determine what to do. In a surreal moment he found himself questioning the man.

"Where do you live?"

"About forty-five miles from here, southwest on Indian reservation land."

"What do you do for a living?"

"We have a few cows and goats. I do some mechanic work for friends to make some extra money."

"Do you get a government check each month?"

"Yeah, that helps too. We're never caught up. After he did this the last time, I got drunk and came for my truck. He threw me in jail for two weeks. I have to pay those charges too. It was everything I could do to scrounge up this money, and now he won't give me my truck."

"We try so hard," the woman said. She had a wrinkled but kind face. Her eyes looked like the saddest eyes Tanner had ever seen.

"What if I helped you out? Help me understand why it won't happen again next month or a few months from now."

"It won't," the man said. "I stopped drinking. We go to church now."

"Come back in the store with me," Tanner said.

Tanner walked through the lobby and approached the counter that the family had stood at minutes before. "How much do you need to get his truck back?"

"I told him twelve hundred. What, you're gonna be a hero?"

"Let me see the invoice." Tanner glanced at the document, a computerized invoice listing the business and customer name and a list of associated charges.

Fred's Auto & Truck
"Reliable Transportation for Thirty-Five Years"
1225 Mountain Heights Lane
Santa Fe, New Mexico 87502
555-505-1515

Alvin Yazzie
P.O. Box 1389
Kewa Pueblo, NM 87052
Invoice # 0946
October 22, 2021

August:	$400
September:	$400
Tow Operator:	$300
Accrued Interest:	$ 50
Miscellaneous Fees:	$ 50

"You're Fred, I assume," Tanner said.

"All sixty years of my life."

"Twelve hundred catches him up, right? When's the next payment due?"

"Ten days from now. He's over sixty days delinquent. You gonna be back here on the first of the month? Looks like you'll be spending a lot of time in my store."

"How did he accrue one hundred dollars interest and fees in sixty days? I don't believe that's legal, Fred."

"Look, buddy. I don't owe you an explanation for anything. He can run it by his attorney if he has one. You can run it by yours. I don't give a dang. I got things to do. What are we doing here?"

"Hold on, give me a second." Tanner walked over to the couple and said quietly. "I want to help. I won't be around in the future. I hope it makes a difference."

"If we have our truck, I can make a living. I'll pay you back."

"You have eight hundred, right?"

The man pulled out a brown tattered billfold and removed eight one-hundred-dollar bills. "You want the money?"

Tanner took the funds, walked back to the counter, and pulled out a credit card. "I have eight hundred in cash. Put eight hundred on my card. Twelve hundred pays his bill, the other four hundred is this month's invoice. You won't need another payment until November, right?"

"November first. I'll see you then," Fred said with a broad, sardonic smile.

"Here's my card. Hand me the keys."

Tanner motioned for Alvin. "Can you identify the keys?"

Five minutes later, Tanner and the family stood in a parking lot across the street, the truck parked in a spot Alvin had driven to after it was released from a fenced area at the back of the dealership. The little boy and girl were dancing on the sidewalk with happy expressions often seen on a schoolyard playground. The woman smiled warmly. "Thank you, sir. We will never forget your kindness."

"I'll pay you back," Alvin said.

"It's a gift. You don't have to pay me back. Stay sober. Take care of these guys," Tanner motioned to the man's wife and the two kids who were now holding their mother's hands. "You have a nice family."

Johansson's income was limited, he really didn't have the excess funds, but Amara said later, "You did the right thing. I'm proud of you." Why was he in the store that morning? He had stopped for directions and then "just happened" on the scene as it unfolded. He was there at the exact moment needed. He always felt there was something providential in the encounter.

His thoughts turned to another incident. On a cold winter night in Gallup, New Mexico, Tanner had finished a late interview with a local politician, grabbed a quick bite to eat at a diner on Coal Avenue, and was driving along E Historic Highway 66 toward the interstate on-ramp when he passed a man hitchhiking. The man was standing under a streetlight and it appeared his left leg was amputated below the knee. He was wearing a stocking cap but no coat. The temperature was twenty-three degrees, windchill minus five. Tanner pulled his car onto the shoulder of the road and waited as the man hobbled toward the vehicle.

"Where are you going?"

"Tucumcari," the man replied. "Anyplace east of here will help."

"The temperature is below zero with windchill. Why don't you wait until morning?"

"I don't have anywhere to stay."

"What were you doing here?"

"Visiting a relative, but we got into an argument. I just need to get home."

The two drove along old historic Route 66 for about a half mile, Tanner having slowed down to twenty miles per hour as he tried to determine what to do. He could take the man as far as Albuquerque and hope he got a ride the rest of the way. But it was late. He'd be taking I-25 North and leaving the man at a busy intersection at midnight. Maybe he'd get a ride, maybe not, he thought. Tanner pulled the car into a small motel parking lot on the east end of Gallup. "Look, I hate to see you hitchhiking at midnight. I'm going as far as Albuquerque, and I'll drop you off there if that's what you want to do, but I'd be glad to put you up at this motel for the night. You can take a hot shower, get some sleep, and head out in the morning. I've also got some extra clothes in the trunk you can have. What do you think?"

The man looked down and nodded.

The men walked toward the entrance of the motel

and entered the small, dimly lit lobby. Tanner reached for the silver desktop bell and pressed the button. An elderly woman appeared.

"How can I help you, gentlemen?"

"Do you have a room available?" Tanner asked. Five minutes later after paying the bill, Tanner stood in the doorway of the motel room and handed the man a box with two pairs of jeans, two shirts, undergarments and socks, items that had been boxed up to be dropped off at a clothing bank in Santa Fe, but the facility had been closed when Tanner left town that morning.

"Good luck to you," he said to the man.

Tanner thought he saw tears in the man's eyes as the door closed.

The passenger car seat was stained when Tanner opened the car door the next morning, but any obsessiveness that generally lent itself to an organized office, tidy garage work area, or immaculate car interior was put aside. There was a satisfaction that he done something for someone in need.

In the ensuing years, Tanner had often wished he had more stories like that. How can I be so consumed with my own needs and desires? he thought.

The next morning as Tanner walked along the boardwalk, there was another text from Ezra with two more passages from Proverbs:

"Keep my commandments and live,
And my teaching as the apple of your eye."

(Proverbs 7:2 NASB)

"Buy truth, and do not sell it,
	Get wisdom and instruction and
understanding."
(Proverbs 23:23 NASB)

Just wanted to give you a reminder and encourage
you to read God's Word.
Ezra

Chapter Fifteen

Tanner scanned through snippets of Mitch's summary page, brief subject titles listed in bold:

Tagged with digital identifier;

Diametric Data Transmission;

Nanotechnology Engineering;

Measurement and Transmission of Biometric Data to 3rd Party Analytics Center;

Quantum String Theory;

AI Neuralink technology breakthrough.

"We're moving too fast, Mitch. Unless you're a nuclear physicist, biologist, or computer scientist, you're not going to get it."

Mitch was emphatic. "Most of this is racing along at breathtaking speeds, and the American people don't really have a voice in it. Like the sentient robot we read about."

"You're right. Good job, Mitch. Just keep it tight. I don't want to lose everyone."

"Understood, sir."

Tanner closed the week's show with the words, "There's a handful of Silicon Valley technocrats making all the decisions about where we go with Artificial Intelligence. There are extreme dangers, to be sure. Not even the government has jurisdiction over this. You will never hear me advocate for greater government control, but we need a myriad of voices from every sector of society debating, planning, and determining how far and how fast we go with AI. The discourse needs to begin immediately. I'm afraid we're fast approaching a point of no return. Then the entire country will ask, 'Who authorized this? Who approved these decisions? How did we get here?' At that point, friends, it may be too late."

The following week, Tanner began his monologue by addressing audience members who had written or called into the station.

"A viewer wrote, 'Explain the Federal Reserve. How does it work? Where does it get its money?'

"Good question, Bonnie. Economic theory is certainly complex, but there are components within that theory that are straightforward and easy to comprehend. The problem is they fill the definitions with jargon, legalese, and other gobbledygook so that nobody has a clear understanding. The Federal Reserve was created in 1913 with the purpose of protecting the banking system. It prints money and then buys bonds from the Treasury Department who then uses the cash to sell bonds to corporate America. What's the result? A huge influx of currency into the money supply. What's the result of that? More dollars are now chasing the same available inventory of products and goods in the marketplace. Consequently, supply and demand are altered. When the demand is greater than the supply, what happens? What happens is the price of those goods increase. When you raise the price of oil, for example, transportation and production costs increase. Manufacturing and distribution prices go up, wholesaler prices jump, and the consumer pays more at the retail level. This was one of the biggest drivers of the inflation spike that began in 2021, and I hear almost no one talking about it. Biden declared war on fossil fuels day one, and this is the outcome three and a half years later.

"Will Thomas writes in, 'Do you think there should be age limits governing presidential candidates? Secondly, do you trust anyone, Johansson?'

"Good question, Will. Let me ask you, how old do you have to be to run for president?

"I'll answer that for you, Will. You need to be thirty-five years or older to be a presidential candidate. Why is that? Because our founders determined that thirty-five was the minimum age needed to give a person the maturity, knowledge, and wisdom required to hold the highest political office in the land. Conversely, Will, we all reach an age where we're no longer in the prime of life. Our faculties are diminished, both mentally and physically. Have you ever seen an eighty-year-old man playing quarterback on an NFL team? Or participating in an Olympic world championship wrestling match? How about a professional boxing title fight? We know they're not on the front lines in hand-to-hand combat—the physical strength is simply not there. But let's shift gears, Will, and approach this from an intellectual standpoint. How many eighty-year-old men design missile technologies or are put in charge of developing an aeronautics curriculum for new aircraft? Virtually none. These projects are given to men and women in the prime of life.

"I'm not disparaging anyone for their age. I'm simply explaining reality. We all slow down, Will. Eighty years old is not the optimum age to be making decisions involving our nuclear arsenal."

Moments later, a montage of portraits of former Soviet Union Politburo leaders from the seventies and eighties—Leonid Brezhnev, Andrei Gromyko, Konstantin Chernenko, Yuri Andropov—flashed across the screen. "They all look like they're one hundred years old, Will. Does anyone remember what happened to the USSR?

"To answer your second question, I'll tell you where I don't place my trust, and that's with bureaucratic institutions or political parties.

"Another viewer writes in, 'Tanner, you've been

conspicuously silent on the Trump-Biden presidential debate and ensuing fallout. What gives?'

"The debate and changes within the Democratic Party have been reported on by every major news outlet in the world, Nate. Nothing fresh to add at this point, but I will say this: No one watching conservative media clips for the past two years was the least bit surprised by the president's debate performance. I take no pleasure in saying that we've been viewing this decline for some time now.

"I disagree with this administration on virtually every significant policy decision they have made to date, but I won't attack an aging process that affects most people that live into their eighties. What I do take umbrage with is the failure of the president's staff and cabinet—people that were aware of this decline on a daily or weekly basis—to be transparent on behalf of the American people. Remember, on an international level both our allies and our enemies have had some level of awareness of the president's cognitive decline. For too long, the mainstream media in the United States failed to report on the problem. Yes, they are 100 percent complicit. Unequivocally, they bear responsibility.

" 'Tanner, it seems like there's no loyalty in the Democratic Party,' Tony Andrews writes in an email. 'As soon as Biden lost his usefulness to them, they turned on him. Talk about circling the wagons!'

"I couldn't agree more, Tony. Not a group you'd want to be in a foxhole with. More on this later, but there is one thing I'll add: President Biden being shown the door by the party's powers that be, and the ensuing rise of Kamala Harris to the Democrat's presidential nominee, is a textbook marketing and propaganda campaign unprecedented in American politics. To go from castaway vice-presidential notoriety to celebrity status in less than a month defies imagination. One more example of what a corrupt media can do.

"Another viewer writes in, 'Tanner, I listen to the talking heads on the right—night after night they're all saying the same thing. Then I listen to the talking heads on the left—they're all saying the same thing too. Sometimes one side or the other will create a montage of their competition using identical phrasing to describe a current event that's unfolding. It's clear to me these people have been given directives from corporate management and, above them, from the ownership of the station. Basically, I see different faces on different days—with only slightly different personalities, I might add—with the same messaging from the right and the same messaging from the left. Then I do an online search and find out how much money these people are making. Hundreds of thousands of dollars a year minimum, millions of dollars a year in some cases. Then the whole thing makes sense: the media participates in the ultimate play for pay scheme. My question is, Why would I think you're any different from the rest? Yours truly, Evan McCormick.'

"Well, Evan, I've addressed this in the past. At this stage of life, I'm not in the income bracket you're describing. As far as being a mouthpiece for corporate America,

I think if you listen to my shows, week after week, you'll realize I'm a lot more like you than I am them."

"Hi, Tanner. Zach Whittier from Bridgeport, Connecticut. I like your show, even though you come across as very abrasive sometimes. Maybe a new hair style might help. Try parting your hair on the left side like other influential figures."

"When I was a kid, I parted my hair on the left side with a thin, straight line—like every political despot on the globe. And yes, I'm including U.S. politicians. What do we get from these celebutantes? Jagged, crooked legislation, not straight lines. As soon as I was old enough to see who I was resembling, I changed my hairstyle, Zach."

"Hello, Mr. Johansson. Eduardo Jimenez from Tucson. Who are your favorite commentators in the media world? Is there anyone in particular that you admire?"

"I have no favorites, Eduardo. I don't look up to any of my peers, and, frankly, I hope they don't look up to me. How do I describe myself? I'm like every other American who is disgusted by what the radical leftist progressives are doing to our country.

"Tim Rollins writes in, 'Johansson, I listen to your reporting and get one perspective, but then I read or hear the facts from reputable, long-established journalists and realize you've been pulling the wool over my eyes. I think you're the one who engages in fake news. How do you respond to that assessment?'

"You're gullible, Tim. What else do you want me to say?

"Friends, in five months I've been called every foul name imaginable, but always 'conspiracy theorist.' The difference between me and well-known, so-called conspiracy theorists is that I don't speculate about the future. I only report on what's already happened. As far as whether or not current, real-time conspiracy theories are true or not, you decide. Just remember the old adage, 'Where there's smoke there's fire.'

"Those of you who have watched my show, know that I name names. I tell you what happened and who the people were that conspired to orchestrate this event or that. Obviously, there are a lot of people who aren't happy with me. So, I want to leave you with this: I'm young, healthy, and have no adverse medical conditions. I eat a Mediterranean diet, exercise regularly—I jog three or four miles several times a week with a long run on the weekend—get regular checkups, the whole kit and kaboodle. If anything happens to me, it's not a coincidence. If you read that I was taken in an unresponsive state to a hospital and the medical examiner said that hallucinogenic mushrooms or fentanyl was found in my bloodstream, know this: I'm not without fault or vice, but I've never smoked a cigarette in my life, and I don't take illicit drugs. The report won't be true.

"If you hear on the news that Johansson's Charger went up in flames, or if an eyewitness testimony states, 'I saw Johansson's body lying on the boardwalk near Miami Beach,' or a group of teenagers report that they found me lying face down in the sand ten feet in from the water, show some discernment, folks. Something's afoul in Miami."

Tanner closed the segment by saying, "I just present facts to you, friends. And within those details there's usually a storyline that paints an unsavory picture. Accept it, reject it, or spin it to fit a narrative that fits your belief system. That's your decision. Until next week, signing off, this is Tanner Johansson."

Chapter Sixteen

S o, tell me your story," Tanner said, as the men sat at their usual spot on Saturday morning. It was a splendid morning, and a colorful blend of reddish-orange hues settled just above the eastern line of palm trees beyond the pond as the sun made its rise to an early September day.

"Well, I've shared bits and pieces over the past few months. If you're interested, I'll try to fill in some of the gaps. I told you about Esther's passing. We were holding hands, and she was smiling; and then she just closed her eyes, and she was gone. We always understood that we'd see each other again, that we'd be reunited in heaven. We knew that. We had that faith our entire lives together. The Lord gave us that peace years ago.

"I have two daughters. They're as different as night and day. The oldest one went to college and now works as an administrator for a large hospital. The youngest graduated from high school and was married a year later. That's Rachel, she has three kids. Her husband is a civil engineer and makes a good salary, so, thankfully, she didn't have to work outside the home, but the kids kept her busy. She was a straight A student in high school—the oldest daughter was, too, and close to 4.0 in college—but never feels she's missed out on anything. My oldest daughter, Deborah, loves being in a professional environment, although it was challenging for her and her husband when their boys were young. Of course, all my grandkids are grown up. I have four great-grandkids at this point.

"I was a sales manager for RTD Manufacturing. Robert Thomas Downey owned the company. We were a midsized manufacturing company that built bookcases, china cabinets, staircase ornaments, and other decorative items for fancy homes. I had half the country at the peak of my career. The company had thirty-five sales reps nationwide. I had about fifteen direct reports, regional managers who reported to me. Push, push, push. The same standard for myself. My dad used to tell me, 'Don't get too puffed up. You're only as good as your last per-formance.' Mine was never good enough, or so I thought, so I kept pushing.

"I had a lot of ambition as a young man. 'Be the best you can be; be all that you can be.' Whatever the mantra was from the top motivational speakers at the time, I bought into it hook, line, and sinker. Work to achieve my full potential in everything I did, I felt that was what God wanted me to do. Climb the mountaintop; ski down the highest slope; down by three, bottom of the ninth, bases loaded and two outs—give me the bat, put me up to the plate.

"I went to church every Sunday morning, Sunday evening, and when I was in town on Wednesday nights. But I was so driven that half the time my mind was thinking about my work performance when I should have been listening to the sermon. No one in the organization needed to motivate me. I always held high expectations for myself, but in reality, in my mind, I never met those standards.

"There was a time in my life when a particular dream was really important to me. This was during a time when there were some struggles I was going through. I was experiencing some financial problems, and there were issues at work with my job. I went through a really challenging time. My numbers were bad. The metrics they used to gauge performance were suddenly unsatisfactory. The results weren't there. Things eventually turned around, but it was tough for a while.

"Looking back, it seems like we either have time or money. In our younger years we work so hard that even though we have money, we have no time. Or if something happens to our career, we have time but no money. Then you retire, and you're left with yourself. You have more time, but it's not the same.

I came to realize that if I had a beach home in the Caribbean and millions of dollars in the bank, I'd still be left with myself, with all the questions of fulfillment and inner peace, if you will, that I had when I had very little in terms of material possessions. I remember requesting prayer to a group at church about some struggles we were having. A man later wrote to me telling me he was blind, but he had been at the service when I shared my concerns. He told me he had been praying every day and that he knew God was going to help me. After I read the letter, I started crying. To think that my business concerns would warrant a blind man's prayers, was beyond humbling.

"There was another time when I really needed to hear a word from the Lord. Esther was a prayer warrior. She prayed fervently, and I got an answer. She later told me she had been praying for days, that she knew something was wrong even though I hadn't shared anything with her.

"There's a verse in Hebrews that talks about Jesus saving those who come to God through Him, and that He is always interceding before God on their behalf.

There was a time when I went through the deepest depression I had ever experienced. I remember waking up in the early hours of the night feeling in my spirit that someone had been praying for me and that the Lord had been interceding for me at the right hand of God the Father.

"I've learned that life is not a self-fulfillment exercise. Sacrifice doesn't mean giving up things to better yourself. It means surrender.

"As a young man I was very driven, much like I imagine you are. Even when things were going well, I was always striving. That drive carried into every work project I was a part of, even into my home life. When I stopped working and stopped getting an income, I felt like I was missing out on something. My daily existence seemed incomplete. And then I realized what an incredible blessing it was to be able to get up in the morning, spend time in prayer, read the Bible, and reflect on how good the Lord has been to me. There was a contentedness. I no longer look for the home runs. I've learned that progress comes in small, incremental steps, that life goes forward in sometimes unassuming ways that might seem insignificant. It's like building a house. You start with the foundation and then you build the frame. You lay the pipes, wiring, and electrical outlets before you complete the flooring and walls, otherwise you've covered up the access. Everything has a sequence.

"I think about the planning that was needed to coordinate a Billy Graham crusade. People came to hear Billy Graham, but what many people don't realize are the countless hours that went into preparing for the crusade. The commitments needed, all of the support activities from volunteers—men and women manning the gates, ushers, counselors, the janitorial staff, emergency medical technicians on standby, security personnel, and countless other activities performed by people in the background—and then, after all of that, Billy Graham preaches for thirty minutes and invites folks to surrender their lives to Jesus Christ. It was a great team effort led by God Himself. William Randolph Hearst—I don't know where he stood with the Lord, but he was used in a mighty way by God when he sent a telegraph wire to his reporters throughout the country, saying, 'Puff Graham.' The Los Angeles crusades exploded after the publicity that followed.

"I was at the crusade in 1975 in Jackson, Mississippi, when Ethel Waters sang, 'His Eye Is on the Sparrow.' I was a young man, twenty-five, twenty-six maybe, and it was something I'll never forget. I just happened to be in Jackson for my job, and Esther urged me to go. There were organizers at every level. Pastors worked together to get the word out to the greater metroplex where the crusade was being held. People distributed posters throughout the city. All the activities needed to be coordinated. Somebody spearheaded the drive to enlist and train all the support workers needed to answer phone calls seeking information. Marketing representatives called radio and television stations and local newspapers to get media coverage. I wish we had that level of coordination today in organizing prayer gatherings on a national level.

"Otherwise, without turning to God, there is no uniting the country. Politically, ideologically, philosophically, most importantly, spiritually, the divide is so wide that it's impossible to bridge. The only hope for our country is to turn to God in repentance.

"I've enjoyed writing since I was a young man. I recently published a collection of short stories with the keynote story having the same title as the book. That's the story in the book that's closest to my heart. It's called, *This Time Next Christmas.*"

"What's it about?" Tanner asked.

"It's about a man who has a goal to clean up all the clutter and distractions in his life. He's tried for years, unsuccessfully I might add, to get completely caught up

. . . his desk clear, files organized, nothing to catch up on, no pending projects, just a clean slate. But he's lost the energy. No matter how much he tries he just can't seem to get there. Basically, he's just tired. Not tired *of* life but tired *in* life. So, his son and daughter—both professional people, he's a civil engineer, she's an administrator at a large hospital—each one is married with a couple of kids, teenagers, so their lives are full. They devise a plan where they'll come and stay a week, if it takes that long, and work with him step-by-step to help him complete the project. In the end it takes four days. Lots of memories, laughter, a special time for the man and for his son and daughter. When they're done, they each get on a plane and head back to their respective homes."

"So, it's your story?" Johansson asked, intuitively.

"Yes. With some embellishments here and there that you generally have with fiction.

"I loved reading the American classics when I was in high school and college. It was only in recent years that I read *The Scarlett Letter* and *Uncle Tom's Cabin.* You know, when you read a work like that by Harriet Beecher Stowe, when you read the lofty prose and nuance and depth of feeling, it's humbling for a writer. I realize that I'll never write a piece of classic literature that captures that eloquence. So, I just accept the talents God has given me and write what He puts on my heart.

"Famous author? I suppose that would have been pretty neat fifty years ago. When you're seventy-five years old, it doesn't matter whether or not you're a famous author, a business owner, a CEO of a Fortune 500 company, or President of the United States. What matters is your relationship with the Lord.

"If Christianity isn't true, then there are no absolutes. If I were to ever reach that point, I wouldn't need help from a man's philosophy to explain life. I can come up with my own opinions by myself. But let me say this clearly: I believe with all my heart that Christianity is true.

"I appreciate being able to send you verses. I'm a serious Christian . . ." Ezra paused and looked intently at Tanner. "I hope I'm not coming across as self-righteous in any way. I'm not a perfect man. I've never pretended to be. I'm very flawed, actually. I pray for those I've hurt, and there are many instances where I've hurt people. Basically, just living for myself.

"Another passage in Hebrews speaks of 'the sin that so easily entangles us,' some translations use the word 'ensnares.' Sin is such a corruptive force. It led to man's fall from a perfect fellowship with his Creator, Almighty God, and led to him being cast out of a garden of paradise—the most idyllic, beautiful setting man has known in this world. More magnificent than the splendor of mountains, the splendor of the oceans and seas, the Grand Canyon, the rain forest, or any other awe-inspiring place in nature. Sin led to millions of deaths in World War I and World War II, the atrocities of Nazi Germany and Soviet Russia, the horrific genocides . . . you report on some of this.

"On a personal level, when I think about the seriousness of my sin, the recognition that I'll never be worthy, I can only say, 'Jesus is my righteousness.' It's staggering to think about the ramifications of sin, but He paid the price for me, dying on a cross for my sins so that I could have eternal life.

"I often pray, 'Thank You for sparing me so much pain. Please give me a grateful heart, every day and every hour.' Don't get me wrong. I've experienced grief and loss, certainly regret.

"What were the sins? Pride, ego, worry, fear, lust of the flesh, lust of the eyes, and the pride of life. Selfishness with my time, not being as loving as I should be. Some of the common sins of everyday man, but I'm more sensitive to them now than when I was younger."

"Why didn't God stop it?" Tanner asked.

"He created man in His image, to love Him, to fellowship with Him. He didn't create robots. Once sin entered mankind, a propensity toward wrong, a bent toward evil, entered humanity. But, in reality, He has intervened, time and time again. Had He not, man would have destroyed himself."

Ezra closed his eyes, bowed his head for a few moments, and then looked back at Tanner. "God has let me down easy. I'm beyond grateful.

"Even into my sixties, I used to say, 'I'm too young to get old.' Now I'm not so sure." Ezra smiled at Tanner. "The years go by faster than you can ever imagine. I remember when I was a young man, in the early years of our marriage, a woman at church telling me, 'They'll be gone before you know it.' The girls were about four or five at the time. When you hear a message like that when you're in your twenties, you can't even remotely comprehend how quickly the years will pass.

"Sometimes you hear people say, 'If I could do it all over again, I wouldn't change a thing.' Well, I would change a lot of things. I have deep regrets for the people I've hurt. Sometimes, the older you get, the more acutely you're aware of the pain you've caused others. I was so consumed by my own pursuits I rarely thought about the impact some of my decisions had on the people around me. It took me years to be readily and willingly available for the Gospel.

"Forgive me for rambling. I probably told you more than you wanted to know."

"No, not at all. I'm honored that you would share with me. You've given me a lot to think about. Thank you so much."

Ezra had shared a small portion of his life's story, a colorful patchwork, a tapestry intersecting the past and present with future hopes and dreams not yet abandoned, in the end a seamless mosaic of struggles and faith.

Velvet-colored horizontal lines formed across the pastel sky, and jagged streaks of light flashed across the ocean waves as the sun inched up over the horizon, brightening the blue waters and sending shimmers of light across the sandy beach. Tanner pulled his car into the parking lot, checked his phone for messages, and then strapped the phone to a Velcro sheath on his left tricep. He exited the vehicle, leaned against the upper driver-side door rail, and stretched both legs.

Johansson drove a black 2018 Dodge Charger, but he had grown up around Fords. His dad had restored a 1963 Thunderbird—complete with electric windows and a sliding steering column—rebuilding the engine and painting the exterior to its original salmon color. A couple of years later he restored a 1967 Thunderbird, complete with electric seats and a tilt steering wheel to give the driver more room to exit the vehicle. Roland Johansson loved the early year Thunderbirds, and though he never owned one of the classic year cars, he had a photograph of a 1955, 1956, and 1957 T-Bird on his office wall. His dad could fix anything, Johansson used to tell kids at school when he was growing up, and Tanner appreciated the hands-on mentoring he received in an apprenticeship role helping his father. Their final project was restoring a 1967 Mercury Montego MX and rebuilding the 351 Windsor engine. The car was aqua blue with a white vinyl top and the first car Tanner drove in high school before selling it and buying a 1979 Pontiac Trans Am Firebird. Old, classy cars by millennial standards that would have set some teens apart, elevated to an esteemed platform, combined with a celebrated athletic prowess in two sports, would have offered a distinction and prestige of popularity for most seniors, but Johansson rarely left the isolation of his rapidly evolving aspirations which had pushed aside the typical inclinations and enticements of many of his classmates.

It was a splendid morning, and the colorful blend of reddish-orange hues settled just above the western line of palm trees bordering the walkway as Tanner Johansson began a ten-mile run along the Miami Beach boardwalk. Eighty minutes later, after a strong eight-minute-mile run, Tanner slowed to a walk and removed his phone from the sheath strapped to his arm. He had put the phone on silent when he started his run. Four voice messages waited, two of the four from Aggie, who had also sent a text message after each call, both referencing scheduling changes for the upcoming week. There was also a text from Ezra. Tanner opened the message from Ezra and read the verse he had forwarded:

> "The law of the LORD is perfect, converting the soul;
> The testimony of the LORD is sure, making wise the simple;
> The statutes of the LORD are right, rejoicing the heart;
> The commandment of the LORD is pure, enlightening the eyes;
> The fear of the LORD is clean, enduring forever;
> The judgments of the LORD are true and righteous altogether."
> (Psalm 19:7–9 NKJV)

I just wanted to give you some perspective.
Ezra

As Tanner reflected on the passage, another verse populated on the screen:

"Thus says the LORD:

'Let not the wise man glory in his wisdom,
Let not the mighty man glory in his might,
Nor let the rich man glory in his riches;
But let him who glories glory in this,
That he understands and knows Me,
That I am the LORD, exercising lovingkindness,
judgment, and righteousness in the earth.
For in these I delight,' says the LORD."
(Jeremiah 9:23–24 NKJV)

"Now acquaint yourself with Him, and be at peace;
Thereby good will come to you."
(Job 22:21 NKJV)

I'm praying for you.
Ezra

Chapter Seventeen

Ezra Townes sat quietly in his prayer corner as the sun worked its way up in the early morning hours, glistening through the palm trees on the eastside of his property, and casting shadows through the window panes onto his dining room table. Across town, a marching band section of trombones, trumpets, and other brass and percussion instruments rehearsed at the football field of the high school five miles to the east. The years had gone by too fast—faster than he could have imagined as a young man—but now it made sense. He had shared his story with Tanner Johansson but barely scratched the surface of some of the trials and challenges that he too often reflected upon. He thought about one of the stories he had touched on with Tanner. He remembered when the girls were young, ages five and four, and he and Esther had attended a Missionary Alliance church in a small town in Iowa. An older woman at the church had said to him, "Make the best of these years. They'll be gone before you know it. You'll wake up and they'll be scattered all over the country raising their own families. You'll wonder what happened to the years." It never registered at the time. Thankfully, the girls were both nearby.

An oak-colored lectern, a gift from a pastor friend many years before, sat stately in the corner of his office. A King James Bible he had been given fifty years before sat on the lectern with the curled yellowish pages opened to Psalm 91. The Bible had a solid black cover and spine, about an eighth of an inch thick, with the title Holy Bible written in cursive on the front lower-right corner. Ezra cherished Scripture. He loved the divine symmetry seen from the Book of Genesis to Revelation, an amazing tapestry, a mosaic of truth, reaching and connecting events and people to the Creator of a vast universe, revealed wisdom of the triune God, inspired by the Holy Spirit in an overarching, magnificent plan covering eternity past and looking on to eternity future with Him.

Ezra wore an old pair of jeans, faded from the years, loosely fitting—a testament of a thin frame, fifteen pounds lighter than before retirement. He had alert, kind eyes, sometimes bright and joyful, other times filled with sadness. He still had a full head of hair, thick, silvery-gray waves pulled straight back in the front and on the sides but curled in places and swirling in a number of directions when he didn't have an appointment to keep, which was most of the time.

Ezra thought about his wife and wondered once again, where had the time gone? He moved his desk chair in front of the window and looked at the bird feeder mounted on a wooden post in the corner of the flower garden. Esther had so much enjoyed working in the yard, planting flowers, cultivating the soil, watering the plants, filling the bird bath with water, and then watching as species after species descended on the basin, some to drink, others to bathe.

What happened to the years? he thought. Life had been so vibrant, so filled with dreams and pursuits, in the past always planning, but now, no longer visionary, albeit at times his former sense of vision would have seemed grandiose to him in these moments. Some days were spent meticulously organizing books and papers and other items that at this point in his life required little attention of any kind. He would catch himself spending far more time on these activities than they warranted, and then he would leave the house, go for a walk, drive to the park, maybe grab a bite to eat at a restaurant on the way home. He missed Esther terribly, but he knew they would be reunited. Through the challenges of old age—wondering what to do, how to fill the hours, the occasional loneliness, and these concerns had not escaped him—his faith was strong.

Ezra had long had an unspoken dream that he believed God had put on his heart. The year before, it finally came to pass. He used to pray, "Why did it take so long?" But he knew the answer. He was too consumed with the cares of this life to handle the blessings that came with the answered prayer.

He had never been able to reconcile his blessings with

the struggles of so many suffering people throughout the world. His life had been more than comfortable, luxurious even, compared to the tragic stories facing so many hungry men, women, and children in impoverished nations. He lived in a nice home, enjoyed a beautiful garden, ate—by his standards—gourmet foods, marveled at the sunrise in the morning and the sunset at eventide, sat in a lovely park each Saturday morning, and enjoyed what seemed to him a botanical garden of nature's beauty.

Oftentimes, these thoughts carried over to his prayer life. When he considered the comforts of the life he had enjoyed for so many years and then contrasted those comforts with the pain and suffering and turmoil of war-torn places; when he thought about hungry children in Third World countries; when he thought of people with life threatening health conditions, it was difficult for him to ask for anything more. All of his concerns seemed so trivial in the face of so much suffering. His life had been showered with blessings at every turn. He felt like a child who been given lavish material gifts year after year and then, suddenly, he was told there would be nothing more given. What had been given was enough. "Enjoy what you have and be thankful," was the message. Yet he knew he served a heavenly Father who was the giver of glad surprises. He accepted the Bible's precious words, "Casting all your care upon him; for he careth for you" (1 Peter 5:7). And, in the midst of his loneliness, Ezra had learned to be thankful for the gray days.

Ezra marveled at the wisdom of God. He remembered

Tanner telling him that his father had been an engineer. Ezra often thought about some of the engineering achievements from the last millennia and beyond. He marveled at the design and structure of bridges and skyscrapers and levees and canals in contemporary times, the architecture of mountaintop castles, and the mystery of the great pyramids. Praise God for His wisdom and the insight He gives! he thought. He wondered what a child or even an adult from undeveloped nations might think when viewing pictures of twenty-first century America.

Ezra was amazed at the awesomeness of God.

When he was a child, he would look at a fire and ask, "Why do the flames dance and dart about?" He imagined every child had asked the same question, but he never heard the answer. He was always curious. Where do birds go to die? he wondered. They were rarely seen in their final resting state.

Ezra glanced through the room. He looked through the glass doors of the pecan-colored buffet on the dining room wall, still adorned with the same blue plates of English countryside settings. Collector plates sat on top of the buffet, and antique dishes, cups, and saucers decorated the shelves. It was understood that after his passing, any collectibles and ornaments would go to his daughters, but why wait he thought. Let them have the treasures while they were young enough to enjoy the memories they represented. But the sentiment was too much for Ezra to part with, so he hadn't followed through with emptying the cabinet, and they sat unmoved from the last spot

Esther had placed them in.

Impressionist pen and ink drawings, colored-pencil pictures of pastel colors, had not been moved from their place on the wall, remaining a testament to Esther's decorative touch; but she was also the artist, having drawn many colorful scenes that adorned the living room walls of their home and the homes of their daughters. A picture of a meadow bordered by a broken fence with an old red barn in the distance, a white country church with a cross on the steeple, a field lined with trees and a small brook with an embankment on either side winding into the distance, were among Ezra's favorites.

In the early years of their marriage, it seemed like there was no money and no time. As his career gained steam there was money but no time to enjoy it. Then you retire and you're left with yourself, he thought. You have time, but it's not the same.

"Please restore the wasted years. Please pour out special grace on those that I've hurt. On those who I could have been kinder to," Ezra prayed.

There was a vivid dream that Ezra could never shake from his heart and mind. He was walking through snowdrifts with Esther. Blinding snow hurtled at them from every direction to the point they could hardly see in front of their path. Ezra clutched her hand and held her arm to make sure she didn't fall behind, but it was becoming harder to walk as the snow kept getting deeper. Suddenly, he saw a small house in the distance. Somehow, he knew in the dream that he had the key that would unlock the door and take them into warmth and safety. They approached the steps to the door, and he reached into his pocket for the key. As he lifted his arm toward the keyhole, he stumbled in the snow and fell, losing his hold on the key, which fell from his hand and disappeared into a snowbank. Ezra frantically dug through the snow but was unable to find the key. The storm became even fiercer, and the temperatures dropped further, as he and Esther stood outside the house unable to open the door. And then he awakened. He knew the meaning of the dream. His life had been too easy, too focused on himself, too absorbed by the pursuits and self-achievements of a life centered on self. He resolved to do better with God's help. Ezra now spent more time praying for family, his daughters, his grandchildren and great-grandchildren, his friends, and others at his church who requested prayer for needed life-changing circumstances. At times he would fast, as God laid people and needs on his heart.

His mind wandered to places he and Esther had gone to in the early years of their marriage. They had always been adventurous, in their twenties once taking Amtrack from Osceola, Iowa, to New York City with no advance planning for a hotel, which they eventually found after walking the streets of Midtown Manhatton for two hours after getting off the train at Grand Central Station. Over a span of four days and four nights they climbed the crown staircase of the Statue of Liberty, ascended to the observation deck on the 86th floor of the Empire State Building, visited Chinatown, Greenwich Village, Central

Park, Saks Fifth Avenue, Tiffany's, Carnegie Hall, Radio City Music Hall, and a host of famous museums and attractions. Ezra had a special affinity for trains, and a decade later he and Esther had taken Eurail from Paris to Zurich to Salzburg to Vienna, through Prague in The Czech Republic and on to Warsaw, Poland, which served as a base for tours of Auschwitz and Treblinka and a walking tour of the Warsaw Ghetto, before flying home from Warsaw Chopin Airport to Frankfurt to Chicago. Taking a leg of the Venice-Simplon Orient Express, perhaps from Brussels to Geneva, or more adventurous yet from Budapest to Istanbul, and then embarking on a guided tour of the seven churches described in Revelation chapters 3 and 4, had long been a goal when he was younger. But now his energy level would hardly allow for an overnight stay in Orlando or Siesta Key, a favorite beach on the Gulf Coast near Sarasota.

Sometimes in the evening, he would watch a show about places in the world that he always thought he wanted to visit. "I went all over the world in a years' time, and still got to sleep in my own bed every night," Ezra would tell friends with a sparkle in his eyes.

Ezra's gaze returned to the garden outside his dining room window and the palette of colorful plants and flowers he somehow managed to maintain each year. "You've been so good to me, Lord," Ezra prayed quietly. And then he began singing, in a soft and reverential tone. "Morning by morning, new mercies I see. All I have needed, Thy hand hath provided. Great is Thy faithfulness, Lord, unto me."

Ezra bowed his head and whispered, "Thank You for Your mercy in my life, Lord. Thank You for Your grace."

Chapter Eighteen

Friends, do you know who Kendra Kingsbury is? She's a former FBI operative from Garden City, Kansas, who was given a 46-month prison sentence for having classified documents in her home. She pleaded guilty to the charges, and to be sure, over a span of years she had multiple documents at her home that were of a highly classified nature. I'm not excusing these violations; we don't want government officials randomly taking sensitive, classified information to their personal residences. We have laws in place to protect the security of these documents. What I am arguing for is equal application of these laws, which I'm dismayed to say, we do not have. In others words, these laws are enforced selectively. Hillary Clinton had over thirty-three thousand classified documents stored on a personal server—not files on the approved government secured hard drive, but rather highly classified information hanging out in cyberspace on a private sector operating system independent of the government's authorized server. Once it was discovered that she had these documents—illegally, I might add— she deleted thousands of the emails, BleachBit the hard drive of the computer in question, and then had aides take a hammer to the phones that contained some of these documents. They destroyed the evidence, and everyone who has followed this story for the past eight years, knows that it's true. What happened to Mrs. Clinton as a result of this breach? Legally, nothing; there were no legal consequences for her actions. Joe Biden had classified documents at the Penn Biden Center for Diplomacy & Global Engagement, at his home in Greenville, Delaware, and before that at a rental home in McLean, Virginia, where classified documents were exposed to his ghost-writer in the course of working on his memoir. A Special Counsel was appointed who, in his final report, said that a jury would likely find Mr. Biden too old and forgetful to hold him accountable for his actions, hence no criminal charges were filed. In contrast, former President Trump is being prosecuted for having documents at his home even though many legal scholars would suggest that this falls under the Presidential Records Act. By the way, in case you've forgotten, former President Obama had thousands of documents stored at his presidential library in Chicago for an extended period of time before they were turned over to the National Archives and Records Administration.

"On another note, friends. What if I told you that the NSA had built a database that included every phone call you had ever made, where you made the call from, who you called, how long the conversation lasted, and, that in some instances, there was a recording of the call on file? I imagine you'd be outraged. What if I told you that American troops indiscriminately unleashed fire on a group of civilians in Haditha, Iraq, killing twenty-four Iraqi civilians, and the U.S. Government covered it up? Are you aware that over 280 thousand Iraqi civilians died in this war? What if I reported intelligence data that suggested that Julian Assange was set up by our own government? My guess is that most of you would say this is information the American people need to know.

"Edward Snowden reported on the database of calls made by American citizens, and he's now branded a traitor and exiled in Russia. Julian Assange exposed war crimes and, until his recent release, was fighting extradition to the United States where he would surely have lived out his remaining years in prison.

"Folks, the Founding Fathers didn't construct a government for the purpose of spying on American citizens, they didn't give government powers to enforce regime change in sovereign countries, and they didn't give any branch of government the power or the authority to conceal these actions from the American people. Our bureaucracy has become a government within a government, answerable only to themselves.

"Edward Snowden is an American hero; Julian Assange is an international patriot. These men exposed corruption at the highest levels of government, and now they're outcasts, traitors, criminals of the worst sort.

Alexei Navalny died a tragic death in a Russian prison for speaking out against a corrupt regime. Don't let that happen to Assange or Snowden. Call your congressional representatives and demand that charges be dropped against these men, that Assange have his charges expunged, and that Snowden be released from exile. Military industrial complex neocons are not the arbiters of right and wrong and good and evil. They're also not the guardians of our Constitution. You, the American people, have authorized government to protect the populace, not persecute people. Let your voices be heard!"

Johansson suddenly paused his monologue, stood erect, pulled his head back, and feigned shock. "I feel darts being hurled at me through cyberspace. The endless-war, Patriot Act architects are saying, 'Johansson's a domestic terrorist; Johansson's dangerous. He supports insurrection and political upheaval!' No, I simply don't believe we're all serfs, here to serve the globalist monarchy on Pennsylvania Avenue. Our government does not have a right to spy on the American people. Whistleblowers that expose these crimes should not be exiled or end up in prison and have their lives destroyed and turned upside down."

The next week, Johansson, never shy, was particularly emboldened. "The Democratic Party of 2024 is the most disgraceful, shameful political party since the Democratic Party of the Ku Klux Klan era, and before that the Democratic Party of the Civil War period. The Progressive Left today is far more radical than the

McCarthy-era Communist Party, which was opposed by politicians in both parties. And yet, Republicans, the most inept, incompetent group of legislators since, frankly, I can't remember when, treat these people as if they were all elementary students on a grade school playground. Republicans are like the English who fought gentlemanly rules during combat. Friends, you don't win a fight by taking turns going on the offensive—not when the other side is street fighting. Do you remember "Gentleman" Jim Corbett? James J. Corbett was Heavyweight Champion of the World from 1892–1897. To use a sports analogy, the Republican Party today would be like Jim Corbett, while the Democratic Party would resemble the top UFC fighter in the world. What if they were both put in the ring but allowed to fight under UFC rules? It doesn't take an expert in pugilism to understand how quickly that fight would end."

Tanner closed by saying, "We're being run by a government of incompetents."

"One more thing. You mentioned Sean Davis earlier. So, what happened to him?" Tanner asked the next week, as the two men approached their cars in the parking garage a block from the Emerald News Media building. They had spoken once before in a setting not unlike today, at a similar time and in the same proximity to their cars, a brief cursory exchange scarcely above greetings, unplanned, coincidental, or so Tanner thought, with the well-dressed man suddenly asking Tanner about the ages of his wife and children. Today, he shared a story about a former reporter who had disappeared from public view. His story about government surveillance sounded eerily similar to the narrative Art Goodrich had outlined in describing the surveilling activities surrounding another journalist who had dropped out of view and been forced to take on a new identify.

"They were shadowing every move he made, monitoring him through his car and phone, all the standard tracking devices and then some. They were following his spouse, bugging his house, etcetera. Most people don't last long when those things start happening."

"He's safe now? In hiding?"

"He has a new identity."

"Do they know where he's at?"

"They don't care at this point. He's out of sight. Neutralized. No longer in the game."

"Did he have a past?"

"No worse than most, but enough to cause embarrassment at minimum, career change at worst."

"Their methods were illegal, right?"

The man looked at him with a blank stare. "Of course, they were illegal. You still don't get it, do you? Let me explain this in a way you can understand. First, there's a large group of underlings within the bureaucracy carrying out the tasks."

"Low-level employees, in other words?"

"Not necessarily. You have middle managers, lawyers, bankers, any number of people in the professional class entrusted to carry out the directives they've been given."

"What's their position on the policies?"

"They like some of the directives; they don't like others. It really doesn't matter. That's their job. They live in the suburbs, they have mortgages, car payments, some of their kids go to private schools. They do their jobs so they can keep paying their bills and maintain their lifestyle. Nobody wants to lose anything, even if they disagree. So, they carry out the orders that are issued by the idealogues—these are the people who truly believe in the cause.

"The next group has sold out. They don't have any real convictions, but they can be bought. They want the money, the power, the prestige that comes with being at the top. Above them are the lieutenants giving directives from the puppet masters.

"The cabal issues statements like, 'For the betterment of the global community at large and the well-being of the common man,' or some other song and dance word smorgasbord that crosses all the t's and dots all the i's of responsible public discourse. The real root of the message is too dark to share. I've said enough."

"So, who are the puppet masters? Tell me, you've gone this far."

"Use your imagination. You've been meeting with the old man. He can tell you."

"What are you talking about?"

"Is that a serious question? You're asking me how I know about the old man? I gotta go, Johansson. Stay safe."

With that, he was gone.

Chapter Nineteen

After an hour-long visit with Amara's mother on Friday evening, Tanner and Amara sat down for dinner at Damasia's, a quaint paladar in Little Havana. After each ordered a Cubanos and small bowl of frijoles colorados, Tanner started talking. "I've been doubting myself. What if all this is what my antagonists say? 'It's a conspiracy theory!' I hear the words screaming at me in the wee hours of the night. Last night I woke up in a cold sweat. I was in the crosshairs of an assassin, red dots darted off the walls and then settled on my chest.

"I'm standing in the line at the grocery store, and someone glances at me and smirks. I know what he's thinking: 'There's the guy who thinks the whole world is out to get him. What kind of an upbringing did he have?' Sometimes it's a cynical smile I see. Usually, it's more of a smirk. I'm weary. I can't even go to the store without someone wanting an autograph or a picture, or, if they don't like me, they create a scene. The other night, a guy got in my face and unleashed the most hateful, expletive-filled diatribe that I wouldn't wish on my worst enemy, and then he challenged me to a fistfight. I thought we were going to end up in a fight when the guy suddenly backed away. I looked over my shoulder and saw a police officer enter the store. The officer was a fan. He walked over and said, 'Thanks for everything you do, Mr. Johansson.' The guy who wanted to fight disappeared."

Tanner sighed, pursed his lips, and gazed thoughtfully toward the mural on the opposite side of the dining room, a picture of a matador standing gallantly in a large coliseum, taking in the cheers of an animated crowd as he awaited an unknown fate. "It's that kind of stuff, ranging from adoration—which I don't need, by the way—to hostility from people I've never seen before, at this point, day in and day out it seems. It happens more often than it used to. It didn't bother me early on, but now it's getting to me."

"Maybe God has something else for us, Tanner. We don't need the new contract. I'll get a part-time job if need be."

Tanner reached out and took Amara's hands. His eyes revealed a sense of fear he had felt frequently as of late, an emotion he had despised and resisted throughout much of his life. "I don't know what's true anymore," he said softly.

That Sunday, unable to sleep, he arose at 5:00 a.m., left Amara a note, drove to a public parking area near Indian Beach Park, walked a block to the boardwalk, and then set out on a five-mile run in the darkened early morning, the only lights coming from the lampposts situated along the boardwalk every twenty yards or so. After five miles, he slowed to a walk and removed his phone from the sheath on his arm. There were no voice messages, but Amara and Ezra had each sent a text.

The whole world's up early, Tanner thought. Well, at least the ones I lean on the most.

Tanner looked at the note from Amara.

We'll be leaving for the early service a little later, and then over to Ama's. See you this afternoon. I love you! Amara

Three red hearts were placed prominently between "I love you!" and "Amara."

The text from Ezra said:

When we met yesterday, you were asking about truth and wisdom. I think you said, "In the end, who really knows what's right?" I wanted to share a well-known Bible verse with you:

"The fear of the LORD is the beginning of wisdom,
And the knowledge of the Holy One is understanding."
(Proverbs 9:10 NASB)

I like the way *The Living Bible* paraphrases this

verse:

> *"For the reverence and fear of God are basic*
> *to all wisdom. Knowing God results in every*
> *other kind of understanding."*
> (Proverbs 9:10 TLB)

I hope this helps.
Ezra.

Tanner scrolled up on his phone and realized there was an earlier text from Ezra he had missed.

Please see the Scripture passage below. A warning but also a blessing. God has made Himself known to man.

> "For the wrath of God is revealed from heaven
> against all ungodliness and unrighteousness of
> men, who suppress the truth in unrighteousness,
> because what may be known of God is manifest
> in them, for God has shown it to them. For since
> the creation of the world His invisible attributes
> are clearly seen, being understood by the things
> that are made, even His eternal power and
> Godhead, so that they are without excuse."
> (Romans 1:18–20 NKJV)

In the depths of our being, deep in the soul, every man or woman knows there is a God who created the universe.
Ezra

Tanner read the verse a second time. There were incidents from the past that he couldn't explain. He remembered driving through a blinding rainstorm just south of Emporia, Kansas, when the kids were young. He had taken Amara on a vacation and revisited the news station in Topeka where he had gotten his start in the news business. At one point, the rain was coming down so hard he was afraid the car would hydroplane or that he would lose control and go off the embankment. Out of the corner of his eye he caught Amara, head bowed, clutching Flor's hand, and faintly heard the words, "Please help us, dear God." Moments later, the rain stopped.

On a stretch of I-80 between Lincoln and Grand Island one night, trying to make an assignment he should have postponed due to well-broadcast weather alerts, he was caught in a blizzard with near whiteout conditions. With almost no visibility, he lost sight of the center line but was afraid to attempt navigating to the shoulder for fear of driving into a ravine. Out of nowhere, it seemed, a small exit ramp appeared with an abandoned service station and canopy at the end of the off-ramp. Tanner pulled his car under the canopy as the storm raged on for the next several hours. He had fallen asleep and was awakened by a tap on the driver's-side window.

"Are you okay?" the man yelled.

Tanner edged the window down. The storm had let up some, and a highway worker bundled in coveralls and a stocking cap covering his face stood awaiting his reply. A strobe light flashed from the orange snow plow in a lane adjacent to the canopy.

"I couldn't see. Thankfully, I found this place. I'm trying to get to Grand Island."

"The interstate is closed east of Grand Island, but you can follow my plow to Aurora a few miles ahead if you'd like," he yelled in a muffled voice through the wind.

Tanner followed the plow to a town five miles away and found a small motel that had one remaining

room available. Over the next year, he traveled that section of the state on three other occasions but was never able to locate the off-ramp, abandoned station, and canopy that provided shelter that night. On one occasion, he inquired about the canopy with a resident of the town he had stayed in.

"I remember the storm. I've been through a lot of 'em over the last fifty years I've lived here. I think you're turned around in your directions, Mr. Johansson. There's never been a service station five miles east of Aurora."

But there were doubts. "Maybe he was wrong," Tanner had told Amara.

"It was a miracle, Tanner," Amara said. "The man had lived there all his life. In God's providence, He provided a shelter for you from the storm."

The phone dial lit up as Tanner looked at the screen:

"How can anyone know if he's going to heaven?" you asked me last week. I felt led by the Lord to send you this verse.

> "Because if you acknowledge *and* confess with your mouth that Jesus is Lord [recognizing His power, authority, and majesty as God], and believe in your heart that God raised Him from the dead, you will be saved."
> (Romans 10:9 AMP)

You can be assured of salvation. You can be certain you're on your way to heaven.
Ezra.

As Tanner was reading the verse a second, then a third time, a new text from Ezra came over.

> "How blessed is he whose transgression is forgiven,
>   Whose sin is covered!"
> (Psalm 32:1 NASB)

I like the way *The Living Bible* describes Psalm 32, verses 1–2:

> "What happiness for those whose guilt has been forgiven! What joys when sins are covered over! What relief for those who have confessed their

sins and God has cleared their record."
(Psalm 32:1–2 TLB)

I'm praying for you.
Ezra.

Chapter Twenty

W hat else have you been working on, Mitch?"

"I put together a montage of interviews we haven't run. Here are the interview notes, sir. I have expanded footage if anything jumps out."

Mitch handed him a binder, each section carefully laid out by interview date, subject, name and title of guest, along with concise talking points.

Tanner gleaned through the files, settling on an array of questions and answers from recent weeks of guest interviews.

"Here's the flash drive, sir, if you're interested in watching. If anything gets your attention, I'll get you the full exchange. Combining several of the expanded versions, along with your commentary, will give us a complete show. Another idea I had, is maybe we could run the entire montage in more of a sound-bite format. The voices I've compiled are fairly diverse. We could couch the show in a specific theme." Mitch hesitated. "I hope I'm not overstepping my bounds by suggesting that."

"Not at all. Did you have a theme in mind?"

"I did, sir. I anticipated you asking me that. I thought the opening could say, 'Our panel today is comprised of several leading evangelical voices, who I've asked to share with our audience what they believe is the greatest threat facing our nation.' The excerpts have been collated to provide that symmetry."

Mitch paused for a moment and then said, "I know you said you've been distracted. I'm just trying to help, sir."

Tanner placed the flash drive into a USB port on the side of his computer and began watching the interview with a panel of leading Christian ministers.

"Pastor Whitefield, please tell us your greatest concerns about the state of America."

"These are dark days, Tanner. An Antichrist will emerge who will deceive countless people. A whole generation of young people have been indoctrinated with lies. Sadly, they were brought up in homes where their liberal parents told them to find their own truth, which many of them did through secular humanism teachings, so we now have two generations—the Millennials who were born between 1981 and 1996, and Generation Z who were born between 1997 and 2012, who are illiterate when it comes to the Bible."

Another voice entered the discussion. "When our country was founded, the Bible was taught in school. Biblical stories, ideals, principles, and truths were taught to young people from the time they entered grade school until they left their formal education to work and care for their families. Some of the most prestigious colleges of today—and I use that description with tongue in cheek—were founded as schools of divinity. Over time, the entire concept of separation of church and state was turned upside down by a liberal academia and media who, sadly, have been successful in distorting the original meaning of the First Amendment when it comes to the church's role in society," a Christian podcaster noted.

"I don't mean this disrespectfully, but there seems to be a divide between people of faith and those in higher education. Just saying," a man by the name of Jorge Villanueva interjected.

"I agree. A lot of college educated people seem very gullible," the podcaster, Walt Buchanon, said.

Johansson laughed. "Ouch."

Buchanon continued. "Many young people go off to college and fall for the propaganda being pushed by leftist progressives. It doesn't take long before the indoctrination is entrenched into the minds of otherwise very talented, bright young people—the next generation of leadership in our once great country. Lots of commentators are reporting on this. You're talking about concerns shared by millions of Americans."

A professor from a leading Christian university spoke next. "The heretical teaching in the church is so pronounced that even churches that at one time were beacons of sound biblical doctrine have now embraced a type of woke theology, sensitive to today's culture more than the fundamental teaching of Scripture."

Pastor Kenneth Matthews followed: "I'm not an isolationist. Jesus said, 'To whom much is given, much is required.' I believe that the United States, as the leader of the free world, has an obligation to help those in need, to feed the hungry, to rescue the oppressed, to free the captives. It's a sad day, Tanner, when the United States is no longer a beacon of hope to the world, and I'm afraid we've reached that place at this time in history."

Johansson turned to a leading evangelical he had interviewed the prior month. "From Egypt, Yemen, Iran, and Saudi Arabia in the Middle East to North Korea and China in Asia, and Somalia, Sudan, and Nigeria in Africa, Christians are being persecuted for their faith. In many instances, they lose their homes and livelihoods; in other settings they're killed. Why are we giving aid to governments that support and turn a blind eye to these oppressions? In the United States, not only are other faiths allowed to gather for religious services, they are also allowed to criticize and protest government policies. Are Christian missionaries in Sudan allowed to lead protests against the mistreatment of women or on behalf of home church services? I think we both know how that would go down, Tanner. To sum this up, we've lost our moral fortitude, which is why these dichotomies exist. I fear for our nation."

The segment ended, and the montage switched to short, edited segments from a potpourri of topics and viewpoints, for the most part, conservative voices.

The Senior Editor for *Lighthouse Harbor* said, "Our

subscribers deserve to know the truth. Our readers are given a dose of relevant, eye-opening news stories that the mainstream media won't report on."

The topic switched to climate change. Tanner greeted his guest, an eccentric looking man with an avocado-colored Tyrolean hat and unusually large, dark-rimmed glasses that one might see on the set of a futuristic, sci-fi movie set.

"Mr. Shillingsworth, tell us your views on climate change, please."

"Thanks for having me, Mr. Johansson. Let me start by commenting on the climate change deniers who think they can poison our planet and get off scot-free without paying a price for their criminality. How many people are they protecting? I think they should be locked up before they destroy any hope for future generations."

The next guest mentioned Klaus Schwab.

"Tell us about him," Johansson said.

"He heads up the World Economic Forum. His famous quote, is 'You will own nothing, but you will be happy.' I'm sure I know who *will* own something, Tanner! Obviously, 'we the people' aren't included in that group."

Another guest chimed in: "The only thing his utopian vision for humanity will accomplish is more privilege for people like himself. Inequalities will continue and the masses will suffer. It's beyond me, how anyone could give even a moment's credence to his amphigory."

"How does he have the influence he does?" Tanner asked. "Why would anyone allow it?"

"Because his guests are world leaders who themselves are sociopaths. He strokes their enormous egos and makes them feel as if they're at the vanguard of global transformation. They're blinded by their own sense of power."

"Who are 'they?'" Tanner asked.

"We have a corrupt, radical-leftist government running our country who will go after anyone who tries to break their stronghold on the ruling authority they think was vested to them—by whom, we can only guess. Socialism is a term bandied about that makes the unaware think there's a group of kind benefactors who will take care of you when you're sick, allow you to work thirty-hour weeks, and, in some places now, assist you when you want to die. Socialism is a segway to communism, Tanner. Young people who think European socialism is superior to the republic we love so well, are, unfortunately, products of an academic state that produces the likes of Schwab's donors."

The topic switched to the Federal Reserve and the Treasury Department: "Like the term 'transitory' to describe inflation. No matter how ridiculous it sounded, they hoped that if they said it enough, a segment of the population would believe it. I think that segment is getting smaller," the guest added.

"No doubt. Thank you, Jonathan," Tanner said.

The footage switched to Tanner talking with a leading conservative voice from *Manifest Now.*

"And what about the pundits, Hollywood types,

corporate America, and leading voices in academia? How would you describe these people?"

"Puppets of the state, Tanner. And sadly, for the rest of us, most of them still don't get it. You could feed them every vaccine-incriminating piece of data available—and at this juncture in our research, the evidence is overwhelming—and they'd still be looking at the same screenplay, still be working out of the same playbook, and still be singing from the same songbook. The scary thing is that next time they'll be more dangerous. They figure they had us the last time, and they still can't believe they let it slip away. To use a sports analogy, as I know you like to do from time to time, it's like the boxer who's way ahead on the scorecards after eleven rounds. There's one round to go. He's cruising to victory and the fight's not even close. All he needs to do is dance around and not make a mistake, but he gets sloppy and drops his gloves. He leads with his chin. The other guy throws a lucky punch and knocks him out. All he needed to do was stay with the fight plan, but he blew it.

"They won't make that mistake again," he continued. "And next time they'll make it impossible to pull out a win. I'm not saying that there's not naïve voters out there that think the Democratic Party is the same 1960s party that once looked out for the working-class men and women of America. We have a lot of gullible people that make up our voting rolls. It's like the store manager who had an exorbitant retail shrink month and in the course of the investigation, said, 'None of my employees would ever do that.' He's getting ripped off blind by internal theft, and he doesn't have a clue. Same thing with a number of the people that make up the Democratic Party of today. Some of them don't realize they're supporting the most radical, progressive arm of politics our country has ever seen."

"That's what the progressive left does best, Raymond," Tanner said. "They're masterful propagandists. They gaslight and call you conspiracy theorists and then two years later the whole world realizes that the so-called conspiracies were true. By then millions of people have been deceived. Then they start all over with the next gaslighting campaign, hoping that everyone forgets the last one. They told you it was going to be a sunny day, but when it wasn't, they changed the forecast they had given you the day before. When exposed, they create a new narrative and then rewrite history. You knew it rained yesterday. You knew your clothes were wet by the time you got from the store to your car. But they told you that you were imagining things."

"Here's a perfect example of gaslighting, Tanner. When Democrats say that Trump, DeSantis, whoever— fill in the blank—will be the end of democracy, they're making that statement on the platform of the most totalitarian government our country has ever seen. They're nefarious actors, Tanner. We have a fascist government! If things continue down this road, we'll soon be living in a police state."

The screen flashed to an earlier show on the government's immigration policy. "When I hear talk about the Biden administration getting things done, I think to myself, 'Do you really believe that? That's the most outlandish, revisionist history statement imaginable. Nothing but pure propaganda,' Johansson began.

"Let's talk about what they didn't get done, folks, and then you can weigh the evidence on a scale: The State Department and top brass of our military pulled out of Afghanistan in a whirlwind of incompetence that will go down in infamy. The Biden Administration declared war on fossil fuels and unleashed the worst inflation the country has seen since the 1980s. They reversed Trump's 'Stay in Mexico' policy and rescinded a total of ninety-one border security regulations including reinstituting 'Catch and Release.' What was the effect of this open border policy? It opened the floodgates of illegal immigration to the point that we have no idea who's here, where they're at, or what national security risk they may pose.

"For those of you living in Neverland, Avalon, the Land of Oz, or some other fantasy world, the fact that you're unaware of these incriminating details in no way lessens the veracity of their claims. It simply means that you're uninformed, friends. It's all public record. Accept it or deny it, that's up to you."

Tanner's monologue was followed by a guest, Antonio De La Rosa, a leading voice in immigration reform. "I've read that you have a Cuban wife, which is puzzling to me because you come across as very anti-immigration. What gives, Johansson?"

"I'm not anti-immigration, Antonio, but I do have

what many would classify as an unconventional view on the subject. Notwithstanding what I just said in my monologue, I do believe there needs to be a level of amnesty for at least some of the immigrants who are here illegally. If they've been here for fifteen or twenty years, they don't have a criminal record, they're paying their taxes—in other words, no legal issues—they should be given an immediate path to citizenship. Here's the requirements: Pay a fine; there has to be a penalty. Require the individual to learn English, renounce their citizenship from the originating country—no dual citizenship—and then pass the naturalization test. Having said all that, the border needs to be closed immediately. Three reasons: An open border is a national security risk. We have no comprehension of the bad actors with malevolent intent who are crossing our borders and settling into cities and states indiscriminately. We have enemies abroad who hate everything this country stands for. Is anyone naïve enough to believe that none of these people have entered the country illegally? Secondly, Antonio, the country is broke. Financially, the well's dry. How are we going to pay for the services these folks require when we can't even fund our own legislation without printing money? Finally, and this is very important. Take a look at our major cities. Have you noticed the homelessness, poverty, and drug addiction prevalent on the streets of America all across the country? We haven't come up with solutions to take care of our own people. How can we fund the problems of millions of people entering our country illegally? We can't, Antonio."

The topic switched to transgender athletes: "Has it occurred to you that the United States is at the vanguard of this insanity?" a guest asked.

"Yes, it has. But share with our viewers, if you will, why that is," Tanner said.

"Because we've been overtaken by radical leftist ideologues who are bent on destroying the traditional Judeo-Christian values this country was founded on. If your daughter was an athlete who participated in what were at one time traditionally male sports like wrestling or boxing, would you want her competing against a biological male? This is beyond craziness, Tanner.

"Ten years ago, no one had even heard of the terms, 'gender affirming care,' or 'gender studies,'" the man continued. "Health professionals who believe this nonsense should be barred from the medical field. It's insanity!" he exclaimed. "Male boxers and wrestlers competing against women is pure lunacy!

"These are the same people who believe that a woman has the right to a late-term abortion, which is the definition of evil! They have a worldview that's contrary to everything our Founding Fathers stood for. And now they're steering the ship. I wouldn't put anything past these people," he added.

The montage switched to a new screen. "Tonight we're going to talk about 'election integrity,'" Tanner said, emphasizing the title with utter derision. "We've invited a panel of leading constitutional lawyers, political pundits, and commonsense Americans to answer the glaring question, Was the election stolen in 2020, and what's on the horizon in 2024?

"Joe Black is the senior attorney for Black's Center for Legal Justice with offices in Nashville, Atlanta, and Tallahassee. Mr. Black, answer the question for the American people, How can we trust that the current system will give us honest election results?"

"The current system won't give us that assurance, Tanner. Unless we eliminate ballot harvesting, illegal drop boxes, and the ability to vote without producing a valid identification card, we'll get more of the same. A number of states have made progress since the last election, but there's no time to lose in putting these controls into place."

"I couldn't agree more," a second man said. "Ballot harvesting and mail-in voting were rife with fraud. Something else that has failed to get the attention it deserves involves the tabulating of votes. States that can't count their ballots on election day should have to relinquish the administration of their voting polls to states like Florida or Iowa that have their votes tallied the night of the election. It can be done, regardless of what they tell you."

A third guest spoke up: "I have a very cynical view of election results. I think they would actually justify fraud saying they have the best interest of the country in mind. Tanner, I'm not a MAGA Republican, and I don't want to see a second Trump term, but I believe his opponents are the real threat to democracy. I think the indictments were a total sham. A to Z, every last one of them. I think these people will do anything to stay in power. Would they cheat to stay in office? Absolutely, in a heartbeat. They wouldn't think twice about it. And even when they get caught, they'll gaslight the findings and turn it back on the other side. It's a precarious place we've found ourselves in."

"Who do you like for president?" Tanner asked.

"Nothing's changed. I came out for DeSantis early on after he announced his candidacy. I think he has the executive skills needed to clean house. Unfortunately, he's no longer a candidate.

"Democrats like to use the term 'election integrity' as if it's some type of sacred vow. Are you kidding me? Election results aren't anything sacred. The term is an oxymoron. With the ideological stakes at play, you don't think people would cheat? Of course, they would. People cheat on taxes, in sports, in just about every aspect of society. Why do retailers require an ID to buy cigarettes? Because the law has determined that an individual must be twenty-one years old to purchase tobacco products. Why don't retailers simply take a person's word for how old they are? Because there's a recognition that someone will lie in an effort to buy cigarettes, or alcohol for that matter. It's ludicrous that we would even be having this discussion. Of course, people will cheat if there's no safeguards in place. That's the demise of common man. So, what's the answer? You need strong checks and balances in place to prevent cheating, just like every good business in the country has. The term 'election denier' has become the most castigated term in the English lexicon.

"So, yes, I believe there was cheating and fraud. Saying that falls under the First Amendment, but with this regime you never know. I'm looking over my shoulder a lot these days, Tanner."

"Thank you, Samuel. Closing thoughts, Mr. Black?"

"This is a watershed moment, Tanner, a critical time in our history. We have an intel community who is active in this affront against the American people. They truly believe they're protecting American democracy by shielding the public from an existential threat. They believe they're preventing the election of someone who they think is a threat to American democracy, and they use lies, propaganda, cover-ups, media outlets, and corporate America to perpetrate their cause. The one problem is, that's not their job. Their job is to gather intel and report that information to the legislative and executive branches of government. The intel community doesn't make laws. Intelligence agencies have no authority under the Constitution to interfere with elections."

"Final thoughts, Gracie Ann."

A kindly woman about sixty, with a cheerful face and sparkling eyes, smiled at the camera. "Thank you, Tanner. As I think you know, I've been the director of Fearfully and Wonderfully Made for twenty years now. For the sake of your viewers, I'd like to read the biblical passage this title was taken from. I'm reciting Psalm 139 verses 13–15 from the New International Version of the Bible:

'For you created my inmost being;
   you knit me together in my mother's womb.
I praise you because I am fearfully and
wonderfully made;
   your works are wonderful,
   I know that full well.
My frame was not hidden from you
   when I was made in the secret place,
   when I was woven together in the depths of
the earth.' "

Gracie Ann's face turned from the monitor back to Tanner. "I'm reading verse sixteen from the Complete Jewish Bible because I believe the phrasing in this translation magnifies the realty of this precious life we're talking about.

" 'Your eyes could see me as an embryo, but in your book all my days were already written; my days had been shaped before any of them existed.'

"Tanner, I believe that God has sanctioned human life and that abortion is one of the great evils of the twentieth and twenty-first centuries. Thank you for expressing pro-life views on your show. It's not lost on me that I'm sitting on a panel that's been convened to talk about election related issues, so I'm going to pose a hypothetical to your viewers that I think will be illuminating.

"Here's the question I'd like to ask each member

of your audience: If an election came down to the last vote, and you were the person given the responsibility of tabulating that final, deciding vote, and once you had posted that vote the ballot would immediately be tossed in a furnace—in other words, no one in the world would know what you had read on that final ballot—and that vote meant a ban on abortion or it meant no abortion restrictions, would you tabulate the vote correctly and honestly, or would you lie depending on your ideology?

"Tanner, I'm a nice person. I try not to cast aspersions on people. But I've been spit on, had food thrown at me, had water poured over my head, and listened to the worst vitriol imaginable just for standing and praying in the vicinity of an abortion clinic. I've been told, 'I wish your mother had aborted you,' 'You're the reason abortion should be legal,' and 'You should never have been born.' I've been called, 'despicable,' 'loathsome,' 'disgusting,'—and those are the adjectives I can repeat on national television—simply for saying I believe that an unborn child has the right to be born and to live a fruitful life.

"I agree with what your earlier guest said. In the final analysis, a person who would vote to allow a woman to abort a baby up to the moment of birth is capable of anything."

The montage ended, and Tanner looked at Mitch approvingly. "Nice job."

"Anything you want to use?"

"I think so. See if the guy from *Manifest Now* is

available. And Gracie Ann also. Maybe we can book them again as we get closer to the election."

"Yes, sir. I'm on it, sir."

Chapter Twenty-One

Tanner looked at the bullet points. "What else, Mitch?"

"Official government information is available online at vault.fbi.gov which takes you to 'FBI Records: The Vault.' The site gave me some information to review, including a number of email messages relating to the case. I should note that some of the recipient names or email addresses in the 'From' and 'To' sections are redacted on a good number of the emails, so there's a lot of missing pieces in the report. After compiling info from multiple sources, here's the nuts and bolts of the case: In effect, the FBI spied on the Trump campaign after acting on an alleged tip that the campaign was colluding with Russia. The operation revealed all kinds of bias against Trump, which has been well publicized in conservative outlets. On December 18, 2019, the U.S. Department of Justice Officer of the Inspector General released the 'DOJ OIG FISA Report: Methodology, Scope, and Findings,' which we refer to today as the Horowitz report. The document details the report Michael Horowitz gave Congress. Horowitz had a number of recommendations for the FBI following the discovery of operational failures that took place in the investigation."

"Operational failures?" Tanner interjected. "Did the FBI accept that characterization?"

"They probably had a euphemism for the word 'failures,' but they claim to have implemented over forty 'corrective actions' as a result of the report. I could say that time will tell if they were serious or not, but given intel's overreach since then, it's clear we have more of the same.

"Speed forward to May 2023. The Durham report was even more incriminating of the FBI. The Attorney General had appointed a Special Prosecutor, John Durham, and after four years he issued a 306-page report detailing systemic abuses by the FBI. The FBI's response was that these operational deficiencies were addressed following the Horowitz report. All of this might be forgivable if they weren't now targeting pro-life demonstrators and conservatives in general."

On Friday night's show, Johansson's cynicism—and confidence—was on full display. "Government propaganda is ongoing and pervasive. Most people don't have a clue that they're being fed lies on the most routine of matters. Endless propaganda. Lies for the sake of lying. At one point they lied to protect their turf. Now, it's lies just to lie. In the end, friends, what's happening in the United States is no different than what happened in Athens, in Rome, in Petrograd, or in Shanghai, and every other corrupt ruling class throughout history. An elite group of aristocrats, who fancy themselves as kings, oversee the bourgeois, the peasants, the proletariat—or another way of putting it, the farmers, the auto workers, the roofers, the plumbers, and every man, woman, or child who labors with their hands for the betterment of society—to enrich themselves and their fellow monarchs. Call it totalitarianism, dictatorship, or communism—or a host of other unsavory terms. In the end, there are no 'comrades,' just serfs and nobility. What's different today lies in our perception of the United States. Some of you didn't believe it could happen here, and as a result of your denial, it has only allowed the ruse to unfold faster than it would have otherwise.

"Allow me if you would, to backtrack for a moment and expand on government surveillance, specifically FISA 702. Let's start with the definition of FISA, friends. FBI.gov writes, 'Congress enacted the Foreign Intelligence Surveillance Act (FISA) in 1978 to provide oversight of foreign intelligence surveillance activities while maintaining the secrecy necessary to effectively monitor national security threats.' The website goes on to say, 'In 2008, Congress enacted Section 702 of FISA, which authorizes targeted intelligence collection of specific types of foreign intelligence information—such as information concerning international terrorism or the acquisition of weapons of mass destruction.'

"Imagine you're entrusted to start an intel agency.

You tell the group, 'Okay, go out and gather intelligence and keep us safe from foreign and domestic adversaries.' Suddenly, you find out information that requires a follow-up meeting with the group. You sit down and tell the head of the agency, 'Wait a minute. I hired you to keep us safe. That doesn't mean I wanted you to spy on me. That doesn't mean I wanted you to tell social media platforms who can say what. That doesn't mean I wanted you to go to the New York Times and Washington Post and manipulate news coverage.'

"My first question is, Who authorized this governmental agency to have this level of surveillance oversight? Well, surprise, surprise. It came from none other than the Congress of the United States of America, the same group of lawmakers who fund the agency year after year. And some of the same group of congressional leaders who hold sham public hearings with the FBI in a round of fiery questions that are almost always met with vague, opaque responses, deflecting substantive answers by saying, 'I can't really comment on that due to the ongoing investigation.' Demand change, friends, or, better yet, send these litigators back to their home states.

"Friends, the intel community has become a government within itself. It's disheartening to think that your country is the freest nation on earth and suddenly realize your government has been lying to you for decades.

"Ladies and gentlemen, what I've presented to you is inculpatory evidence of wrongdoing by our government, whether elected officials or deep-state actors who are part of the nation's ruling class—I'm talking about unelected bureaucrats—who have conspired, always for personal gain, to thwart the will of the American people, and who have put this country on a course that in less than a decade will be unrecognizable.

"At this point, it's directed at conservatives. But mark my words, folks. The overreach will soon affect everyone. Black, white; young, old; male, female; conservative or liberal, it won't matter. The plans underway would cause most people to panic, but the problem is, most people are blind to what's going on.

"We've had two tiers of justice, which everyone sees at this point: The Clinton emails; Crossfire Hurricane; Holder defying Congress but Navarro and Bannon being thrown into prison; rioters at the Capitol Building in May 2020 being let off scot-free, but January 6 protesters being locked up for years; BLM rioters getting away with anarchy in Minneapolis, Portland, Seattle, and other cities, but pro-life activists being persecuted for standing up for unborn children. We have the Russian hoax and Russian collusion perpetrators operating with complete impunity. In December 2019 the Horowitz report was published, an incriminating accusation against our leading domestic intel agency. Before that we had the Mueller report that failed to uncover evidence of collusion, and finally, most recently, there was the Durham report, which was nothing less than an indictment against the FBI.

"Were these reports enough to acquit the former president in the eyes of his enemies? No, once he crossed the line, he was done. Maybe not today, maybe not tomorrow, but before it's over, they'll find a way to destroy him. For all of his flaws, and there are many, the fact remains that he's an unacceptable leader in the eyes of the establishment. They hate him so much that they'll do anything within their power to destroy him.

"Along the way, we get reports of the Mueller team wiping Apple phones clean.

"We have news organizations that perpetrated the Russian collusion hoax for three years. Can you believe that these people still use the phrase 'journalistic standards?'

"Speed forward to 2024. The Hurr report listed locations where Biden kept classified documents, which included his home and the Presidential Library at the University of Pennsylvania, but failed to mention there were records stored at his attorney's office in Delaware. Hmm . . . I wonder why that was.

"And then our intel community is brazen enough to go before Congress and request more money. After violating FISA 702, after being an arm of the Democratic Party engaged in a witch hunt of their political opponents, after being utterly inept in protecting our southern border from terrorist cells, not to mention the health dangers some of these immigrants might pose. They'll throw you out of the military for not getting the jab but turn a blind eye to millions of unvaccinated migrants crossing into the United States.

"Of course you have the right to know! Who do you

think is paying these people?"

Johansson closed his remarks by saying, "Friends, we don't have a democracy. We have a system that's as rigged as a heavyweight title fight during the championship reign of Primo Carnera. The American people know when the fix is in."

The following morning his post, 'There's no such thing as objective journalists, the term is an oxymoron. These people are just mouthpieces for someone's radical progressive agenda,' had gotten over 500 thousand likes on the network's X account, but the critics lambasted him with every known conspiracy theory moniker listed in the public domain, and some unprintable labels as well.

Nonetheless, Johansson was in an uncharacteristically good mood when he sat down at a table in the executive meeting room near the production studio for his morning meeting with Mitch. He glanced through Mitch's briefing, and said, "Now you're cookin oysters."

"Cooking oysters, sir?"

"*Cookin* oysters, not *cooking* oysters. It's one of my dad's old sayings. He was kind of zany at times. It means, 'Great job. Now you're on to something.'"

The infrequent, insouciant, lighthearted moment was interrupted by a voice from outside the meeting room.

"What the blankety-blank is going on, Johansson?" Ed Collins yelled, as he stormed into the room and moved rapidly toward the two men. Aggie, silent and somber looking, stood a step behind him with her lips pursed and her hands crossed.

"You wanna overthrow the government, Johansson, you gotta pay the piper," he said loudly. "Let me ask you a question. What's the definition of sedition?" Collins asked. "Exactly! Exactly what I'm talking about with these insurrectionists!"

Tanner had yet to speak but now stood up facing Collins. "I'm glad you said that. So, you agree with me that Adam Schiff and James Comey and every other government official that was involved in perpetuating the Russian hoax lie, should be indicted on federal charges and thrown into prison for perpetrating these lies to the American people, right?"

Collins looked angrily at Tanner and waved his arms as he spoke. "You think you got me, don't you? Everybody knows that's not the same thing!"

Tanner made no effort to hide the arrogance he felt, on full display this morning in front of his boss and her boss. "I memorized the definition for a moment just like this. Here's Wikipedia's definition of sedition: 'Overt conduct, such as speech or organization, that tends toward rebellion against the established order.' I would say that we have congressional members and intel bureaucrats who are guilty of that very thing. What type of prison term do these people deserve?

"Prominent Democrats spent thirteen million dollars of taxpayer's money, went on every mainstream television show that would have them—which by the way, was every last one—lied countless times to the American people when they knew they were engaged in subterfuge at the highest levels, kept the country off-balance for three years, and you think that's okay?

"By the way, do I call you daddy or just dad?"

"Ed, let's go." Aggie placed her hand on Collins's shoulder and turned to leave.

"You're going in the wrong direction, Johansson," Collins said angrily, as the two abruptly left the room.

The next morning at nine o'clock, Tanner walked into Aggie's office and sat down. "I'm starting to think that Ed doesn't like me," he said with biting sarcasm.

"Are you trying to get fired, Tanner? Are you trying to get me fired?" she said in an exasperated tone. "Aubrey won't always have your back. Just like Troy Elkhart before you. He'll tell Ed, 'Do what you have to do.' Why are you always so confrontational?"

"No, the questions are, Why is he so defensive? What's he afraid of? Who's he afraid of?"

"He wants a balance, Tanner. So do I. So does Aubrey. You can be confrontational. Be brash, be a little bit audacious even, but don't be so impertinent."

"Now I'm impertinent?"

"That's putting it mildly. You're disrespectful to everyone who challenges you. Ninety percent of the media world thinks you're a radical, right-wing extremist."

"Well, the other 10 percent like me. And so do the ratings."

That night, long after Amara had gone to bed, Tanner sat at his office desk staring blankly at the computer screen, the only light in the room other than two black, flexible arm lights positioned on the top shelf of the desk, each creating a spotlight on the folder situated in front of him. For a moment the screen blurred, and his head nodded ever so slightly. He closed his eyes, leaned forward, and dropped his chin. Just for a minute, he thought.

"Honey, come to bed." Tanner lurched slightly and turned to see Amara standing in the doorway.

"I'm sorry, sweetie. I'll be along shortly."

"I'm worried about you, Tanner."

"Please, don't be. I'm just up to my neck. I have a show to tape tomorrow, meetings before and after. It just seems like there's never any time. Give me a few more minutes, and I'll wrap things up."

"Promise?"

"I promise, sweetie."

Amara closed the door leaving Tanner alone, musing about which conspiracies to air in the weeks ahead. Tanner looked at the memorandum from Mitch titled, "Too Extreme? You Decide."

The outline started with a reference to the moon landing and a link to a video with the words, "How did Apollo 11 get through the Van Allen radiation belt?"

The next line in the outline referenced "Bohemian Club" with a paragraph saying, "The group, basically a malevolent galère of Republican panjandrums and other business leaders, meets every August in a forested area called Bohemian Grove near Monte Rio, California. Footage shows a bizarre ceremony in which participants sacrifice an effigy before a statue resembling Molech, a pagan deity referenced in Leviticus in the Old Testament that heathen people sacrificed their children to. I watched the entire documentary, Tanner. All of my research supports that there is indeed an annual event that takes place, although the 'who's who' dignitary list isn't as prominent as it used to be. (Note: I should have omitted the word dignitary from the last sentence. I hate to use any derivative of the word dignity when referencing this group.)

"The two-weeks-long gathering is off-limits to the press. No one in the media reports on these activities. Basically, no one wants to touch it. I was sick by the time I got done watching the video."

Tanner gleaned through the next two Roman numeral headings on the list:

"Antarctica, Flat Earth Confirmation - New Evidence."

"Combustible Engines Run on Water - Developer Dies Mysteriously."

Tanner hit "Reply" and typed a message to Mitch: "Let's shelve these, Mitch. Not because there's no smoke here. Just no time. If the world ever calms down for a minute, maybe we can revisit. For now, let's focus on the avalanche in front of us."

His thoughts turned to his conversation with Mitch earlier in the day. "It's more than our audience can handle. They're overwhelmed. They know they're being lied to, but what can they do? They feel powerless. At some point, survival mode means blocking everything out. I'm personally seeing deception at every turn, and it's more than I can process most days. We need to stay focused on the most important issues facing our audience today. They're in information overload mode, forgetting critical news because the next item hits them so fast and hard they can't see straight."

A short time later, his phone dial lit up. Tanner unplugged the charger, picked up the phone, and glanced at the text message icon showing one new message. It was from Ezra. He's up late, Tanner thought, and then clicked on Ezra's message.

"He is the image of the invisible God, the firstborn over all creation. For by Him all things were created that are in heaven and that are on earth, visible and invisible, whether thrones or dominions or principalities or powers. All things were created through Him and for Him. And He is before all things, and in Him all things consist."
(Colossians 1:15–17 NKJV)

"You alone are God. You have made the skies and the heavens, the earth and the seas, and everything in them. You preserve it all; and all the angels of heaven worship you."
(Nehemiah 9:6 TLB)

" 'Not by might nor by power, but by My Spirit,'

says the LORD of hosts."
(Zechariah 4:6 NASB)

I just wanted to remind you who was in charge.
Ezra.

Tanner sat quietly at his desk, his mind fixated on the verses on the screen, and then he breathed deeply and slowly exhaled. His thoughts shifted to his last conversation with Ezra.

"There are a million outlets for alternative voices that want to be heard. It's hard to keep secrets anymore. Fifty years ago the government could cover things up. It's a lot harder to do today," Ezra had said. "It's not like the old days. Today, the internet doesn't let you cover these things up for long. You know that better than I do.

"We're in agreement. Many of these cover-ups represent actual conspiracies, not theories. There's no shortage of dishonesty in our society, and I do appreciate your work," he continued. "I'd rather know what's happening than be in the dark. But in the end, it's not the most important thing."

"What do you mean by that?" Tanner asked.

"In the end, we're talking about distractions from the most important question in life: Is your soul saved?"

Tanner closed his eyes, let out an audible sigh, and pushed himself up from the chair, faltering for a moment before steadying himself against the desk. He then turned off the lights and walked slowly to the bedroom, Ezra's question still burning in his mind.

Chapter Twenty-Two

On Monday morning, Tanner walked into Aggie's executive office suite and glanced up at the ceiling. "Do you think the lights are bright enough in here?" he said with his customary tone of sarcasm.

"They match my personality, Johansson," she said. "Sit down, Tanner. What are you reporting on this week?"

"Why? Since when do you micromanage my shows, other than every show?"

"Because an hour ago, a little bird perched on my shoulder and told me to walk through the news room. I heard a rumble that you were going to talk about the Twin Towers and 9/11. Let me see your notes, Tanner."

"Haven't we met our quota for meetings this week? We met yesterday, remember?"

"We're not doing the 9/11 piece. Don't spend any more time on it."

"Are you joking with me? What do you mean, we're not doing the 9/11 piece? We've spent a ton of time on the story already. The viewership will be off the charts."

"I don't have time for a debate this morning, Johansson. We're not doing the piece. Period. Final. What don't you understand about the word 'no'?"

"Okay, let's start over. What happened? Think back to what you said last week. Let me remind you: After looking at my outline, you said, 'I'm sure your audience will love the story. Captivating.' Your words, not mine. That's what you told me a week ago. This is the second story you've squashed in the last month. Talk to me, Aggie. What's going on?"

"It's not my call. I have no say in the matter. Ed said no. What more do you need to know? Let's cut this short. I have a busy schedule today."

"Tell me why."

"He didn't tell me why. Maybe he wants you to stay alive."

"Wait a minute. When we spoke about this last week, you said the leadership in our intel agencies acted with, quote, unquote, 'utmost integrity.' If that's the case, what's to worry about?"

"Quit nitpicking, Tanner. We're not running the story. Bring me something that won't have you and everyone else around here ducking for cover every time we turn around."

"I take it that 'everyone else' includes you?" Johansson said with a smirk. "I thought you were the iron lady."

"Of course, it includes me. If I were made of steel, I wouldn't be dodging bullets with Ed every time you air a new show. You think I have no sense of self-preservation?

Besides, I have three grandkids. One of my resolutions this year is to get to know them better. My youngest granddaughter can't say grandma, so she calls me bama."

"So, you see them regularly?"

"Over the phone. We FaceTime. But that's going to change this year."

"I'm impressed with your maternal instincts."

Aggie gave a blank stare and motioned for him to leave. "We're done. I'm not talking about it anymore. We're not running the story. Have a good afternoon, Tanner."

"So, Ed won't cover this because they're holding something over his head?"

"Maybe. Probably. So what? The whole world has secrets, Tanner." Aggie stood and motioned impatiently with her hand. "Run anything else you'd like, but, and I repeat, we're *not* running the intel slash 9/11 story."

Agnes Martindale reached for the phone, answered an incoming call, and motioned for Tanner to leave, but as he stood up, she put the phone on mute and said, "Don't spend any more time on the story, Johansson. That's an order."

With that she removed her glasses, turned toward the window, and with her back facing Johansson, said, "Good day, Tanner."

The following week, Tanner sat down in a plush, velvet-colored chair across the desk from Aggie.

"How many backup tapings do you have in the queue?"

"Three, four, why?"

"I just watched the new taping for Friday's show. We're not running it."

"What do you mean we're not running it? You're squashing three consecutive stories?"

"We're not running the story, Johansson. Aggie's just doing what she's told. The directive came from me."

Tanner turned to see Ed Collins standing in the doorway. "I didn't think they let you out of the ivory tower at this hour."

"You're not gonna talk to me that way, Johansson. The decision is final. It was made by Aubrey."

Undeterred from his typical cynicism, Tanner began Friday's show with a somewhat altered narrative. "Folks, if changing election rules in the eleventh hour—changes that predominantly benefited the Democratic Party, by the way—if that doesn't concern you, there's one major event that unquestionably swayed the election. Tune in next week, friends, because what I'm going to share is a bombshell. I'm going to give you undeniable proof that the election was stolen.

"And now, as I end this segment, I have a message for the naysayers out there in cyberland. I'm speaking directly to you: We have people running the country who think it's okay to abort a baby up to the moment of birth. Who think it's okay to chemically alter a grade school child's anatomy in an effort to—and I say this tongue in cheek—'change his or her sex,' without even notifying the child's parents, in some cases, and these people have the mainstream media behind them. You honestly don't understand that this is a battle of good versus evil? You want to diminish the argument with the term 'conspiracy theory?' This isn't a conspiracy theory; it's an actual conspiracy! Wake up! You remind me of a man on opiates!

"In closing, friends, so you still think it couldn't happen here? You'd probably accept waking up to a global dictator from the ranks of the WEF running the country and rationalize that it was in the best interest of humanity. You remind me of the retail manager who says, 'None of my employees would ever do that.' If you believe that, you've got your head in your—"

The following Monday, Collins stormed onto the production set and in front of the entire crew shouted, "What the heck were you doing swearing on prime-time television?"

"Armpit. Head in your armpit. Last time I knew, that was still safe." Johansson rolled his eyes and glanced at Aggie. "What's he doing here? Again! I thought you were supposed to have free rein."

"Tanner, stop! Ed, he wasn't swearing. Nothing close to what I hear from you every time the numbers are bad."

"You're crossing a line, Johansson!" Collins screamed, in front of not just Aggie but no less than eight production personnel who had stopped what they were doing and stood mesmerized by what was unfolding.

"Something needs to change, Aggie," Collins shouted and stormed off toward the hallway.

Chapter Twenty-Three

S everal months ago, a coroner came out with a new report on George Floyd's death. A number of pundits have weighed in. Do you want a brief on the updates?" Mitch asked.

"I saw the reports and watched the video again. If a six foot, 185-pound man pressed his knee on my neck for nine minutes, if I didn't suffocate to death, I'd probably die of a heart attack. I get sick every time I watch the footage. I stopped watching it at night. Every time I played the scene, every time I watched the officers standing on the sidelines, every time I listened to the cries for help, every minute that went by and they didn't simply shackle his ankles and cuff his wrists, I could hardly refrain from screaming out at the top of my lungs. Every pore of my being was overcome with grief.

"I agree there were other complications. Mr. Floyd had a lot of serious problems. And the prison sentences may be too long in light of those issues. I hope the courts get it right in regard to sentencing, but I have nothing to add—other than a sense of overwhelming sadness. My heart goes out to Mr. Floyd and his family, and for everyone else involved. What else do you have?"

"That's the third story in the past month that you've turned down, sir. Are you disappointed in my research?" Mitch asked, slumping slightly in the chair, his countenance giving way to a sullen expression.

"Mitch, not at all. You've done great work; you're doing great work! Don't ever think otherwise."

"It just seems—"

"No, no," Tanner interrupted. "It's not you, Mitch. With one of the recent stories we didn't run, I just felt there was enough out there already. Everybody had weighed in. On a couple of the others," Johansson paused, looked down, seemingly contemplating his next words, and then continued. "I don't know. I'm struggling lately. I feel conflicted. Like I'm stirring the pot but not adding the right ingredients. It's like I'm on a battlefield with not only no path to victory in sight, but I also have a sense that the entire mission has been wrong from the beginning."

The following Tuesday morning, Mitch was back in Tanner's office. "I have the report, sir. Five pages typed and ready to load to the prompter if you approve the script."

Tanner took the pages and began reading:

State attorneys general in Michigan, Pennsylvania, and Georgia have all enacted election clauses that directly violated the state's legislative body. For example, in Pennsylvania the state legislature says that no election laws can be changed without the state legislative body passing legislation allowing those changes. This did not happen in the course of the 2020 election, but rogue attorneys general came down with rulings that allowed changes to mail-in balloting laws. Basically, they bypassed their state legislatures with these moves.

"Who would have imagined?" Tanner mused.

"It makes you wonder what they'll do this time, sir."

That night, Tanner and Amara sat at a corner table of Versailles Restaurant on Calle Ocho, a plate of quesitos in the center of the table and cups of espresso coffee at each place setting.

"Thank you for coming with me to see Ama. She's always so happy to see you."

Tanner smiled and took Amara's hands in his. "I'm glad your mother's close by. We need to spend more time with her. I'll do better."

"This reminds me of that little diner on Camino Cabra we used to take the kids to. The décor, the way the tables are laid out, especially the atmosphere. It brings back memories. Those were good years. Sometimes I miss Santa Fe, but I'm happy we're near Ama."

"You seem so worried all the time, Tanner. Please tell me what's been going on. I know something is wrong."

"I've been under fire at work. I don't know . . ." Tanner's voiced trailed off for a moment. "It's not just the critics. Aggie, Collins, who knows, Aubrey maybe."

"You have the number one weekly show. You said the advertising profits are setting new records."

"I'm crossing a line. Everybody is on edge. I present what I believe to be true. Most of my audience is in lockstep with me. As far as Emerald, who knows what any of them really believe.

"I'm putting together a segment on the World Economic Forum. WEF is the acronym they go by. They're headed up by a guy by the name of Klaus Schwab, the son of a Nazi industrialist during World War II, although nobody in the mainstream media ever reports on that. He reminds me of a sinister figure out of a James Bond movie, although in a Bond movie you know the good guys are going to win. With this group, you tend to fear for the worst. They're the prototypical organization calling for a new world order. It's happening faster than most people could ever imagine. It will sneak up on the average person. Most people will be shocked when it happens.

"I ask myself, 'Shouldn't we warn them? Don't we need to tell them the truth?' I'm beginning to realize that some people don't want to know the truth.

"I had a news competitor call me and tell me he'd been offered a special press pass to Davos, Switzerland, where they meet every year. He asked me if I was going. I wouldn't get within a hundred feet of those people. Not that I'd be invited.

"It's not just Schwab and his ilk. The World Health Organization wants centralized power to declare global health emergencies. They want the ability to issue health edicts to the entire global community. In other words, they want oversight over every member state of the United Nations—193 sovereign countries. Who in their right mind would grant this organization power over their own independent national sovereignty? My belief was that not even radical leftists would support such lunacy. Well, I was wrong. No one will accuse most world governments of being in their right mind."

"I pray every day for God's direction for our family, Tanner. He has a plan."

The two men greeted each other and then sat down at their familiar spots on the bench.

"I just sent you a text," Ezra said. "We were talking about Israel when we met last Saturday. I read these verses in a devotional this morning."

Tanner pulled out his phone, clicked on messages, and silently read the text:

"Did any people ever hear the voice of God speaking out of the midst of the fire, as you have heard, and live? Or did God ever try to go and take for Himself a nation from among the midst of another nation, by trials, by signs, by wonders, by war, by a mighty hand and an outstretched arm, and by great terrors, according to all that the Lord your God did for you in Egypt before your

yes? To you it was shown, that you might know that the Lord Himself is God; there is none other besides Him."
(Deuteronomy 4:33–35 NKJV)

Two things I gather from this passage: 1) God has chosen and supported the nation of Israel; 2) God's divinity is unquestionable.
Ezra

Tanner looked at Ezra, inquisitively, waiting for his thoughts.

"Someone asked me the other day what I thought about Zionism. I said, 'I've been a Zionist since I was seventeen years old.' My dad suggested I read *Mila 18* by Leon Uris. You probably know this, but the book is about the Jewish uprising in the Warsaw ghetto during World War II. They smuggled guns and people in and out of the ghetto through underground drainage pipes and by other covert means. A group of Polish Jews held off the Nazis for sixty-three days. I believe it was the divine intervention of God that strengthened the resistance.

"On April 15, Iran fired over 300 drones and missiles at Israeli territory. Thirty-six days later the president of Iran and the foreign minister were pronounced dead, killed in a helicopter crash. The Bible says, 'It is a fearful thing to fall into the hands of the living God' (Hebrews 10:31)."

"So, you believe the deaths were God's judgment?"

Tanner asked.

"I do believe that. Yes, that is my belief," Ezra said with conviction.

"After *Mila 18,* I read another Uris book, *Exodus,* about the Jewish emigration from Russia to the modern State of Israel. A Christian, spiritual aspect to the Jewish homeland in modern-day Israel came about when I read *The Late Great Planet Earth* by Hal Lindsey after the book was published in 1970.

"I consider myself a student of World War II, a historian of sorts. In 1934, General Rohm of the SA was arrested at night and executed by the SS. The SS broke into the homes of ten other SA officials who were also assassinated. No public hearings, no witnesses, no trials. The Nazi propaganda machine announced that traitorous enemies of the state had been eliminated. Over a decade of Nazi war crimes went by before World War II ended. And though a committed number of Christians harbored Jews at the expense of their own lives, and even as rumors of Jews being taken by train to death camps filtered through society, the masses largely, or at least tacitly, accepted the state-run media propaganda.

"We always say that it could never happen again. Or it least it could never happen here. *The Hidden Persuaders* by Vance Packard was published in 1957. It was read in hundreds of current events classes throughout the sixties and seventies. The book exposed some of the subconscious messages we were getting from corporate America through media advertising. It was an interesting book, but I propose to you that the manipulation taking place then was child's play compared to the propaganda we get today.

"Jim Crow laws were in effect until the Civil Rights Act of 1964. Imagine being a Black teenager, growing up in Tupelo, Mississippi, in 1955. In school you learn about the early immigrants coming over from Europe, seeing the dramatic flame of the torch on the Statue of Liberty, reading the words, 'Give me your tired, your poor, your huddled masses,' but then on the way home from school you pass a drinking fountain that has a sign differentiating between 'White' and 'Colored,' or you want to use a bathroom that points one direction for 'White,' and the other direction for 'Colored.' This was close to one hundred years after the Civil War ended.

"Early in a democracy, our government leaders become a reflection of us. They become reflections of our own hopes and fears, but when too much power sets in, they no longer represent the people. At that point, they've committed their lives to a different cause, which is power. Sometimes it's just power for the sake of power. Other times they want a change in government that they believe is a better way for the country, like a type of European socialism for example. They consider themselves the arbiters of this change, not the people. If they would repent and turn to God and submit their lives to Him . . ."

Ezra closed his eyes and bowed his head before straightening up and continuing. "But they won't. They view the world as an international stage, as some sort of giant war game.

"I heard you cite a public opinion poll showing that only 12 percent of Americans trust our political leaders, an all-time low. Too often this mistrust in public officials has paved the way for even more nefarious actors to emerge and gain power. I pray often that God will send revival to America.

"This past October, when the Hamas atrocities against Israeli civilians were being reported, I was up in arms, distraught over what was happening. All of my plans and aspirations seemed so vain. As I reflect on that, and on so much suffering throughout the world, all of my striving seems pointless. You know what Jesus said about the last days, don't you?"

"I'm listening."

"Jesus said, and I'm paraphrasing, that His return will be just like the days of Noah before the flood. People will be eating and drinking, marrying and giving in marriage. Jesus said they didn't understand what was happening until the flood came and took them all away. He compared that time to His coming."

"Do you think we're in that period of history?"

"Yes, I do. The content on your show proves me right."

"So, you believe we're in the last days? The biblical end times?"

"Jesus said in the last days there would be wars and rumors of wars, that nation would rise against nation, and kingdom against kingdom, that in various places there would be famines and earthquakes. In 2 Thessalonians we read that there will be a great falling away. Some believe this is referring to the rapture of the church; others believe it's referring to a falling away from the faith. I do believe that apostasy will be widespread. The Bible talks of a world leader coming on the scene. A global leader will emerge who the world will unite behind. His emergence will probably be somewhat sudden. It may follow global, international unrest. Many of the political leaders internationally, will unite behind his agenda. This man is referred to as the 'Man of Sin,' and the Antichrist. This man opposes Jesus and ultimately proclaims himself to be God.

"In 1 Corinthians chapter 15, the Apostle Paul, under the inspiration of the Holy Spirit, writes that the Lord's return will happen in a moment, in the twinkling of an eye. I'm looking forward to that day, and, only God knows, but I believe it could happen in my lifetime.

"I wouldn't be surprised to suddenly hear sirens blaring, turn on the TV, and hear an emergency broadcast saying that nuclear missiles were headed toward the United States and that we had twenty minutes before they were going to strike.

"Just because someone isn't expecting it, doesn't make it any less plausible. What do you think people in Hiroshima were doing the day before the United States dropped the first nuclear bomb? They were going about their business, buying and selling, socializing, working, carrying out a host of day-to-day activities, and suddenly disaster struck. I fear for the future of our country.

"Today we have an entire generation of young people, many who attend prestigious colleges, that are immersed in social media apps. TikTok, Facebook, Instagram, what have you, and they have no clue what's going on in the world. They're checking how many hits their latest post got, perusing through the scores of games for their favorite sports teams, FaceTiming with friends. It's not just young people. We have an older generation of people anesthetized by alcohol and so-called medical marijuana, not to mention the filth coming out of Hollywood.

"There seems to be a great delusion over our country. We play the Star-Spangled Banner at sporting events, we pledge allegiance to the flag, but all of that seems like a mirage, like we're living in a land of make-believe, oblivious to the tragedies unfolding in so many places around the world. Close to my heart is the suffering that so many Christians endure in countries opposed to the Gospel. In China, the true church meets in underground churches, house churches, and covert meeting places for fear of the authorities. In Muslim countries, Christians are persecuted and thrown into prison and oftentimes killed. Believers don't enjoy the same privileges in these places that non-Christian faiths are allowed in the United States. Why does our government allow that?

"The Antichrist will require that everyone receive a mark on their right hand or forehead. Without that mark, a person will not be able to buy or sell in the world economic system.

"The mark will be embraced by most people. Think about that. With one quick scan all of your personal information can be accessed. Basic personal identification information, medical history, financial payment processing capabilities, and the like. If there's an emergency and you end up in a hospital, unconscious, they can immediately see your name, where you live, who your emergency contact person is, what previous medical conditions and treatments you've had. You won't need to carry credit cards—payment transactions will be made and processed with a barcode type scan. You won't have to worry about identity theft. Each person will get a chip with a dedicated code specific to them. With that said, the Bible gives a strong warning about the consequences of receiving this mark. You would think that after the rapture occurs people would realize the truth, but the Bible says they'll believe a lie. They've been conditioned to believe that portals, quantum physics, theories about a parallel universe, the matrix, or any number of fantastical theories are responsible for the disappearance of millions of people. Tragically, they'll believe anything but the truth.

"It's not so hard to believe that this will happen. Sweden has been implanting microchips for identification purposes since 2015. At this point, the chips act as basic identification tools. You can scan your hand and get into a corporate building, for example. Some are also transactional. They can be used to purchase items from a vending machine that has interfacing software. It's happening in the United States as well. In 2017, a company in Minnesota gave its employees the option of receiving a radio frequency identification device implant for vending machine payments and computer logins.

"People see that the world is out of control. It may only take one cataclysmic event to usher in this world leader. Tragically they'll embrace the Antichrist and this new world order, hook, line, and sinker.

"Your viewers recognize the system is broken. I couldn't agree more. Irreparably broken, actually. The whole world sees it.

"There are places in Colorado where you're driving through the mountains on windy roads with no guard rails. Just because someone's not paying attention to a steep drop-off in the road ahead doesn't mean the danger isn't there.

"For the sake of my grandkids, I keep hoping things will return to normal."

The old man looked at Tanner. There was a sadness in his eyes. "But I don't think they will," he said.

"I think you're right," Tanner said softly.

"When I was a child, I used to pray that God would show me the truth. That I wouldn't go through life and miss the meaning of what life was all about. Even as a child, I was horrified to think that I might be deceived and miss the most important thing in life—truth about eternity and my eternal soul."

The old man looked intently at Tanner. "It's not surprising that so many are deceived on this. A man or woman who has missed the most important truth in history—that Jesus is God Incarnate, the One who came into this world to die for the sins of all who would put their faith and trust in Him—would believe all manner of deception."

Tanner had sat mesmerized, taking in every word, when suddenly a myriad of thoughts engulfed him, like a man submerged in a massive current, powerless against a riptide that had left him paralyzed, unable to move. The phrase, "missed the most important truth," crashed through his mind like a runaway train approaching a section of unfinished railroad tracks with a deep ravine just ahead. Ezra had continued talking, but Johansson could think of nothing but the notion that all of his efforts, all of his attention and focus and impassioned convictions had missed the mark, had failed to capture the ultimate duplicity. He had neglected to cover the unalloyed truth about life itself.

"I probably told you more than you wanted to know," Ezra said.

"On Thursday night, I'll be sharing a message at the small church I attend in Pinecrest. I'd be honored if you came."

"Yes, of course. Amara and I will be at the service," Johansson managed.

Chapter Twenty-Four

It was 6:55—they were five minutes early for the 7:00 p.m. service—when Tanner, Amara, Matt, Flor, and Vernisha sat down in a pew in one of the front rows of the small, nondenominational church, Grace Bible Church, just inside the Pinecrest city limits. An elderly couple sitting to their right smiled, and the man leaned over and shook each of their hands. A young man on the other side of the aisle waved at Tanner, and a distinguished looking woman with white hair turned from the row ahead of them, extended her arms, and took Amara's hands in hers. "We're so glad you're here tonight," she said warmly.

A few moments later, Ezra turned from the front row where he was seated and spotted Tanner. A bright expression came over his face as he braced himself on the back of the pew, stood up, and walked over to Tanner, who whispered to Amara, "It's Ezra."

The couple stood as Ezra leaned over from the aisle and embraced Tanner first and then Amara, giving each an awkward but gentle hug.

"I'm so happy to meet you, Mr. Townes," Amara said. "Tanner has told me so much about you. I feel like you're part of our family, even though we're just meeting for the first time." Amara's eyes sparkled as she spoke.

"It is my pleasure, Mrs. Johansson. You are even lovelier and more gracious than Tanner said you were, and believe me, he places you on a very high pedestal every time your name is mentioned."

"Thank you, Mr. Townes," Amara said.

"And this must be Matt, Flor, and Vernisha," Ezra said, beaming at the three children who had been seated but now stood respectfully and smiled at Ezra. "Your father, and I know your mother, too, are immensely proud of each of you. And seeing you in person, I can understand why."

"Thank you, Ezra," Tanner said.

Ezra left the couple and sat down at his seat, and a short time later Pastor Brown appeared and greeted the congregation. Ezra had told the pastor that Tanner and his wife would be present, and Pastor Brown took a moment to welcome the couple. "We have some guests with us tonight, Mr. and Mrs. Johansson, Tanner and Amara, and also, I'd like to introduce Leif and Gin Ellsworth who are sitting toward the back on my left side. Could I ask each of you folks to stand up and allow the congregation to see you?"

The couples stood up and were met with kind expressions and a few audible 'bless you' greetings from members of the mostly elderly congregation.

"At this time Tom will come and lead us in singing from our hymnal."

The song leader, Tom Roberts, came forward, smiled at the small choir already assembled on the platform, greeted the congregation and then said, "Please stand, if you would, and lift your voices to the familiar song, 'My Jesus, I Love Thee,' in worship to our Lord and King."

A pianist began playing, and Tom lifted his arms motioning the congregation to begin singing.

"My Jesus, I love thee, I know thou art mine;
for thee all the follies of sin I resign;
my gracious Redeemer, my Savior art thou;
if ever I loved thee, my Jesus, 'tis now.

"I love thee because thou hast first loved me
and purchased my pardon on Calvary's tree;
I love thee for wearing the thorns on thy brow;
if ever I loved thee, my Jesus, 'tis now."

The chorus subsided, and Tom said, "Please open your hymnal to page 437 to the song, 'This Is My Father's World.' "

The pianist played the final four lines of the first stanza as an intro to the melody, and then Tom began singing, his baritone voice resonating through the small sanctuary as he led the choir and parishioners in the familiar hymn.

"This is my Father's world,
And to my listening ears
All nature sings, and round me rings
The music of the spheres.
This is my Father's world:
I rest me in the thought
Of rocks and trees, of skies and seas—
His hand the wonders wrought.

"This is my Father's world:
O let me ne'er forget
That though the wrong seems oft so strong,
God is the Ruler yet.
This is my Father's world:
Why should my heart be sad?
The Lord is King: let the heavens ring!
God reigns; let earth be glad!

"Our next song is the wonderful hymn, 'At the Cross.'
Join me in worshipping our blessed Savior."

Tom again lifted his arms and began directing the small choir, the congregation standing in reverence at their seats.

"O Jesus, Lord, thy dying love
Hath pierced thy contrite heart;
Now take my life, and let me prove
How dear to me thou art.

"At the cross, at the cross, where I first saw the
light,
And the burden of my heart roll'd away,
It was there by faith I receiv'd my sight,
And now I am happy night and day."

Tom's announcement of the final hymn, "I Have
Decided to Follow Jesus" was met with "Amen" and
"Thank You, Lord," exclamations from the small flock,
and then the assembly began singing:

"I have decided to follow Jesus;
I have decided to follow Jesus;
I have decided to follow Jesus;
No turning back, no turning back.

"Though none go with me, I still will follow;
Though none go with me, I still will follow;
Though none go with me, I still will follow;
No turning back, no turning back.

"The world behind me, the cross before me;
The world behind me, the cross before me,
The world behind me, the cross before me;
No turning back, no turning back."

Tom graciously nodded toward Pastor Brown, signal-
ing the end of the worship time, and Pastor Brown walked
back to the podium. "Thank you, Tom. And thank you,

congregation, for your wonderful praises to our King. Bless you all and please be seated."

The songs reminded Tanner of the small Baptist church where he attended vacation Bible school one summer as a child. Amara took his hand and whispered, "That was so wonderful."

"At this time," Pastor Brown announced, "I'd like to introduce our guest speaker, who will be delivering the message this evening. Each of you know Ezra Townes, a longtime member of Grace Bible Church, who will be sharing a message the Lord has laid on his heart. God bless you, Brother Townes. Ezra, come, please, and share what the Lord has laid on your heart."

Ezra walked to the podium and placed his Bible and some papers on the lectern facing the congregation. "Thank you, Pastor Brown. It's a blessing to be here tonight, and I'm grateful to the Lord for allowing me the honor and privilege of sharing from the pulpit tonight.

"The title of my message this evening is, 'Drawing Near to God in Perilous Times.' We live in uncertain times, brothers and sisters, and it is imperative that we stay close to the Lord and have our eyes set on Him. That we are resting in the shelter of our precious Lord.

"Jude 21 says, 'Stay always within the boundaries where God's love can reach and bless you. Wait patiently for the eternal life that our Lord Jesus Christ in his mercy is going to give you' (TLB).

"In Proverbs Chapter 4, verses 26–27, we read, 'Ponder the path of thy feet, and let all thy ways be established.

Turn not to the right hand nor to the left: remove thy foot from evil.' The Living Bible translation says, 'Watch your step. Stick to the path and be safe. Don't sidetrack; pull back your foot from danger.'

"And we know that as we set out to serve and obey the Lord Jesus, that there is danger in our Christian walk. In Ephesians 6, verses 10–18, Paul, under the anointing of the Holy Spirit writes, 'Finally, my brethren, be strong in the Lord, and in the power of his might. Put on the whole armour of God, that ye may be able to stand against the wiles of the devil. For we wrestle not against flesh and blood, but against principalities, against powers, against the rulers of the darkness of this world, against spiritual wickedness in high *places*. Wherefore take unto you the whole armour of God, that ye may be able to withstand in the evil day, and having done all, to stand. Stand there-fore, having your loins girt about with truth, and having on the breastplate of righteousness; and your feet shod with the preparation of the gospel of peace; above all, taking the shield of faith, wherewith ye shall be able to quench all the fiery darts of the wicked. And take the helmet of salvation, and the sword of the Spirit, which is the word of God: praying always with all prayer and supplication in the Spirit, and watching thereunto with all perseverance and supplication for all saints.'

"Philippians 4:7 says, 'And the peace of God, which passeth all understanding, shall keep your hearts and minds through Christ Jesus.' But this peace and safety comes by staying in the 'secret place of the Most High.'

"We're to live holy lives, sanctified, set apart for His service, consecrated unto Him. It was never intended that we become part of the culture, but rather that our salt, our light, our testimonies, push back the darkness and positively impact society for good. There is a wrath of God that is poured out upon all who reject the forgiveness He offers in Jesus. God took sin so seriously that He sent Jesus as the Sacrificial Lamb to atone for the sins of all who would put their faith and trust in Him.

"A friend once told me, 'We're not shadow boxing; we're in a full-scale war.' This is serious business, saints, with life-and-death consequences for so many persecuted believers throughout the world."

Ezra was a good speaker, steady, composed, his voice at moments a bit gravely due to age, only occasionally interrupted by a slight cough or clearing of his throat, but there was a kindness in his tone that reminded Tanner of his grandfather. It was a fluent message, somber in its warning, but there was a tranquility to his words that gave way to hope.

Following the sermon on spiritual warfare, Ezra closed with a prayer: Lord God, we remember the persecuted church throughout the world. Those suffering for the Gospel of Jesus Christ, men and women who have lost their homes, their families, people who have endured beatings and cold prison floors. In the epistle to the Corinthian church, Your Holy Spirit inspired Word, dear Lord, Paul writes about Christian believers being, 'Persecuted, but not forsaken; cast down, but not destroyed' (2 Corinthians 4:9). We pray for strength for our brothers and sisters in Christ. Lord, we're not blind to the enemy's schemes. Please help us to be alert and watchful. In the name of Jesus, we pray. Amen."

On the Saturday morning following the Thursday night service at Grace Bible Church, Tanner pulled his Charger into the parking lot and walked to the bench he and Ezra frequented. He glanced at the time displayed on his phone. It was 7:35—twenty-five minutes before his usual arrival time, but this morning he had foregone his usual three-mile run, anxious to talk with Ezra.

"I'm just spinning. My life goes from one story to the next, one conspiracy report after the other, rating's meetings, my home life . . . I'm feeling overwhelmed. My youngest daughter asked me the other night, 'Dad, do you have another house you live at sometimes?' Even when I'm home, I'm not attentive to Amara and the kids. How do I refocus on the important things. How do I prepare?"

"Let go of everything," Ezra said. "Prepare for eternity.

"My dad was in the oil and gas industry. He used to say, 'In business, there are two kinds of pressure—when everything's happening and when nothing's happening.' He'd go on to say, 'I'll take the first one anytime.' But there's a caveat to that saying. You need to be grounded in the Word of God.

"When I was younger, before I gave my life to the Lord, I was a skeptic, much like you, I imagine. A friend of mine challenged me to read the Bible. He probably didn't know I'd latch on to the challenge for all the wrong reasons. Basically, I was looking for inconsistencies. Well, I pored through the Bible, and God spoke to my heart. There are doctrinal positions that even after years of study I don't understand, but I trust that He is a holy God, perfect in all His ways.

"I approach God's sovereignty with utmost humility. I know He's just and righteous.

"There's a great deal of heresy in the church today, teachings fraught with liberal theology and metaphorical lessons. If there is no resurrection, there is no Christian faith. But I believe with everything in my being that God gave man an eternal soul.

"It took me a long time, years in fact, to let go of the past. The Apostle Paul wrote, under the anointing of the Spirit of God, 'Forgetting those things which are behind, and reaching forth unto those things which are before, I press toward the mark for the prize of the high calling of God in Christ Jesus' (Philippians 3:13–14).

"I was well into my thirties when I finally learned what it means to 'redeem the time, number our days, and occupy until the Lord returns.' I still have a long way to go, but I prioritize my time for the things that matter much better than I did when I was a young man."

Ezra looked at his watch. "I'm sorry; I need to run. I have a sit-down scheduled with an insurance agent for nine o'clock this morning. I really can't miss the appointment, and I need to get a couple of things done before he arrives at the house.

"Would you mind if I prayed for you before I go?"

Tanner nodded, and the old man began to pray:

"O God! What deception clouds the world! Pour out truth on this man, please, Lord! I pray that You would bless him and his family with knowledge and understanding and wisdom and discernment. Help them to know the time and season we're in. In the mighty name of Jesus, I pray. Amen."

The October vacation had been planned since early August. Tanner spent the week catching up on a number of personal tasks from his to-do list, including writing a will, which he had long procrastinated on. He read through the New Testament in its entirety, reading the book of Revelation three times, as well as prophetic writings from Psalm 83, Daniel chapters 7, 8, and 12, and Ezekiel chapters 37–39.

That night at dinner after the kids had excused themselves from the table, Amara looked at Tanner and said softly, "Your thoughts?"

"Every story I had ever heard about Jesus in grade school and junior high, flashed across my mind in what seemed like an instant. Stories about Him feeding five thousand men with five loaves and two fish, and then later feeding four thousand with seven loaves and a few small fish; healing the man who had been blind from birth; healing the ten lepers, and only one came back to thank Him; raising Lazarus from the dead; stories about the empty tomb and Jesus appearing to hundreds of His followers; His ascension into heaven and the promise of His return.

"I don't know how I strayed so far from the truth."

"Please listen to this song tonight," Amara said. "I know God is working in our lives. We may not understand everything right now, but He has a plan."

That night in his office, Tanner sat at his desk and listened to the song, "Which Way the Wind Blows" by 2nd Chapter of Acts, a haunting but beautiful melody first released in 1974, fifty years before. As he lay in bed the words rang through his mind over and over:

"You don't know which way the wind blows, so
how can you plan tomorrow?

"Jesus knows which way the wind blows, so give Him
your tomorrow."

He remembered Ezra saying, "Everybody's selling something. The question is, Are you selling the truth?"

For most of Johansson's adult life, he held little empathy for anyone who didn't agree with him. In fact, he often disdained those with opposing views. To say that Johansson didn't love his friends would be mischaracterizing the relationships he had cultivated over the course of his adult life. He had many colleagues, professional acquaintances, and business associates but few genuine confidantes. There was virtually no one in his life outside of Amara and his parents, and in recent months, Ezra, who he would trust with struggles, doubts, uncertainties, or misgivings governing his work, certainly not with personal fears of any kind. Most of these concerns were consciously vanquished, or, at minimum, cloaked in an air of primacy, buried deep into his subconscious before ever gaining traction.

In his work, pejorative words or phrases were tools, operating mechanisms, an offensive ordnance or weaponry used to dismantle opposition.

A thread of sin seemed woven in so much of his life. Self-righteousness, pride, a competitiveness that had no compassion for people who he viewed as not merely sports opponents or fellow competitors—or, in the professional realm, respected rivals—but rather, too often, his colleagues and peers were adversaries, people with the wrong ideals and the wrong vision for the country. He imagined his sin to be much more serious than that of Ezra, who he recognized as a man remorseful and sorrowful for his wrongs.

"I remember when I was a young man," Ezra had said. "Esther and I woke up in the wee hours one morning to the most beautiful rendition of the Lord's Prayer I had ever heard. We had a clock radio in those days—this was about fifty years ago, I guess—I'm not even sure why the radio went off. There was no reason we would have set it for four-thirty in the morning. We laid in bed and listened to the most wonderful voice and symphony I could ever imagine. It was Kate Smith singing. Another time I had a dream. I must have been in heaven, although I don't remember much beyond the music I was hearing and the most amazing assembly I had ever seen. There was a heavenly choir of angels, an assembly I can only describe by saying that I was looking at a stadium from a distance and seeing multitudes filling an arena. The most amazing song, voices, and accompaniment, unlike any music I had ever heard, filled the heavens with reverence and adoration to the Lord Jesus." Ezra paused and looked off into the distance. "I don't have words to describe the heavenly choir, other than to say it was the most magnificent sound I had ever heard. I've never forgotten those stories. Sometimes, in these small moments in time, it seems like the Lord is reaching out to us, giving us an understanding and awareness that He's here with us."

Before going to bed, Tanner read a Scripture verse from Hebrews:

> "And without faith it is impossible to please God, because anyone who comes to him must believe that he exists and that he rewards those who earnestly seek him."
> (Hebrews 11:6 NIV)

Johansson heaved forward, his face grimacing, his eyes glistening in a swirl of tears like a man overcome with self-examination who had questioned everything he stood for and suddenly concluded that his life was nothing more than an exercise in vanity and pride. A heaviness came over him, like a crushing, burdensome weight on a frail man's back, pressing him downward until he finally collapsed to his knees. Or, like a man caught in the turbulent swirling of a crosscurrent, pressing him lower into the water, unable to rise. And then, for an instant, he fell asleep, forearms resting on his quads, fists clenched, his chin pressed against his chest.

Tanner jerked up, gasping for a breath of air, and then composed himself. He looked at the clock in the lower right-hand corner of his computer—2:14 a.m. Tanner turned off the office lights, walked into the bedroom, noticed the silhouette of Amara, motionless on her side of the bed, removed his shirt and jeans, and laid down, Ezra's question still piercing his mind.

"Lord, there's so much I don't understand, but I believe in You," he prayed in a small whisper. "Dear God, I echo the words of the man who told Jesus, 'Lord, I believe; help thou mine unbelief' " (Mark 9:24).

Chapter Twenty-Five

The following week, Tanner proceeded with his long-planned, follow-up Covid broadcast, this time complete with a symposium of leading health officials. His guests included Dr. Mark Ashcroft, a renowned epidemiologist who had been studying virology at a leading university in the greater Seattle metropolis, but after speaking out against Covid protocols, his research grant had been revoked and his work censured by every prestigious medical journal in the country.

"I've been shut out of submitting peer-reviewed papers from the entire medical community, Tanner, but I refuse to be silenced."

Dr. Ashcroft raised his eyebrows, looked intently into the camera, and tapped his fingers together as if he were beginning a lecture. "Your earlier guest asked me why I didn't take the vaccine," he said, his eyes glistening, his mouth forming a wry smile. "Let me start by saying, I don't trust the messengers. And why would I? Throughout the entire pandemic . . ." Ashcroft's smile turned to a sullen smirk as he emphasized the word *pandemic.* "The NIH, CDC, and WHO, and I suspect most of the apologists convened here tonight, didn't formally endorse even one alternative therapeutic for COVID-19. Not budesonide or any other mild steroids, although many doctors prescribed these with great success. Not hydroxychloroquine or ivermectin, which doctors worldwide successfully prescribed to their patients in spite of both drugs being maligned and vilified by the mainstream media. Zinc and vitamin D were proven to be effective supplements, but they were ignored. Thousands of doctors throughout the world successfully prescribed these therapeutics, but our leading health agencies failed to endorse even one. Instead, what was their guidance? Stay at home, rest, and if you reach a certain point of illness, come to the hospital. What did they do when you got to the hospital? They gave you remdesivir, induced a coma, and put you on a ventilator. Most of the time there was no coming back."

With each phrase, Dr. Ashcroft's intensity increased. He looked like a prosecuting attorney who after a methodical series of clever questions had just trapped the defendant in a lie. "I asked a colleague the other day, What percentage of patients who were put on a ventilator survived?

"He shrugged and said, 'Fifty percent, maybe.'

"So, patients get put on remdesivir, which is being litigated in the courts, by the way—it's a recently developed drug proven to attack a number of organs, one of those organs being the kidneys. What happens when your kidneys fail? Your lungs fill up with fluid, and you suffocate. You're given remdesivir, put on a ventilator and, in most cases, you're dead within a month. All of this following no therapeutics. None, nada, zilch. 'Wait until you're sick enough,' you're told, 'and then come to the ER.' They should have said, 'And then come to the ER to die.' Our governing body health officials are guilty of the worst medical malfeasance in the history of the United States.

" 'We recommend the vaccine. It's proven to prevent ER visits,' the CDC said.

"Mr. Johansson, this was an experimental drug. Nothing has changed in that assessment. We still don't have a full picture of what spike proteins do to the body's immune system.

"Given the almost zero health risk the virus posed to young people, it was nothing short of malpractice to impose the vaccine on school children. There was even a push to vaccinate infants. This was criminal in light of the fact that mRNA technology was untested. It's no surprise that an overwhelming percentage of the population has refused the latest Covid shots. At this point, I don't think the American people believe anything these people say."

Tanner ended the broadcast by saying, "So, there you have it, folks. Over the past seven months, I've painstakingly delineated key aspects of this story that our legacy media voices refuse to cover. Line-by-line, point-by-point, time frame-by-time frame, I've exposed statements and actions that cast a deep shadow over the official government narrative. Embrace the facts or reject them—that's your decision. With that said, I know that some of you still aren't convinced. After all, we live in a political landscape shaded with gray; things are no longer black or white. So, for those of you who still have doubts, I'd like to seize this moment and present an opportunity: I'm involved with a developer who has hundreds of acres of land adjacent to Everglades National Park in the southwest part of the state. The property may appear to be nothing more than Florida swamplands, but just last week large deposits of uranium and platinum were discovered. It's a rare find, and we're looking for investors, but you need to act fast.

"There's more to come, folks, trust me. Until then, this is Tanner Johansson signing off. See you next week, friends."

Aggie had gotten up from her desk, walked across the room, and was sitting in one of the leather arm chairs near the window when Tanner arrived for their nine o'clock meeting. She had a worried expression on her face and didn't say anything when Tanner sat down on a chair opposite hers, the two chairs separated by a lustrous mahogany-colored table, its surface shiny and clear other than Aggie's hands, which were clenched into a fist position and placed squarely in front of her. She didn't greet Tanner, nor did she look up when moments later Ed Collins stormed into the room screaming, "What on earth are you doing, Johansson, telling half the country that ventilators killed Covid patients?"

"What are you talking about?"

"Don't play with me, Johansson. Here, let me read it for you in case you've forgotten what was said on Friday night's show. Quote: 'I believe remdesivir, induced coma, and being put on a ventilator was a death sentence.' "

"That was his opinion. The last time I checked, we still had a First Amendment."

"Do you know how many phone calls I got this morning? Do you know how many federal agencies weighed in on this? And yes, Aubrey was getting calls. And guess who he called at five o'clock this morning?"

The meeting was short-lived. Aggie had lifted her hands from the table and pressed her fingertips together forming a motionless crown. As Collins spoke, she stared vacantly out the window, lips tightly compressed, with an otherwise pained look in her eyes. Collins unleashed a five-minute diatribe, directed mostly at Tanner, but neither did Aggie escape his wrath.

"Get your boy under control, Aggie," Collins shouted angrily, as he abruptly turned, walked the length of the room, and then slammed the door as he left.

"Please, leave. I need some time to myself," Aggie said, without changing her position or looking away from the stationary gaze she held while Collins was speaking.

Johansson, uncharacteristically shaken, left Aggie's suite, walked briskly to his office, called Cynthia from his desktop phone and asked her to forward any messages for the rest of the day to Mitch, grabbed his attaché case from its position on a small table by the coat rack, and left the building.

Long after Amara had gone to bed, and well past midnight, Tanner sat in his office, his mind racing from one topic to the next—the week's events, Collins's rage, the abrupt ending of his meeting with Aggie, his last conversation with Ezra, the concern evident in Amara's eyes and in her voice when they were at dinner—when his cell phone, situated neatly on the desk, suddenly lit up. It was Aggie. Why is she calling me at twelve thirty, he thought?

"Aggie? Emergency?" he spoke softly, not wanting to wake Amara up.

"No, Tanner. But we need to talk."

"The whole house is in bed. Let me walk out to my car. Hang on a second."

Tanner quietly walked through the house, locked the door behind him, and got into his Charger.

"I'm here."

"I couldn't sleep. I want to clarify a few things. You still don't get it, do you?"

"Get what? What are you talking about?"

"There are no good guys," she stated matter-of-factly.

In an uncharacteristically poignant moment that revealed she knew far more than she normally let on, Agnes Martindale turned the script and began to lecture Tanner:

"You think you're a knight in shining armor, an ideological warrior opening people's minds to what's happening in a corrupt government. You're simply a pacifier, Johansson. You're just a conduit for people to channel the anger and discontent they feel every day for any number of reasons. They listen to you and funnel their rage accordingly.

"Do you think Aubrey is aligned with the far right? Do you think he's independent in any way? Of course, he's not. He's in it for the money. They all are."

"Wait, wait . . . wait a minute. You're telling me that Aubrey has no stake in the ideological divide one way or the other?"

"Absolutely, I'm telling you that."

"I don't believe it."

"Really? So, you think you're making a difference? What kind of difference? I'll tell you what kind of difference. You're making *zero* difference. All you're doing is preventing real action. Don't you understand that half the country disdains the left's policies, and without a balancing voice they would probably revolt at some point? All you're doing is putting a damper on an uprising! Your audience, and the audience of every anchor on every news platform, liberal or conservative, lives out their frustrations through your voices. They're like the parent who regrets not pursuing athletics during their misspent youth. What happens as soon as their kid is old enough to play sports? He's signed up for every sports league mom and dad can find. The parents get to be star athletes living vicariously through their kids. Maybe it's not a perfect analogy, but you get it. Everybody in the country is a star commentator with you at the helm.

"First of all, 90 percent of the population doesn't know what's going on, and they don't care enough to find out. They're too consumed with trying to survive and keep a roof over their heads, put food on the table, buy school supplies for their kids without racking up too much in credit card debt that they never seem to get ahead of, trying to please the boss and not lose their jobs—you get the drift, you talk about it in one form or the other every week. The remaining 10 percent, half of them don't care. They're resigned to the fact that they have a corrupt government. As long as they're left alone, they couldn't care less what these people do. So, you're left with 5 percent of the population that's informed and cares enough about what's happening to make their voices heard—5 percent standing up to a bureaucracy that controls every decision Washington makes. What do you think the odds are that they're going to win?

"It's just like in World War II when Rockefeller financed both sides of the war. Who do you think controls every conservative and liberal media outlet in the country, Johansson? I'll tell you who: wealthy financiers that give their support to both parties at any given time, depending on which one is in power. And why do they do that? First of all, money. Second of all, they're trying to provide equilibrium. Ultimately the effect on the masses is detachment and indifference because the resentment they feel is lived out vicariously through the media host. We have a uniparty, Johansson. I don't need to tell you that."

"I had a disconcerting conversation a few weeks ago with a guy by the name of Richard Davies. He knew a lot more about me than I would have ever imagined. Who is he? A counterpart of Max Bennet?" Tanner asked.

"Ten steps above Bennett, Johansson. At his level, they all blend together."

"Then who does he report to?"

"The illuminati, the Council on Foreign Relations, heads of the International Monetary Fund, the WEF, the deep state, a cabal of Washington insiders, whatever you want to call them. The name doesn't matter. They have the money, they control the programming, the narrative, the policy decisions, who gets elected. It's not that hard when you stop and think about it."

"They came out of our ranks, didn't they?"

"Our ranks?" Aggie laughed, in a taunting, belittling, condescending tone as if she were talking to a child. It was a laugh Tanner had never heard from her before.

"No, they didn't come from *our* ranks, Johansson."

"I didn't think you had any ideology. You come across as if you've thought all of this through."

"Far more than you know, Johansson."

A long silence ensued. "Don't say I didn't look out for you, Tanner." And then the call was disconnected.

No, 'Goodbye,' no, 'See you in the morning,' just silence in a dark, starless Miami night. Tanner felt he had just been blindsided by a three-hundred-pound linebacker. He got out of the car, walked unsteadily to the front door, and then went back to his office where he slumped into his chair and closed his eyes, Aggie's words ricocheting through his mind like strands of jagged light flashing through a black cosmic universe, and then, in moments, he was asleep.

Chapter Twenty-Six

On Saturday morning, Johansson rose early, gave a gentle kiss to Amara who was still sleeping, drove his Charger to the park, and then set out on a brisk three-mile run along the walkway. Ezra, who almost always arrived first, was waiting on the bench when Tanner reached the end of his run, slowed to a walk the last fifty yards, and then leaned against the top side of the bench where he stretched for a minute as the men greeted each other.

"I appreciated your show last night," Ezra said. "Can I add something to the narrative?"

"Please do. I'm always interested to hear your take," Tanner replied.

"I love our country, but I'm also mindful of the atrocities we've committed along the way. From the, 'Go west young man,' and the American Indian carnage that followed, to the democracy-building wars and the international death toll that's become a part of history, to the racial discrimination and lynching, to the modern-day child sacrifice under the name of women's health care, we can blame this on our government—which you so rightly have done in your weekly segments—but ultimately somebody had to appoint these people to office. In the strictest sense of democracy, the voters have to be held accountable for their political leaders' actions. When life is all about pursuing the American dream, all about accumulating financial gain and prosperity, all about fulfilling my needs and my wants, it doesn't leave much time for me to demand accountability from Congress. So, in the end, these people continue unchecked. Whose fault is it? Is it their fault? Of course, it is. But it's our fault equally. I have an old saying: 'People get the leaders they deserve.'

"We need to pray for our government officials. That's not always easy to do when we look at some of the evils unfolding in society, but the Bible says, 'Let every person be in subjection to the governing authorities. For there is no authority except from God, and those which exist are established by God' (Romans 13:1 NASB).

"Events and rulers are woven throughout the pages of history in ways not easily understood, but God has His purposes.

"Love of country isn't the main thing. What did Jesus say the greatest commandments were? He said, 'You shall love the Lord your God with all your heart, with all your soul, and with all your mind' (Matthew 22:37 NKJV). He said, 'This is the first and great commandment' (v. 38). The Lord then went on to say, 'And the second is like it: You shall love your neighbor as yourself' (v. 39).

"In Hebrews chapter 12 we read that we're surrounded by a great cloud of witnesses. Some biblical scholars think this a figurative description, but other Christians believe it's literal. Some might disagree with me, but I tend to believe both. It's easy to imagine a host of viewers, an assembly of onlookers in the unseen world watching us as we live out our faith, cheering us on to greater victories."

That afternoon, Ezra sat in his study reflecting on his conversation with Tanner. For a moment he gazed out the window at the flower garden in the backyard and remembered how much Esther had enjoyed working outside. Even on the most humid days of summer, when many Floridians were inside being cooled by their air conditioners, Esther would irrigate the rows, fertilize the soil, and water the flowers that filled her garden. She especially loved daylilies. Each season in the years since her passing, Ezra would maintain the small parcel, weeding, watering, raking a bit here and there, and today the daylilies were in late-season bloom—mostly yellow and white petals, but purple and pink and red flowers filled the garden as well.

Thank you, Lord Jesus. You are the giver of life, Ezra prayed silently. Ezra glanced at his bookcase, the light, wavy pine-colored streaks running the length of the sides. The shelves were filled with an assortment of titles on Christian living, books on great hymns of the faith, eschatology, and theological dissertations.

England Before and After Wesley, a historical volume of work detailing the societal transformation of England following the Great Awakening, was a favorite of Esther.

Classic devotionals, *Streams in the Desert, Joy & Strength,* and *Apples of Gold*, cherished morning readings of Esther during her early hour's prayer time, had been moved from the living room coffee table to a top shelf in the bookcase along with other prominent Christian titles: *My Utmost for His Highest* by Oswald Chambers, *Morning and Evening* by Charles Haddon Spurgeon, and Ezra's favorite devotional, *100 Portraits of Christ* by Henry Gariepy. A group of other distinguished works rested on one of the six shelves of the seven-foot-high bookcase. *The Gift of the Magi* and *Why the Chimes Rang* brought back memories of Esther reading to the girls when they were young.

Bible Doctrines by P. C. Nelson, and other theological works were laid out on a shelf, sometimes arranged by author, in other instances placed in a symmetrical fashion based on the book's height.

No less than ten Bibles rested side by side, including the *1599 Geneva Bible,* the *Darby Translation,* and the *Orthodox Jewish Bible.* Ezra cherished his Bible collection but was often overcome with a sense of guilt, knowing how privileged he was to have the text of so many translations and study Bibles, while Christians in Communist or Muslim countries were denied even one Bible.

Ezra gazed at the Bibles and then prayed quietly, "Lord, please help the persecuted church."

On the bottom shelf, a secular work, *The World at*

War, narrated by Laurence Olivier, a 26-episode body of work that Ezra considered the definitive and consummate narrative on World War II, was contained in a box of eleven DVDs.

He thought about the Scripture passage referencing the great falling away and the coming of the 'Man of Sin,' 'the son of perdition,' the 'lawless one,' who he knew was the Antichrist in the last days before the Lord's return. Ezra opened his Bible to 2 Thessalonians 2 verses 11–12: "And for this reason God will send them strong delusion, that they should believe the lie, that they all may be condemned who did not believe the truth but had pleasure in unrighteousness (NKJV)."

He felt ashamed that so many years had passed by over the course of his professional career when he had neglected studying Scripture, and again prayed that God would restore the wasted years. Help me to redeem the time, number my days, and occupy until You return, please Lord, he prayed silently. He spent the next half hour praying for his family—each of his daughters, their husbands, his grandchildren, and great-grandchildren—each by name, and carefully referencing any needs he was aware of. He also prayed for Tanner Johansson, asking God to reveal His truth to him, and to draw Tanner to Himself.

"Please, dear Lord," Ezra prayed aloud. "Reveal Your plans to Tanner. Please tell him what you want him to do."

Chapter Twenty-Seven

H e's been here less than seven months and sets new records every month. That's why they're letting him do a live broadcast tonight. Apparently, a lot of viewers were calling in and demanding a live show."

"It's a one-off, but it'll be fun. There won't be a chance to do a retake like we do most weeks. You know how spontaneous he is. I love hearing Aggie say, 'Be nice, Tanner. Softer tone, Johansson.' "

"They're letting him do it with fear and trembling, you can be sure of that," another voice said.

Aubrey Stevens, entrepreneur, founder, and sole principal of Emerald News Media, unknown by appearance to virtually every employee at the station, and even tonight anonymous to the staff other than Ed Collins, Aggie, and several other top executives, stood twenty feet away at the far end of the men's restroom, a fifty-foot-long room of stalls, latrines, sinks, air dryers, and paper towel dispensers, all with hands-free electronic sensors, and listened to the voices in the room.

"I guarantee he's talking about Area 51," a young man about twenty-five said with conviction.

"Or Roswell," said another man.

"Area 51 makes Roswell look like playground stuff," the first man responded.

"JFK, guaranteed. I heard they squashed the story a couple of months ago. This is his chance to stick it to 'em."

Minutes later, Ed Collins sat down next to Aggie in the executive theater room. "I just got the scuttlebutt from Aubrey on what the staff thinks Johansson's gonna talk about tonight. Some of them think he's going to talk about the government's cover-up of UFOs; some think the JFK assassination or 9/11. I hope you have our boy on a tight leash," he said, not trying to hide the disgust he felt.

"Do you want my resignation?" she said smugly. "Do you want to hear about the offer I got last week? And guess what? I go, 'our boy' goes with me."

"I'm too good to you. You're not going anywhere."

"The offer paid twice what, 'you're too good to me,' pays. Don't press your luck, Ed. I don't care if he talks about little green men from Krypto. And if you want your ratings, you shouldn't care either."

A month had passed since Aggie's late-night phone call to Tanner. The call had not been brought up between the two even once since then.

The last time they had met, Aggie was in an exceptionally good mood in the wake of a huge ratings surge following Johansson's most recent Covid broadcast.

"Your ratings are off the charts—again! Where do you go from here? How do we keep the momentum going?" she asked.

"I've got the biggest story of all coming up."

"Seriously? Are you playing with me? Tell me!"

"Mum's the word. I'm afraid it's going to have to be a surprise. I'm on vacation the next two Fridays. You'll have to wait."

"Executive privilege. Tell me."

"Creative license," Johansson replied.

Now two weeks later in the executive movie theater overlooking the broadcast studio, Emerald News Media top brass were gathered for a rare live recording of the station's top weekly show, and this time it was the executives weighing in:

"Can't wait for this one," one of the top marketing reps said. "I'll bet it's about the government cover-up of UFOs."

"No, guaranteed—it's on Antarctica. I'm not a flat-earther, but there's more to the story than we've been told about planes reaching an impenetrable wall."

"Do you know many aircraft have disappeared in the Bermuda Triangle that they haven't told us about?"

"No question it's on the election," another voice said. "Reliable sources tell me that he has incriminating evidence on the Dems."

"I heard the same thing," a man in the front row of the theater said. "Pennsylvania, Michigan, and Wisconsin. They won't be able to pull the same thing this time around," he added.

"Nope," the first voice said. "Too many eyes watching."

"Exactly."

"We'll know by the end of the week."

"Yep, can't believe it's almost here."

"Unbelievable," Collins said with a smirk, and loud enough that the entire room heard him. "You all sound like a bunch of conspiracy nuts."

Moments later the screen lit up, and Tanner Johansson, after a brief introduction, far more conciliatory and gracious than his customary intros, began speaking:

"I've learned a profound truth in recent weeks, a truth I'm ashamed to admit should have been evident in my life years ago. At this point, I can only address my neglect by saying publicly that I'm sorry. I thought I was doing the ultimate public service by spotlighting the abuses of our government, and though I still believe, for the sake of our country, that changes are needed to reverse these infractions, I've come to recognize that a far greater cause deserves my voice, and that cause is what I, and I suspect many others, have taken for granted for far too long. I'm referring to the cause of Christ, which we call Christianity—a far greater ideal than the enterprise of public discourse in the political realm."

Ed Collins glanced at Aggie with a confused look. "Talk to me, Aggie. What's happening here? Help me understand this."

"It may come as a shock to some of you, but democracy is not a biblical word," Johansson continued. "As much as we cherish the term 'republic' and everything it has come to represent, we should recognize that living in a democratic society is not, or at least it should not be, our ultimate objective in life. I will note that early Christian converts lived under a tyrannical Roman government. Christians in the Middle Ages were subjected to the rule of kings; for centuries Christian believers lived under decrees from the papacy, and when church tradition clashed with doctrinal truths from Scripture, persecution followed for those who refused church hierarchy.

"Over the past one hundred years Communist governments have systematically imprisoned and killed Christians, and in contemporary times Christians are attacked and killed in Islamic countries throughout the world. The important thing is that these believers remained steadfast and stayed true to their faith.

"What am I saying in all of this? What I hope I'm getting across is a profound truth I've recently come to embrace, and that is, as much as we cherish democracy, our greater focus should be on the One who the Bible says puts governments in place and who also holds the key to eternal life.

"The Christian cause in society is far beyond an adherence to Christian principles and virtue. The gospel is the proclamation of a risen Savior, Jesus Christ, the incarnate God of eternity past, present, and future. This message supersedes societal outcomes, social standings, affluence and material wealth, television host popularity, and yes, network ratings."

"Taken by surprise," "bewildered," or "startled" were

not descriptive words that would typically characterize Agnes Martindale, her distinguished countenance and demeanor almost always purposeful and controlled, but this morning she sat open-mouthed with a look of incredulity bordering shock, as she turned away from Collins's now penetrating glare. Collins's eyes narrowed, his brow burrowed into a wrinkled frown, and then he glared angrily about the room, looking at no one in particular, but taking in the group at large as if they were all responsible for masterminding a cruel hoax at his expense. His face had the furious expression of a man who had just discovered a truckload of teenagers driving across his well-manicured, immaculately kept lawn.

Suddenly Collins lurched forward and stood to his feet. "What's going on here, Aggie?" he said loud enough that the entire executive team turned and looked at him. Aggie looked aghast.

"Shut it down," Collins yelled through a headset. The screen went blank.

"Contingency!" a producer nervously directed to the production team, and within seconds the screen was alive and a backup segment was being live-streamed over the airwaves.

Johansson rose from his seat behind the silver Emerald News Media broadcast desk, smiled at the production team of writers, producers, camera personnel, photographers, and other technical staff, waved to the stunned group, and said, "I appreciate you guys; thanks for everything you do," and then left the room, Mitch steps behind.

Chapter Twenty-Eight

Tanner glanced at the internet headlines:

> "Conspiracy Theorist Tanner Johansson
> Ousted by Emerald News"

Progressive Insight wrote,

> "LONG OVERDUE: Johansson Wears out
> Welcome at Emerald News Media"

An affiliate's headline read,

> "Not Soon Enough: Tanner Johansson Fired for
> Denigrating Non-Christian Faiths"

The last headline said, "Angry Journalist Taken Off the Air." The article started out, "Surrogate of the radical right thrown overboard without a life jacket."

He had a new job lined up, but said he couldn't start until after the first of the year. His contract with Emerald News Media would have gone into effect ten days after his termination date. A large contract in the pipeline and then he was gone. "Problematic, questionable timing," the attorneys for Emerald News Media told upper management, and Tanner was offered a generous settlement if he agreed to forego litigation.

"With or without a payout, I have no plans to sue," he had told the attorney handling the case.

"Take it and run," the man said. "Just sign the waiver."

Tanner opened his personal email to an inbox filled with messages from colleagues and other acquaintances, and clicked on the one from Aggie first.

Even with all the drama, I didn't want it to end this way. I can't believe someone would start out as well as you did and self-destruct in seven months. Actually, after getting to know you, I do believe it. Let me know if I can help. Aggie

Johansson smiled. She should have fired me the first time I was out of line, which was day one, he thought.

The next email he opened was from Mitch.

I, too, was fired. I thought you might be interested in the summary I was going to send you. (For what I thought would be your last segment. Obviously, I didn't know the timing of this, but I did suspect that something was going down.) I put this together from memory. It was never put in writing during my employ, so I haven't taken anything that belongs to the network. I recorded it for your review. Here it is.

Tanner clicked on the link and watched as Mitch began speaking:

"The title of my piece is, 'Irretrievably Broken: You won't recognize America in Ten Years.'

"Ladies and Gentlemen, longstanding friends, and esteemed guests, my question today is, How do you destroy a democracy with no chance it will ever be rebuilt? Let's begin by elevating a ruling class of monarchs who set out to rule the world. I'm talking about the military industrial complex of the United States of America, autocrats, plutocrats, neocons, call them what you will, but we recognize them as vainglorious narcissists who have exported wars, installed despots to power, and subjugated the will of the people to tyranny and death.

"Add corruption into the mix for a bit of flavor, with failed audits and 50 percent of budgeted Pentagon funds unaccounted for. Unaccounted for? Is that a new term in the English language to replace graft, embezzlement, piracy, or for you wordsmiths out there, peculation?

"In the course of this fraud, why not embarrass ourselves in the eyes of the world by failing to protect our ambassador and his staff in Libya, leading to their tragic deaths, or allowing thirteen servicemen and women to be tragically killed as our troops withdrew from Afghanistan?

"Next on the list, how about bankrupting the nation through incompetence and fraud? Let's destroy our energy infrastructure by claiming that global warming is an existential threat to our survival—until next week when we claim that white supremacy is the biggest threat to our nation. Until the following week, when we define this a little narrower by saying that Christian nationalism is the greatest threat to our nation. How about saying that men can become women and women can become men? Let's throw out thousands of years of recorded history and say that gender is evolving and that anyone who says otherwise is a racist and a bigot, undeserving of having a voice in public discourse. Let's blacklist our opponents from social media, and if that doesn't work, how about a stay in one of the country's glamorous rehabilitation centers? If that doesn't work, let's frighten the masses with a global pandemic. So what if one of our government agencies created the virus! Why quibble about the details? Let's focus on the big picture!

"Since we're talking about life and death concerns, let's create a perception that somehow life is a negotiable contract. Why not hypnotize the masses with the delusion that unborn children are disposable. No matter that our society resembles the ancient Canaanites, who sacrificed their children at the altar of Molech, or other pagan people groups who subjected their infants to diabolical ends. Does it register with anyone that none of these civilizations have survived? Every one of these societies has been relegated to the ash heap of scorn and derision by any decent person who respects that life is a gift from our Creator.

"Inch-by-inch, meter-by-meter, city block-by-city block, town-by-town, yes, state-by-state, and nation-by-nation, the minions will follow along. Like the Pied Piper of Hamelin leading the children astray, an overture of nefarious design will suddenly overtake the hearts and minds of those who once represented a country of worthy dreams and ideals.

"The fourth branch of government, the deep state or shadow government as we know them, comprised of globalists, elitists, technocrats, the illuminati—royalty as they prefer to be called—whatever blackhearted name you want to give these people, and their true identity is more sinister than my description allows, have a nefarious agenda unrecognizable to the undiscerning eye.

"Hollywood actors selling out for fame and fortune, media voices making millions to be the mouthpiece for the official Ministry of Truth government consulate, masterful perpetrators of propaganda and indoctrination—these, my friends, are the guardians of the new America."

Mitch waved his arms like a great orator and statesman of years long past, gazed upward, and then let out a faintly discernible sigh before looking intently into the screen and closing his remarks.

"But though the masses will be deceived, I have learned the greatest truth, and that is that Jesus is the Son of God, the risen Lord, Savior, and King of the universe!"

Mitch relaxed his posture, having completed his

address, and looked into the camera.

"I've been a Christian since I was eight years old, Tanner. I haven't been very bold in my faith. That's going to change."

Tanner smiled, picked up his phone, and speed-dialed a number. The voice on the other end of the call answered immediately.

"Mitch, is that you in there?"

"I always wanted to deliver a monologue. Just once. I feel like I've fulfilled my dream." Mitch paused and then continued. "I'm going to need a job. When you land on your feet, I hope you'll remember me, sir."

"You'll be the first person I call. We'll be in touch soon."

"Thank you, sir."

"Mitch, you don't have to call me 'sir'."

"Yes, sir."

Chapter Twenty-Nine

A pouch of colorful, shiny marbles—cat's eyes, onyx, yellow with purple stripes, solid colors of red, green, and white—caught Tanner's eye as he walked along the sidewalk about a block from the bench he and Ezra sat at. One of the three grade school children, huddled around the cluster of small, circular globes scattered on a bare section of ground just off the walkway, flicked his thumb and careened a silver, steel ball into a black marble six inches away, causing two other marbles to careen off toward the grass.

"That's quite an assortment of marbles. Very impressive," Tanner said with a smile. "How many different colors do you have?"

"Let me show you, mister."

One of the youngsters emptied a parchment-colored marble bag to an assortment of colors, and then as quickly as he had answered Tanner's query, turned his attention back to the contest underway.

Fifteen yards farther along the path, Tanner leaned back and turned slightly, dodging the ball that bounced across the sidewalk in front of him. "Sorry about that," a young boy said, as he raced through the grass to retrieve the ball.

"Johnny, be careful!" a woman called out. "Oh my! Tanner Johansson!" she said as she suddenly recognized the subject of the youngster's company.

A young man who looked to be in his midthirties joined the woman and extended his hand. "Mr. Johansson, Pete Smith. This is my wife, Sally. And you met Johnny. We watch your show every week. Well, we did, anyway." The man looked down, embarrassed for an instant, but then said, "Thanks for everything you do for conservative America."

"Thank you, I appreciate that."

"Can we get a picture? I'll be a hero at work tomorrow," the man said smiling.

Tanner nodded, and the couple and Johnny moved into position in front of and around Johansson. The man extended his arm and took two pictures of the group.

"Thank you, Mr. Johansson. This really made our day."

"Thanks," Tanner said quietly.

"One more request, and I hope I'm not pushing my luck. Will you sign this for Johnny?" The man held out a park and recreation brochure from a nearby information center.

Tanner took the brochure and glanced at the cover

picture displaying a lush green lawn with a pond in the distance.

"On one condition," Tanner said to the boy. Johnny and his parents looked inquisitively at Tanner. "Promise me you'll look up the Bible verse I write down.

"I promise," the boy said eagerly.

Tanner signed the front of the brochure and then wrote, "John 3:16."

"Do you know this verse?" he asked the boy.

Before the youngster could answer, his mother spoke hurriedly: "We're not really church people, Mr. Johansson. Neither one of us grew up in the church, but we believe in God."

"John 3:16!" the boy exclaimed. "That's my name!"

"Did you know that John is the name of one of the disciples of Jesus in the Bible?" Tanner asked.

"We haven't taught Johnny about Jesus yet," the boy's mother said. "We wanted him to learn about God on his own."

Tanner looked thoughtfully at the couple. There was a sadness in his eyes that the father must have detected.

"We've talked about letting him go to one of the youth programs at a Baptist church nearby. Nearby where we live, I mean. You've motivated us to do that." The man looked at his wife and they both nodded.

"I hope you do," Tanner replied softly. "Johnny needs to grow up learning about God. I encourage the two of you to find a good church." Tanner reached in his shirt pocket and pulled out a business card. "Here's the number of a church a close friend of mine attends. It's a good church. My wife and I have been going for the past few weeks. Maybe I'll see you there."

"We'll be there, Mr. Johansson," the man said. "Thanks again for the pictures."

As Tanner resumed his walk, a montage of fragmented thoughts from the election cycle flashed across his mind. The series of events over the past few months had been staggering.

"The Trump assassination attempt all but assures a win in November," the memo from Mitch began. "I may be wrong, Tanner, but the first thing I told my wife when the assassination news was breaking out, was, 'It's over. Trump just won the election.' To use one of your boxing metaphors, Biden was reeling against the ropes after the June 27 debate. The latest news was a knockout punch. I have to believe Democrats all over the country are saying the same thing.

"Then, after the Trump-Harris debate, I said, 'Trump just lost the election. I couldn't believe how badly he underestimated her.'

"But then I switched again. After the JD Vance blowout, I didn't see any way she could come out on top."

"Good observations, Mitch," Tanner had responded.

"With both conventions and three debates behind us, let me know if you want to cover anything on the election," Mitch wrote in his note.

His thoughts turned back to the initial fallout from the

Trump-Biden debate and the Biden coup that followed virtually overnight. The rapidity and celerity of Harris's rise from negligible vice-presidential status to megastar presidential nominee in six weeks was astounding. What an incredible chain of events, he thought.

Days before the election he had reflected on the bedlam that would inevitably follow. What would the headlines say?

Trump Wins
Chaos Erupts

or,

A Media Coup
Harris Edges Trump.

"I won't be voting for Trump," he told Aggie. "I don't trust him."

"Why am I not surprised?"

"I voted for him twice, but . . ." his voice trailed off. "Too reckless sounding," he commented.

"So, you're voting for Harris?"

"Of course not. I would never vote for a Democrat."

In the eleventh hour he wavered and voted straight Republican.

And now the election was over. Tanner glanced at the headline:

Bedlam in the White House!
Trump Wins Second Term!
Trump 45 to Become Trump 47!

Now it was time for the country to face reality. What would the next four years bring? he wondered. Johansson felt numb. Regardless of the fears he had carried around in recent days, and the weight of those concerns had been considerable, he was determined to follow through on a new path. God was in control of national events, and for the first time since he was a child, he was surrendered to God's leading in his life.

Tanner walked through the park and thought about the last message he had received from Ezra and the Scripture passages he had sent:

Sometimes our lives take unforeseen turns, but God knows the future.

"I will instruct you and teach you in the way
   which you should go;
      I will counsel you with My eye upon you."
(Psalm 32:8 NASB)

"For in Him we live and move and have our be-ing."
(Acts 17:28 NKJV)

Regardless of what happens in the future, our identity
is in Christ. Be encouraged.
Ezra

Tanner walked to the edge of the pond and picked
up a handful of thin smooth rocks from the bank. His
third throw skipped five times over the water, each time
creating small ripples that sparkled in the early morning
sun. He turned back toward the sidewalk and saw Ezra
walking up from the parking lot.

"I didn't know if you'd be here today," Ezra said. "I'm
glad you came."

"You obviously heard the news."

"Yes. Are you okay?"

"Surprised, but not shocked. I outlived my welcome."

"What will you do?"

"I accepted an offer from a competitive network. Not
as glamorous as Brickel and Miami Beach but a good
opportunity. Amara and I were praying for God's leading.
We're comfortable this is the direction He wants us to
take. Thank you for your counsel. He used you more than
you'll ever know."

Tanner reached out and took hold of Ezra's right hand.
"I'll always be appreciative. What about you?"

"My oldest daughter's moving to the other side of the
state—Clearwater Beach. It caught me by surprise, but
she said it was a career opportunity she couldn't pass up.
I'll be visiting her frequently, but I'm not going anywhere.
Not sure where you'll be working, but hopefully, we'll

see each other soon."

"We'll be around, no plans to leave. I'll have a longer commute and some travel that I didn't have before, but I'll be here. Take care of yourself."

The last thing Ezra said was, "If I don't see you in this life, I'll see you in heaven."

On an early December morning as Ezra sat on the end of the park bench, forearms resting on his legs, hands held together, head bowed, and praying quietly, a young man sat down on the opposite side of the bench where Tanner usually sat.

The young man looked to be about eighteen, had shoulder-length black hair, and was wearing a navy-blue sweatshirt with the decorative title, "Miami Heat," scripted on the face of the garment. His jeans were torn at the kneecaps and a geometrical impression from his cell phone pressed upward from inside the front-left pocket of his trousers.

"Sorry to interrupt your prayer," he said.

"I had just said, 'Amen.'" Ezra extended his hand. "Ezra Townes. What's your name?"

"Joey. Glad to meet you."

The weather channel had forecast temperatures in the low sixties for the early morning hours, and Ezra had donned a hat and light jacket before leaving the house and driving to the park that morning. He was wearing his favorite ball cap, an Oklahoma City Redbirds hat he had owned for more than twenty years.

"I like your hat," Joey said.

"Thanks. One of my former managers lives in Oklahoma. He gave it to me years ago when I was still working. I think the team goes by Dodgers today."

"Cool."

"What do you do?" Ezra asked.

"I was working at Roccio's as a line cook. I got fired yesterday for not coming to work. Then my girlfriend broke up with me. She said I had too many addictions. I smoke and drink a little. That's about it. Well, pot too, but no big deal. It's legal most places."

The young man proceeded to share his story, touching on the past three years, dropping out of school following eleventh grade, leaving home early, losing four jobs for attendance reasons, and being estranged from his parents.

"I'll get it together. I have lots of time," the young man said confidently.

"What about your relationship with God?"

The young man looked startled but then said, "He's a loving God. He'll wait for me."

"You know what I regret most about my life?" the old man said. "Mistakes I made, sins, to be clear, that could have been avoided if I had submitted myself to God at certain intervals in my life. I've been a serious Christian for many years, but I wasn't serving Him like I should have been when I was younger. Even into my twenties and thirties my life was centered around myself. Once you get serious about your Christian walk, it still takes years sometimes to put the sins of your youth behind you.

It's taken me a long time, years in fact, to let go of the past. The Apostle Paul wrote, under the anointing of the Holy Spirit, 'Forgetting those things which are behind, and reaching forth unto those things which are before, I press toward the mark for the prize of the high calling of God in Christ Jesus' (Philippians 3:13–14). I know God has forgiven me, but I wish I had been more receptive to His voice earlier in my life. I could have avoided a lot of struggles. You're a young man. Why spend years making bad choices and paying for the consequences of those decisions? God will help you, but on your end, you need to repent and turn away from your sin.

"Would it be all right if I prayed for you?"

The young man, who had been listening respectfully, nodded, and Ezra reached his hand out and placed it on Joey's shoulder. He then proceeded to pray for Joey's health, his future jobs, his family, that he would be reconciled to his parents, and that he would put his faith and trust in Jesus.

"I ask for Your divine intervention in this man's life, Lord. Thank You for hearing my prayer. In the name of Jesus, I pray. Amen."

Joey's eyes had teared over when he looked up at Ezra. "I'll do better. I'll call my parents. They raised me in the church. Thanks for praying for me, Mr. Townes."

"I'm usually here at the same time every Saturday."

"I'll come again," Joey said and then rose and walked slowly along the sidewalk until he was out of sight of Ezra's view.

As he looked into the distance, Ezra was reminded of the words of Solomon he had read that morning in his devotional:

> "Remember now your Creator in the days of
> your youth,
> Before the difficult days come,
> And the years draw near when you say,
> 'I have no pleasure in them':
> While the sun and the light,
> The moon and the stars,
> Are not darkened,
> And the clouds do not return after the rain;
> In the day when the keepers of the house
> tremble,
> And the strong men bow down;
> When the grinders cease because they are few,
> And those that look through the windows grow
> dim."
> (Ecclesiastes 12:1–3 NKJV)

"Lord, please help Joey to surrender his heart to You now and avoid so much sorrow in the days ahead," Ezra prayed quietly. And then he straightened up, stood to his feet, raised his arms toward heaven, and began to pray. "O God, even now send revival to a land that has fallen so very far from Your protective hand. We have abused Your mercy and grace. Pour out revival on this nation, I pray. May we turn to You in repentance as Ninevah did in the days of Jonah."

Even with the nation in the throes of judgment, God had still offered His hand of mercy toward Ninevah.

"Lord, help our nation to turn to You while there's yet time," Ezra prayed.

Chapter Thirty

It would soon be Christmas and after that a new year. The small town was bustling with activity—children playing in the park, city workers decorating the stage and hanging lights on the gazebo and banners on the old-fashioned lampposts surrounding the city square—as Tanner walked down Main Street toward Bendicion's, a small gift shop in Harbor Bay. *The Last Supper* portrait by local artist Juan Madera, and one of seven paintings of Jesus and His disciples of close similitude by the artist, had come available three months after Tanner's inquiry.

"Mr. Johansson?" the woman on the other end of the phone said.

"Yes, it is."

"The painting you asked about was just exchanged for another piece of artwork. I can sell it to you for the price we agreed on."

"Wonderful," Tanner had said.

"I'm sorry to say this, but we've . . . well, you know, we're a small family business. We've been struggling as of late. We can't hold it long. Do you know when you would be able to pick it up?"

"I'll be there tomorrow," Tanner said.

The thirty-by-forty-inch oil on canvas painting was as beautiful and majestic as Tanner had expected. Tanner watched as the curator of the shop, a gracious and kind woman who looked to be in her early to midforties, carefully wrapped the portrait in brown paper and then rewrapped it a second time before putting foam guards on the corners of the frame and ever so gently placing the picture and frame in a frame slip and then into a sturdy cardboard mirror box.

Tanner paid the woman with a credit card and typed in an amount of just over 50 percent of the purchase price for a tip.

"Thank you so much, Mr. Johansson." The woman closed her eyes and then wiped away the tears with the sleeve of her blouse. "You don't know how much this will help."

"You are more than welcome. I'll be back in five minutes."

Tanner walked briskly to his car, drove around the block, and then pulled into an open metered parking spot two stores down from Bendicion's.

"Thank you for holding the portrait for me. My wife will be overjoyed. Merry Christmas to you and your family."

Tanner carefully maneuvered the box into the empty trunk of his car and then walked across the street to the park, reminiscent of earlier Christmas seasons. He and Amara and the kids would stroll through downtown Santa Fe, walking along the Spanish cobblestone streets, gazing into storefront windows, sometimes twirling the ristras hanging from storefront beams or lampposts, admiring the vigas running the length of the ceiling or extending out from the exterior of an adobe-styled coffee shop, sometimes sitting on a park bench in the summer, or taking in the spectacle of colorful lights covering the trees in Santa Fe Plaza around Christmastime.

He thought about San Miguel Chapel, the front side of the historic structure surrounded by luminarias, the block wall of asymmetrical stones parallel to the street running alongside the church, the stately oak double doors at the front entryway, the outside chapel yard walkway surrounded by the warming glow of golden lights.

"¡Qué magnífica cruz majestuosa!"— "What a magnificent, stately cross," Amara would say with the softest most reverential tone to the elderly Hispanic doorman handing out candles inside the vestibule before they were seated in the chapel.

It was the same man year after year for as long as he could remember, and then one year a young girl was handing out the candles. "What happened to the nice gentleman I saw for so many years?" Tanner asked a nearby woman after taking his candle.

The woman smiled warmly. "Mateo, Mr. Ramirez, passed away in November. He was a blessed soul. We will see him again."

Always punctual, Amara insisted they be early. Each year they would sit in the same section, midway on the left side facing the front sanctuary, close enough to admire the artwork on the Altar Screen—a restored painting titled, *Christ the Nazarene/Jesus Nazareno,* and portraits of the Archangel Michael, Saint Francis of Assisi, and other venerated and beloved figures.

The Christmas Eve farolito walk on Canyon Road was an annual tradition for the family and for thousands of other families through the years. Pequeña linterna, Spanish for "little lantern," described the farolitos or luminarias that adorned the walkway, giving a gentle winter-night glow reminiscent of so many Christmas celebrations over the past two thousand years since the birth of Christ. The walk began after dark, but the subtle glow from the thousands of farolitos on Canyon Road and nearby streets illuminated the shadowy ridges of the distant Sangre de Cristo Mountains.

As Tanner reflected on past Christmas Eve and Christmas Day celebrations in Santa Fe—good years, he thought, happy times for Amara and the kids—the choir director emerged on the stage of the orchestra shell and began leading an assembly of men and women in rehearsal. Tanner listened as the voices rang out in a cappella.

"All Creatures of Our God and King,
lift up your voice and with us sing,
'Alleluia! Alleluia!'

"Ye who long pain and sorrow bear,
praise God and on Him cast your care;
O praise Him, O praise Him!
alleluia, alleluia, alleluia!

"Let all things their Creator bless,
and worship Him in humbleness;
O praise Him! Alleluia!
Praise, praise the Father, praise the Son,
and praise the Spirit, Three in One;
O praise Him, O praise Him!
alleluia, alleluia, alleluia!"

The next song, "Joyful, Joyful, We Adore Thee," resonated through the park, the small choir singing each stanza of the revered text.

"Joyful, joyful, we adore Thee,
God of glory, Lord of love;
Hearts unfold like flow'rs before Thee,
Op'ning to the sun above."

Stanzas one and five of "O Worship the King all glorious above" followed, ending in the last two lines from the fourth stanza.

"O worship the King all-glorious above,
O gratefully sing his power and his love:

our shield and defender, the Ancient of Days,
pavilioned in splendor and girded with praise.

"O measureless Might, unchangeable Love,
whom angels delight to worship above!
Your ransomed creation, with glory ablaze,
in true adoration shall sing to your praise!

"Your mercies, how tender, how firm to the end,
"our Maker, Defender, Redeemer, and Friend!

The choir director said, "Amen and amen!" and the
ensemble quietly moved from the stage.

Tanner walked slowly toward the center square. In
the center of the park a group of young men and women
had assembled near a gazebo and were lining up in choir
formation when a young man raised his arm and motioned
to the small choir who began singing.

"We will remember, we will remember,
We will remember the works of Your hands;
We will stop! and give You praise,
For great is Thy faithfulness!

"You're our creator, our life sustainer,
Deliverer, our comfort, our joy;
Throughout the ages, You've been our shelter,
Our peace in the midst of the storm.
With signs and wonders, You've shown Your Power;

With precious blood, You showed us Your grace.
You've been our helper, our liberator,
The giver of life with no end.

"We will remember, we will remember,
We will remember the works of Your hands;
We will stop! and give You praise,
For great is Thy faithfulness!"

The word "suddenly" came to Tanner's mind. He remembered Ezra telling him about the return of Jesus and saying that the times would be like the days before the flood, which had prompted Tanner to study the verses as he read through the Gospels during his vacation. In recent days, he had committed to memory the words of Jesus from the Gospel of Matthew:

> "For as in the days before the flood, they were eating and drinking, marrying and giving in marriage, until the day that Noah entered the ark, and did not know until the flood came and took them all away, so also will the coming of the Son of Man be. Then two men will be in the field: one will be taken and the other left. Two women will be grinding at the mill: one will be taken and the other left. Watch therefore, for you do not know what hour your Lord is coming."
> (Matthew 24:38–42 NKJV)

His return will be sudden, Tanner thought. "Lord, help me to be watchful," he whispered.

Tanner thought about a second verse Ezra had referenced:

> "In a moment, in the twinkling of an eye, at the last trumpet. For the trumpet will sound, and the dead will be raised incorruptible, and we shall be changed."
> (1 Corinthians 15:52 NKJV)

Tanner whispered, "Amen. Even so, come Lord Jesus!"

The End.

"The grass withers, the flower fades, But the word of our God stands forever."
(Isaiah 40:8 NKJV)

Appendix

Within the storyline of *Conspiracy,* multiple Scripture passages are quoted or referenced. In some instances, Scripture quotations are accompanied by notations listing the Bible translation, book of the Bible, chapter number, and verse number(s). In other instances, notations are not made. Dialogue in the story in which a character references a Scripture passage, recites part of a verse, or paraphrases a portion of Scripture are examples of this. In addition, some familiar verses may not be listed. Also, please note that some of the references in the Appendix below may include only part of the Scripture verse. The author encourages the reader to continue his or her studies and read each passage in its entirety.

For the benefit of the reader, the following appendix lists the chapter and verse for a number of Scripture passages or paraphrases of Scripture in which complete reference detail is not provided in the text.

The Appendix is divided into two sections:

Appendix A: Scripture passages or references;

Appendix B: Non-biblical references.

Fictional characters and fictional works (book titles, etcetera) are not listed in the Appendix.

Appendix A: Scripture Passages / References

Chapter Seven:
"Jesus told of a man who was delivered of an evil spirit, but later, finding the man unoccupied, the spirit returned with seven other spirits more evil than himself." (Scripture reference taken / paraphrase from Matthew 12:43–45)

Chapter Thirteen:
"In the book of Ecclesiastes in the Old Testament, the writer tells us there is 'a time to every purpose under the heaven: a time to keep silence, and a time to speak; a time of war, and a time of peace.' (Ecclesiastes 3:1, 7–8 KJV reads: "To every thing there is a season, and a time to every purpose under the heaven (v. 1): A time to rend, and a time to sew; a time to keep silence, and a time to speak; A time to love, and a time to hate; a time of war, and a time of peace (vv. 7–8)."

Chapter Sixteen:
"There's a verse in Hebrews that talks about Jesus saving those who come to God through Him, and that He is always interceding before God on their behalf." (Scripture reference taken / paraphrase from Hebrews 7:25)

"Another passage in Hebrews speaks of 'the sin that so easily entangles us,' some translations use the word 'ensnares.' (Scripture reference taken / paraphrase from Hebrews 12:1)

"What were the sins? Pride, ego, worry, fear, lust of the flesh, lust of the eyes, and the pride of life." (Scripture references taken / paraphrase from Proverbs 6:17; Matthew 6:31; 2 Timothy 1:7; Revelation 21:8; 1 John 2:16)

Chapter Twenty:
Pastor Kenneth Matthews followed: "I'm not an isolationist. Jesus said, 'To whom much is given, much is required.' (Paraphrase from Luke 12:48)

Chapter Twenty-One:

"You alone are God. You have made the skies and the heavens, the earth and the seas, and everything in them. You preserve it all; and all the angels of heaven worship you." (Nehemiah 9:6 TLB: verse begins, "Then Ezra prayed, 'You alone are God.')

" 'Not by might nor by power, but by My Spirit,' says the lord of hosts." (Zechariah 4:6 NASB: verse begins, "Then he answered and said to me, 'This is the word of the lord to Zerubbabel saying,")

Chapter Twenty-Three:

"Jesus said, and I'm paraphrasing, that His return will be just like the days of Noah before the flood. People will be eating and drinking, marrying, and giving in marriage. Jesus said they didn't understand what was happening until the flood came and took them all away. He compared that time to His coming. (Scripture reference / paraphrase from Matthew 24:37–39)

"Jesus said in the last days there would be wars and rumors of war, that nation would rise against nation, and kingdom against kingdom, that in various places there would famines and earthquakes. (Paraphrase from Matthew 24:6–7)

"In 2 Thessalonians we read that there will be a great falling away. Some believe this is referring to the rapture of the church; others believe it's referring to a falling away from the faith. I do believe that apostasy will be widespread. The Bible talks of a world leader coming on the scene. A global leader will emerge who the world will unite behind. His emergence will probably be somewhat sudden. It may follow global, international unrest. Many of the political leaders internationally, will unite behind his agenda. This man is referred to as the 'Man of Sin,' and the Antichrist. This man opposes Jesus and ultimately proclaims himself to be God." (Scripture verse referenced is from 2 Thessalonians 2:3)

"In 1 Corinthians chapter 15, the Apostle Paul, under the inspiration of the Holy Spirit, writes that the Lord's return will happen in a moment, in the twinkling of an eye." (Paraphrase from 1 Corinthians 15:52)

"The Antichrist will require that everyone receive a mark on their right hand or forehead. Without that mark, a person will not be able to buy or sell in the world economic system." (Paraphrase from Revelation 13:16–17)

Chapter Twenty-Four:
"But this peace and safety comes by staying in the 'secret place of the Most High.'" ('Secret place of the Most High' Scripture reference taken from Psalm 91:1 NKJV)

The Apostle Paul wrote, under the anointing of the Spirit of God, 'forgetting those things which are behind, and reaching forth unto those things which are before, I press toward the mark for the prize of the high calling of God in Christ Jesus' (Philippians 3:13–14). (Verse 13 begins, "Brethen, I count not myself to have apprehended: but this one thing I do,")

"Lord, there's so much I don't understand, but I believe in You," he prayed in a small whisper. "Dear God, I echo the words of the man who told Jesus, 'Lord, I believe; help thou mine unbelief'" (Mark 9:24). (Mark 9:24 begins, "And straightway the father of the child cried out, and said with tears,")

Chapter Twenty-Six:
"In Hebrews we read that we're surrounded by a great cloud of witnesses." (Scripture verse referenced / taken from Hebrews 12:1)

"He thought about the Scripture passage referencing the great falling away and the coming of the 'Man of Sin,' 'the son of perdition,' the 'lawless one,' who he knew was the Antichrist in the last days before the Lord's return." (Scripture verse referenced is from 2 Thessalonians 2:3)

Chapter Twenty-Nine:
The Apostle Paul wrote, under the anointing of the Spirit of God, 'forgetting those things which are behind, and reaching forth unto those things which are before, I press toward the mark for the prize of the high calling of God in Christ Jesus' (Philippians 3:13–14). (Verse 13 begins, "Brethen, I count not myself to have apprehended: but this one thing I do,")

Chapter Thirty:
Tanner whispered, "Amen. Even so, come Lord Jesus!" (Verse taken from Revelation 22:20 NKJV. Verse 20 begins, "He who testifies to these things says, 'Surely I am coming quickly.'")

Appendix B: Non-Biblical References

Chapter 5:
Project MKNAOMI: CIA, Army Biological Laboratory, Fort Detrick, Maryland; Summary report taken from the National Archives; Internet link, "Summary Report of CIA Investigation of MKNAOMI"— (See National Archives website for additional information: https://archive.org/details/MKNAOMI/mode/2up; Summary report on CIA investigation of MKNAOMI: Free Download, Borrow, and Streaming: Internet Archive.)

Naval Ship Maddox / Gulf of Tonkin: False narrative accelerates U.S. involvement in Viet Nam War. See U.S. Naval Institute; Naval History "The Truth About Tonkin." (https://www.usni.org). Especially incriminating is former Secretary of Defense Robert McNamara's quote: "I learned early on never answer the question that is asked of you. Answer the question that you wish had been asked of you. And quite frankly, I follow that rule. It's a very good rule." (See website for additional information: https://www.usni.org/magazines/naval-history-magazine/2008/february/truth-about-tonkin; The Truth About Tonkin | Naval History Magazine - February 2008 Volume 22, Number 1.)

Chapter Eleven:
"Tanner turned back to his laptop and opened the email:
- Hunter Biden joins Burisma;
- Prosecutor General Viktor Shokin opens investigation into Burisma corruption;
- Joe Biden works with Ukrainian President Petro Poroshenko to get Shokin fired;
- Joe Biden brags about getting Shokin fired;
- 51 intel officers sign off on a document suggesting that the laptop story may be Russian disinformation.

"(Note: For nuanced timelines, financial transactions, and officials named in the report see https://oversight.house.gov/

the-bidens-influence-peddling-timeline/)" (See website for additional information.)

"The timelines are laid out chronologically in an online report from the Committee on Oversight and Accountability." (See website for additional information: https://oversight.house.gov/the-bidens-influence-peddling-timeline/; The Bidens' Influence Peddling Timeline - United States House Committee on Oversight and Accountability.)

"Mitch reached for the manilla folder he had placed neatly on the desk moments before, removed the pages, and began reading:

"Setting: Chapel Hill, North Carolina;
Protagonist: Dr. Peter Daszak, President, EcoHealth Alliance;
Study: Gain of Function research;
Funding Body: National Institute of Health (NIH) headed by Dr. Anthony Fauci;
Synopsis: Allegedly, NIH funded EcoHealth Gain of Function research at the Wuhan Institute of Virology in Wuhan, China. This is the lab where many now believe the Coronavirus (COVID-19) originated. At this point, innumerable voices and organizations, including the FBI, I might add, believe the virus escaped from the Wuhan Lab. The wet market theory espoused by government officials has largely been discredited.
Initial NIH response: Denial.
Recent developments: Emails from Dr. Fauci appear to show NIH's knowledge and complicity. I should note that funding for this research has stopped. Rand Paul has exposed this and asked the DOJ to investigate." (See website for additional information: https://oversight.house.gov/release/hearing-wrap-up-eco-health-alliance-should-be-criminally-investigated-formally-debarred/; Hearing Wrap Up: EcoHealth Alliance Should be Criminally Investigated, Formally Debarred - United States House Committee on Oversight and Accountability.)
"The *Washington Examiner* reported on a recent Johns Hopkins University study that compared Sweden's mortality rate to the United States, showing Sweden with 39.26 COVID-19 deaths per one hundred thousand people; the United States with 29.87 deaths per one hundred thousand." (See website for additional information: https://www.washingtonexaminer.

com/news/1006497/ swedish-coronavirus-death-toll-surpass-es-4000/; Swedish coronavirus death toll surpasses 4,000 - Washington Examiner.)

"On October 8, 2023 the Washington Examiner ran an article with the headline: 'Will Rand Paul get an apology from Dr. Fauci after NIH's latest admission?' (See website for additional information: https://www.washingtonexaminer.com/opinion/beltway-confidential/2750470/will-rand-paul-get-an-apolo-gy-from-dr-fauci-after-nihs-latest-admission/; Will Rand Paul get an apology from Dr. Fauci after NIH's latest admission? - Washington Examiner.)

Chapter Twelve:
"Armenia: The United States Holocaust Memorial Museum website reports on the Armenian Genocide that took place early in the twentieth century: "The Armenian genocide refers to the physical annihilation of ethnic Armenian Christian people living in the Ottoman Empire from Spring 1915 through autumn 1916. The site also says, 'At least 664,000 and possibly as many as 1.2 million died during the genocide, either in massacres and individual killings, or from systemic ill treatment, exposure, or starvation.' " (See website for additional information: https://encyclopedia.ushmm.org/content/en/article/the-armenian-genocide-1915-16-in-depth; The Armenian Genocide (1915-16): In Depth | Holocaust Encyclopedia.)

Chapter Thirteen:
The following quote, "432,093 civilians have died violent deaths as a direct result of the U.S. post-9/11 wars," attributed to "Costs of War, Watson Institute, Brown University." Used by permission. (This entry is also listed on the Copyright page.)

The following quote is used by permission: 'Mao Zedong has rightly been called the greatest murderer of the twentieth century, killing an estimated 65 million Chinese in radical Marxist experiments such as the so-called Great Leap Forward and the Cultural Revolution. Li Rui, Mao's personal secretary, admitted, "The deaths of others meant nothing to him." ' Taken from the article, "A Reminder that China is One of the World's Worst Human Rights Offenders" by Lee Edwards, Ph.D. Printed in The Heritage Foundation on November 2, 2020, the article was originally printed in the *National Review*. (This entry is also listed on the Copyright page.)

"In respect to Norman M. Naimark's book, *Stalin's Genocides,* Princeton University Press writes, 'Between the early 1930s and his death in 1953, Joseph Stalin had more than a million of his own citizens executed. Millions more fell victim to forced labor, deportation, famine, bloody massacres, and detention and interrogation by Stalin's henchmen."

Stalin's Genocides by Norman M. Naimark. Copyright © 2011 Princeton University Press. Princeton University Press quotation used by permission. (This entry is also listed on the Copyright page.)

"In a 2004 report titled, 'An Act,' the 108th Congress reports a compendium of crimes unimaginable to free peoples in contemporary times." (See website for additional information: https://www.gov-info.gov/content/pkg/PLAW-108publ333/html/PLAW-108publ333. htm; govinfo.gov/content/pkg/PLAW-108publ333/html/PLAW-108publ333.htm)

Chapter Twenty-One:
"On December 18, 2019, the U.S. Department of Justice Officer of the Inspector General released the 'DOJ OIG FISA Report: Methodology, Scope, and Findings,' which we refer to today as the Horowitz Report." (See website for additional information: https:// oig.justice.gov/node/16547; Statement of Michael E. Horowitz, Inspector General, U.S. Department of Justice before the U.S. Senate Committee on Homeland Security and Governmental Affairs concerning "DOJ OIG FISA Report: Methodology, Scope, and Findings")

"Official government information is available online at vault.fbi. gov which takes you to 'FBI Records: The Vault.' (See website for additional information: https://vault.fbi.gov; FBI Records: The Vault — The Vault)

"Allow me if you would, to backtrack for a moment and expand on government surveillance, specifically FISA 702. Let's start with the definition of FISA, friends. FBI.gov writes, 'Congress enacted the Foreign Intelligence Surveillance Act (FISA) in 1978 to provide oversight of foreign intelligence surveillance activities while maintaining the secrecy necessary to effectively monitor national security threats.' The website goes on to say, 'In 2008, Congress enacted Section 702 of FISA, which authorizes targeted intelligence collection of specific types of foreign intelligence information—such as information concerning international terrorism or the acquisition of weapons of mass destruction.' (See website for additional information: https://www.fbi.gov/how-we-investigate/intelligence; Intelligence — FBI)

"Here's Wikipedia's definition of sedition: 'Overt conduct, such as speech or organization, that tends toward rebellion against the established order.' " (See website for additional information: https://en.wikipedia.org/wiki/Sedition#:~:text=Sedition%20is%20 overt%20conduct%2C%20such,or%20insurrection%20again- st%2C%20established%20authority. Sedition - Wikipedia

About the Author

As exciting and stimulating, and certainly as important and necessary for the county's democratic ideals as the political debate is today, a more important question faces the hearts and minds of all of mankind: "What must I do to be saved?" The question is answered powerfully with the words, "So they said, 'Believe on the Lord Jesus Christ, and you will be saved, you and your household' (Acts 16:31 NKJV).

R. A. Stokes is the author of *The Nehemiah Project* and *Riches and Prosperity,* which are novels in the Christian fiction genre and part of the two-book Mountain Fire Revival Series.

R. A. Stokes and his wife, Mary Jo, live in Oklahoma.

www.ingramcontent.com/pod-product-compliance
Lightning Source LLC
Chambersburg PA
CBHW020054310726
48970CB00002B/314